The car steadied and he regained control, hearing the snow piled at the side of the road spume upwards as his mudguards hit it. There was just enough room to take the car up the smaller road between the high white mounds. Then, from behind, came the crump of the grenade. A quick glance into the mirror – for he hardly dared take his eyes from the road and the head-up display – showed a dark red flower of flame coming from directly beneath one of the high yellow ploughs. With luck, the grenade would be enough to bog down that plough for ten minutes or so, while the other pushed it, incapacitated, out of the way.

In any case, Bond figured, even along this narrow, dangerous, snow-flanked gulley of a road, he could outrun any snow plough. That was, any snow plough behind him. He had not counted for yet another – dead ahead, spotlights splitting the darkness, dazzling him as it came, seemingly from nowhere. This time there was no place to hide.

John Gardner served with the Fleet Air Arm and Royal Marines before embarking on a long career as a thriller writer, including international bestsellers *The Nostradamus Traitor, The Garden of Weapons, Confessor* and *Maestro*. In 1981 he was invited by Glidrose Publications Ltd – now known as Ian Fleming Publications – to revive James Bond in a brand new series of novels. To find out more visit John Gardner's website at www.john-gardner.com or the Ian Fleming website at www.ianfleming.com

# ICEBREAKER

John Gardner

An Orion paperback

First published in Great Britain in 1983
by Jonathan Cape
This paperback edition published in 2012
by Orion Books Ltd,
Orion House, 5 Upper St Martin's Lane,
London WC2H 9EA

An Hachette UK company

1 3 5 7 9 10 8 6 4 2

A CIP catalogue record for this book
is available from the British Library.

ISBN 978-1-4091-3564-7

Typeset at The Spartan Press Ltd,
Lymington, Hants

Printed and bound by CPI Group (UK) Ltd,
Croydon, CR0 4YY

The Orion Publishing Group's policy is to use papers
that are natural, renewable and recyclable products and
made from wood grown in sustainable forests. The logging
and manufacturing processes are expected to conform to
environmental regulations of the country of origin.

www.orionbooks.co.uk
www.ianfleming.com

# CONTENTS

*For*
*Peter Janson-Smith*

## ACKNOWLEDGMENTS AND AUTHOR'S NOTE

I would like to thank those who gave invaluable assistance in the preparation of this book. First, to my good friends Erik Carlsson and Simo Lampinen who put up with me in the Arctic Circle. To John Edwards who suggested that I go to Finland, and made it possible. To Ian Adcock, who did not lose his temper, but remained placid, when, during a cross-country ride in northern Finland – in early February 1982 – I took him, not once, but three times, into snow-drifts.

My thanks also to that diplomat among Finnish gentlemen, Berhard Flander, who did the same thing to me in a slightly more embarrassing place – right on the Finnish–Russian border. We both thank the Finnish army for pulling us out.

Acknowledgments would not be complete without reference to Philip Hall, who has given me much support throughout.

John Gardner
1983

# I

# THE TRIPOLI INCIDENT

The Military Trade Mission Complex of the Socialist People's Republic of Libya is situated some fifteen kilometres south-east of Tripoli. Set close to the coast, the Complex is well-hidden from prying eyes, screened on all sides by sweet-smelling eucalyptus, mature cypresses, and tall pines. From the air it might easily be taken for a prison. The kidney-shaped area is enclosed by a boundary of three separate, six-metre-high cyclone fences, each topped by a further metre of barbed and electrified wire. At night, dogs roam the runs between the fences, while regular patrols, in Cascavel armoured cars, circle outside the perimeter. The buildings within the compound are mainly functional. There is a low barracks, constructed in wood, for the security forces; two more comfortable structures act as 'hotels' – one for any foreign military delegation, the other to house their Libyan counterparts.

Between the 'hotels' stands an imposing, single-storey block. Its walls are over a metre thick, their solidity disguised by the pink stucco finish and an arched, cloistered façade. Steps lead to a main door, and the interior is cut down the centre by a single corridor. Administrative offices and a radio room extend to left and right of this passage which ends, abruptly, at a pair of heavy, high doors leading to a long, narrow room, bare but for its massive conference table and chairs, together with facilities for showing films, VTR, and slides.

There are no windows in this, the most important room of the

Complex. Air conditioning maintains an even temperature, and a small metal door at the far end, used by cleaners and security personnel, is the only other entrance.

The Military Trade Mission Complex is used about five or six times a year, and the activities within are constantly monitored – as best they can be – by the intelligence agencies of the Western democracies.

On the morning it happened there were, perhaps, one hundred and forty people working within the compound.

Those in the capitals of the West who keep a weather eye on Middle Eastern events knew a deal had been struck. Although the likelihood of an official statement remained minimal, eventually Libya would receive more missiles, aircraft, and assorted military hardware to swell its already well-stocked arsenal.

The final session of the negotiations was to begin at nine-fifteen, and both parties stuck rigidly to protocol. The Libyan and Soviet delegations, each consisting of around twenty people, met in front of the pink stucco building, and, after the usual cordial greetings, made their way inside and down the corridor to the high doors, which were opened, on their well-oiled, noiseless hinges by two armed guards.

About half of the two delegations had already advanced into the room when the whole phalanx halted, rooted in shock by the sight that met their eyes.

Ten identically dressed figures formed a wide crescent at the far end of the room. They wore combat jackets and grey denim trousers tucked into leather boots. Their appearance was made more sinister by the fine camouflage netting which covered their faces and was held in place by black berets, each of which carried a polished silver badge. The badge was that of a death-head above the letters NSAA, the whole flanked by lightning runes.

Incredible, for Libyan officers had checked the room less than fifteen minutes before the two delegations arrived outside the building.

The ten figures assumed the classic firing posture – left legs forward, bent at the knee, with the butts of machine pistols or automatic rifles tucked hard into their hips. Ten muzzles pointed towards the delegates already in the room, and at the remainder in the corridor outside. For a couple of seconds the scene was frozen. Then, as a wave of chaos and panic broke, the firing started.

The ten automatic weapons systematically hosed the doorway with fire. Bullets chewed through flesh and bone in a din magnified by the enclosed surroundings.

The burst of fire lasted for less than a minute, but when it stopped, all but six of the Soviet and Libyan delegates were either dead or fatally wounded. Only then did the Libyan troops and security officers go into action.

The assassination squad was exceptionally disciplined and well-trained. The fire fight – which lasted for some fifteen minutes – caught only three of the intruders while they remained in the room. The remainder escaped through the rear entrance, taking up defensive positions within the compound. The ensuing running battle claimed another twenty lives. At the end, the whole ten-man team lay dead with its victims, like pieces from some bizarre jigsaw puzzle.

At nine o'clock GMT the next morning, Reuters received a message by telephone. Within minutes the text was flashed to the media around the world.

The message read:

In the early hours of yesterday morning, three light aircraft, flying low to escape radar detection, cut their engines and glided in over the well-guarded Military Trade Mission Complex just outside Tripoli, the capital of the Socialist People's Republic of Libya.

An Active Service unit of the National Socialist Action Army landed, undetected, by parachute, within the grounds of the Complex.

Later in the day, this unit struck a blow for International Fascism by executing a large number of people engaged in furthering the spread of the evil Communist ideology, which remains a threat to world peace and stability.

It is with pride that we mourn the deaths of this Active Service unit while carrying out its noble task. The unit came from our élite First Division.

Retribution for fraternisation, or trade, between Communist and non-Communist countries, or individuals, will be swift. We shall cut away the Communist bloc from the remainder of the free world.

This is Communiqué Number One from the NSAA High Command.

At the time, it struck nobody as particularly sinister that the arms used by the NSAA group were all of Russian manufacture: six Kalashnikov RPK light machine guns and four of the RPK's little brothers – the light, and very effective, AKM assault rifle. Indeed, in a world well used to terrorism, the raid itself was one headline among many for the media, who put the NSAA down as a small group of Fascist fanatics.

A little under a month after what came to be known as 'the Tripoli Incident', five members of the British Communist Party held a dinner to entertain three visiting Russian Party members, who were on a goodwill mission to London.

The dinner was held in a house not far from Trafalgar Square, and coffee had just been served when the ringing of the front doorbell called the host from the table. A large amount of vodka, brought by the Russians, had been drunk by everybody present.

The four men standing outside the front door were dressed in paramilitary uniforms similar to those worn during the Tripoli Incident.

The host – a prominent and vociferous member of the British Communist Party – was shot dead on his own doorstep. The remaining four Britons, and three Russians, were dispatched in a matter of seconds.

The killers disappeared and were not apprehended.

During the post mortems on these eight victims, it became clear that all had died from shots fired from Russian-manufactured weapons – probably Makarov or Stetchkin automatic pistols; the ammunition being identified as made in the USSR.

Communiqué Number Two, from the NSAA High Command, was issued at nine o'clock GMT the next day. This time, the Active Service unit was named as having belonged to 'the Adolf Hitler Kommando'.

In the following twelve months, no fewer than thirty 'incidents' involving multiple assassinations ordered by the NSAA High Command became headline news.

In West Berlin, Bonn, Paris, Washington, Rome, New York, London – for the second time – Madrid, Milan, and several Middle Eastern cities, prominent Communists were killed, together with people engaged in official, or merely friendly, discussions with them. Among those who died were three outspoken British and American trade unionists.

Members of the assassination squads also lost their lives, but no prisoners from the organisation were taken. On four occasions, NSAA men committed suicide to escape capture.

Each of the assassinations was quick, carried out with careful planning and a high standard of military precision. After every incident, the inevitable High Command Communiqué was issued, presented in the stilted language common to all ideologies. Each Communiqué gave details of the supposed Active Service unit involved, and the old names, such as the First Eichmann Kommando and the Heinrich Himmler SS Division, brought back ugly memories of the infamous Third Reich. To the world's police and security services, this was the only constant: the one clue. No evidence came from the bodies of dead NSAA men and women. It was as though they had suddenly appeared, fully grown, born into the NSAA. Not a single corpse was identified. Forensic experts toiled over small hints; security agencies investigated their leads; missing persons bureaux followed similar traces. All ended at brick walls.

One newspaper sounded like a poster for some 1940s' movie:

> They come out of nowhere, kill, or die, or disappear – returning to their lairs. Have these followers of the dark Nazi Age returned from their graves, to wreak vengeance on their former conquerors? Until now, the bulk of urban terrorism has been motivated by leftist ideals. The self-styled and efficient NSAA brings with it a new, and highly disturbing, dimension.

Yet, in the shadows of that hidden, and secret, world of intelligence and security communities, people were beginning to stir uneasily as though awakening from bad dreams only to find that the dreams were reality. It began with exchanges of views, then, cautiously, of information. Finally they groped their way towards a strange, and unprecedented, alliance.

# 2

# A LIKING FOR BLONDES

Long before he joined the Service, James Bond had used a particular system of mnemonics to keep telephone numbers in his head. Now he carried the numbers of a thousand or so people filed away, available for immediate recall, in the computer of his memory. Most of the numbers came under the heading of work, so were best not committed to writing in any case.

Paula Vacker was not work. Paula was strictly play and pleasure.

In his room at the Inter-Continental Hotel, at the northern end of Helsinki's broad arterial Mannerheimintie, Bond tapped out the telephone number. It rang twice and a girl answered in Finnish.

Bond spoke in respectful English. 'Paula Vacker, please.'

The Finnish operator lapsed easily into Bond's native tongue: 'Who shall I say is calling?'

'My name's Bond. James Bond.'

'One moment, Mr Bond. I'll see if Ms Vacker's available.'

Silence. Then a click and the voice he knew well. 'James? James, where are you?' The accent was only lightly touched by that sing-song lilt so common to the Scandinavians.

Bond said he was at the Inter-Continental.

'Here? Here in Helsinki?' She did not bother to disguise her pleasure.

'Yes,' Bond confirmed, 'here in Helsinki. Unless Finnair got it wrong.'

'Finnair are like homing pigeons,' she said with a laugh. 'They don't often get it wrong. But what a surprise. Why didn't you let me know you were coming?'

'Didn't know myself,' Bond lied. 'Sudden change in plan.' That at least was partly true. 'Just had to pass through Helsinki so I thought I'd stop over. A kind of whim.'

'Whim?'

'A caprice. A sudden fancy. How could I possibly pass through Helsinki without seeing Paula Beautiful?'

She laughed; the real thing. Bond imagined her head thrown back, and mouth open, showing the lovely teeth and delicate pink tongue. Paula Vacker's name suggested she had Swedish connections. A direct translation from Swedish would make her Paula Beautiful. The name was well-suited.

'Are you free tonight?' It would be a dull evening if she were not available.

She gave her special laugh again, full of humour and without that stridency some career women develop. 'For you, James, I'm always free. But never easy.' It was an old joke, first made by Bond himself. At the time it had been more than apt.

They had known each other for some five years now, having first met in London.

It was spring when it happened, the kind of London spring that makes the office girls look as if they enjoy going to work, and when the parks are yellow carpets of daffodils.

The days were just starting to lengthen, and there was a Foreign Office binge, to oil the wheels of international commerce. Bond was there on business – to watch for faces. In fact there had been words about it, for internal security was a matter for MI5, not for Bond's Service. However, the Foreign Office, under whose auspices the party was being held, had won the day. Grudgingly, 'Five' compromised, on the understanding they would have a couple of men there as well.

From a professional viewpoint the party was a flop. Paula, however, was another matter.

There was no question of Bond seeing her across a crowded room, you just could not miss her. It was as though no other girls had been invited; and the other girls did not like it one bit – especially the older ones and the Foreign Service *femmes fatales* who always haunt such parties.

Paula wore white. She had a tan needing no help from a bottle, a complexion which, if catching, would put all the make-up firms out of business, and thick blonde hair, so heavy that it seemed to fall straight back into place even in a force ten gale. If all this were not enough, she was slender, sexy, had large grey-flecked eyes, and lips shaped for one purpose.

Bond's first thoughts were wholly professional. What a flytrap she would make, he decided, knowing they had problems getting good flytraps in Finland. He stayed clear for a long time, making sure she had come unescorted. Then he moved in and introduced himself, saying that the Minister had asked him to look after her. Two years later, in Rome, Paula told him the Minister had himself tried it on quite early in the evening – before Mrs Minister arrived.

She was in London for a week. On that first evening Bond took her to a late supper at the Ritz, which she found 'quaint'. At her hotel, Paula gently gave him the elbow – king size.

Bond laid siege. First, he tried to impress, but she did not like the Connaught, the Inn on the Park, Tiberio's, the Dorchester, the Savoy, or the Royal Garden Roof; while tea at Brown's she found merely 'amusing'. He was just about to take her on the Tramps' and Annabel's circuit when she found Au Savarin in Charlotte Street for herself. It was 'her', and the *patron* came and sat at their table, towards the end of meals, so that they could swap risqué stories. Bond was not so sure about that.

They became firm friends very quickly, discovering mutual interests – in sailing, jazz, and the works of Eric Ambler. There was also another sport which finally came to full fruition on the fourth evening. Bond, whose standards were known to be exacting, admitted she deserved the gold star with oak leaves. In turn she awarded him the oak leaf cluster. He was not sure about that either.

Over the following years they stayed very good friends, and – to put it mildly – kissing cousins. They met, often by accident, in places as diverse as New York and the French port of Dieppe, where he had last seen her the previous autumn. This night in Helsinki would be Bond's first chance to see Paula on her home ground.

'Dinner?' he asked.

'If I can choose the restaurant.'

'Don't you always?'

'You want to pick me up?'

'That, and other things.'

'My place. Six-thirty? You've got the address?'

'Engraved on my heart, pretty Paula.'

'You say that to all the girls.'

'Mostly, but I'm honest about it; and you know I have a special liking for blondes.'

'You're a traitor, staying at the Inter-Continental. Why aren't you staying Finnish, at the Hesperia?'

'Because you get electric shocks off the lift buttons there.'

'You get them at the Inter-Continental too. It's to do with the cold and the central heating . . .'

'. . . and the carpets. I know. But these are more expensive electric shocks, and I'm not paying. I can charge it, so I may as well have luxurious electric shocks.'

'Be very careful what you touch. Any metals give shocks indoors here, at this time of the year. Be careful in the bathroom, James.'

'I'll wear rubber shoes.'

'It wasn't your feet I was thinking about. So glad you had a whim, James. See you at six-thirty', and she rang off before he could come up with a smooth reply.

Outside, the temperature hovered around twenty-five degrees Centigrade below. Bond stretched his muscles, then relaxed, taking his gunmetal case from the bedside table and lighting a cigarette – one of the 'specials' made for him, by arrangement with H. Simmons of Burlington Arcade.

The room was warm and well-insulated, and there was a glow of immense satisfaction as he exhaled a stream of smoke towards the ceiling. The job certainly had its compensations. Only that morning Bond had left temperatures of forty below, for his true reason for being in Helsinki was connected with a recent trip to the Arctic Circle.

January is not the most pleasant time of year to visit the Arctic. If, however, you have to do some survival training of a clandestine nature in severe winter conditions, the Finnish area of the Arctic Circle is as good a place as any.

The Service believed in keeping its field officers in peak condition and trained in all modern techniques. Hence Bond's disappearance, at least once a year, to work out with 22 Special Air Service Regiment, near Hereford; and his occasional trips to Poole in Dorset to be updated on equipment and tactics used by the Royal Marine Special Boat Squadron.

Even though the old élite Double-0 section, with its attendant 'licence to kill in the course of duty', had now been phased out of the Service, Bond still found himself stuck with the role of 007. The gruff Chief of Service known to all as M had been most specific about it. 'As far as I'm concerned, you will remain 007. I shall take full responsibility for you, and you will, as ever, accept orders and assignments only from me. There are moments when this country needs a trouble-shooter – a blunt instrument – and by Jove it's going to have one.'

In more official terms, Bond was what the American Service speaks of as a 'singleton' – a roving case officer who is given free rein to carry out special tasks, such as the ingenious undercover work he had undertaken during the Falkland Islands conflict in 1982. Then he had even appeared – unidentifiable – on a television newsflash, but that had passed like all things.

In order to keep Bond at a high, proficient level, M usually managed to set up at least one gruelling field exercise each year. This time it had been more cold climate work, and the orders had come quickly, leaving Bond little time to prepare for the ordeal.

During the winter, members of the SAS units trained regularly among the snows of Norway. This year, as an added hazard, M had arranged that Bond should embark on a training exercise within the Arctic Circle, under cover, and with no permission either sought or granted from the country in which he would operate – Finland.

The operation, which had no sinister, or even threatening, implications, entailed a week of survival exercises, in the company of a pair of SAS men and two officers of the SBS.

These military and Marine personnel would have a tougher time than Bond, for their part would demand two clandestine border crossings – from Norway into Sweden, then, still secretly, over the Finnish border to meet up with Bond in Lapland.

There, for seven days, the group would 'live off the belt', as it was called: surviving with only the bare necessities carried on their specially designed belts. Their mission was survival in difficult terrain, while remaining unseen and unidentified.

This week would be followed by a further four days, with Bond as leader, in which a photographic and sound-stealing run would be made along Finland's border with the Soviet Union. After that, they would separate – the SAS and SBS men to be picked up by helicopter in a remote area, while Bond took another course.

There was no difficulty about cover in Finland, as far as Bond was concerned. He had yet to test-drive his own Saab Turbo – 'The Silver Beast' as he called it – in harsh winter conditions.

Saab-Scania hold an exacting Winter Driving Course each year, within the Arctic Circle, near the Finnish ski resort of Rovaniemi. Arranging an invitation to take part in the course was easy, requiring only a couple of telephone calls. Within twenty-four hours Bond had his car – complete with all its secret 'extras', built in at his own expense by Communications Control Systems – freighted to Finland. Bond then flew, via Helsinki, to Rovaniemi, to meet up with driving experts, like his old friend Erik Carlsson, and the dapper Simo Lampinen.

The Driving Course took only a few days, after which – with a word to the massive Erik Carlsson, who promised to keep his eye on the Silver Beast – Bond left the hotel near Rovaniemi in the early hours of a bitterly cold morning.

The winter clothing, he thought, would do little for his image with the ladies back home. Damart thermal underwear is scarcely conducive to certain activities. Over long johns, he wore a track suit, heavy rollneck sweater, padded ski pants and jacket, while his feet were firmly laced into Mukluk boots. A thermal hood, scarf, woollen hat and goggles protected his face; Damart gloves inside leather gauntlets did the same for his hands. A small pack contained the necessities, including his own version of the SAS/SBS webbing belt.

Bond trudged through snow, which came up to his knees in the easier parts, taking care not to stray from the narrow track he had reconnoitred during the daylight hours. A wrong move to left or right could land him in snowdrifts deep enough to cover a small car.

The snow scooter was exactly where the briefing officers said it would be. Nobody was going to ask questions about how it got there. Snow scooters are difficult machines to manhandle with the engine off, and it took Bond a good ten minutes to heave and pull this one from its hiding place beneath solid and unyielding fir branches. He then hauled it to the top of a long slope which ran downwards for almost a kilometre. A push and the machine moved forward, giving Bond just enough time to leap on to the saddle and thrust his legs into the protective guards.

Silently, the scooter slid down the long slope, finally coming to a stop as the weight and momentum ran out. Though sound carried easily across the snow, he was now far enough from the hotel to start the engine safely – after taking a compass bearing, and checking his map with a shaded torch. The little motor came to life. Bond opened the throttle, engaged the gear and began his journey. It took twenty-four hours to meet up with his colleagues.

Rovaniemi had been an ideal choice. From the town one can move quickly north to the more desolate areas. It is also only a couple of fast hours' travel on a snow scooter to the more accessible points along the Russo-Finnish border; to places like Salla, the scene of great battles during the war between the Russians and Finns in 1939–40. Farther north, the frontier zone becomes more inhospitable.

During summer, this part of the Arctic Circle is not unpleasant; but in winter, when blizzards, deep-freeze conditions, and heavy snow take over, the country can be treacherous, and wretched, for the unwary.

When it was all over and the two exercises with the SAS and SBS completed, Bond expected to be exhausted, in need of rest, sleep, and relaxation of the kind he could only find in London. During the worst moments of the ordeal his thoughts had been, in fact, of the comfort to be found in his Chelsea flat. He was, then, quite unprepared to discover that, on returning to Rovaniemi a couple of weeks later, his body surged with an energy and sense of fitness he had not experienced for a considerable time.

Arriving back in the early hours, he slipped into the Ounas-vaara Polar Hotel – where Saab had their Winter Driving Head-quarters – left a message for Erik Carlsson saying he would send full instructions regarding the movement of the Silver Beast, then hitched a lift to the airport and boarded the next flight to Helsinki. At that point, his plan was to catch a connection straight on to London.

It was only as the DC9–50 was making its approach into Helsinki's Vantaa Airport, at around 12.30 pm, that James Bond thought of Paula Vacker. The thought grew, assisted no doubt by his new-found sense of well-being and physical sharpness.

By the time the aircraft touched down, Bond's plans were changed completely. There was no set time for him to be back in London; he was owed leave anyway, even though M had instructed him to return as soon as he could get away from Finland. Nobody was really going to miss him for a couple of days.

From the airport, he took a cab directly to the Inter-Continental and checked in. As soon as the porter had brought his case to the room, Bond threw himself on to the bed and made his telephone call to Paula. Six-thirty at her place. He smiled with anticipation.

There was no way that Bond could know that the simple act of calling up an old girlfriend, and asking her out to dinner, was going to change his life drastically over the next few weeks.

# 3

# KNIVES FOR DINNER

After a warm shower and shave, Bond dressed carefully. It was pleasant to get back into a well-cut grey gaberdine suit, plain blue Coles shirt, and one of his favourite Jacques Fath knitted ties. Even in the depths of winter, the hotels and good restaurants of Helsinki prefer gentlemen to wear ties.

The Heckler & Koch P7, which now replaced the heavier VP70, lay comfortably in its spring-clip holster under the left armpit, and to stave off the raw cold, Bond reached the hotel foyer wearing his Crombie British Warm. It gave him a military air – especially with the fur headgear – but that always proved an advantage in Scandinavian countries.

The taxi bowled steadily south, down the Mannerheimintie. Snow was neatly piled off the main pavements, and the trees bowed under its weight, some decorated – as though for Christmas – with long icicles festooning the branches. Near the National Museum, with its sharp tower fingering the sky, one tree seemed to crouch like a white cowled monk clutching a glittering dagger.

Over all, through the clear frost, Bond could glimpse the dominating floodlit domes of the Upensky Cathedral – the Great Church – and knew, immediately, why film-makers used Helsinki when they wanted location shots of Moscow.

The two cities are really as unlike one another as desert and jungle – the modern buildings of the Finnish capital being designed and executed with flair and beauty, in contrast to the ugly cloned monsters of Moscow. It is in the older sections of both cities that the mirror image becomes uncanny – in the side streets and small squares, where houses lean in on one another, and the ornate façades are reminders of what Moscow once was, in the good old, bad old days of tsars, princes and inequality. Now, Bond thought, they simply had the Politburo, Commissars, the KGB and . . . inequality.

Paula lived in an apartment building overlooking the Esplanade Park, at the south-easterly end of the Mannerheimintie. It was a part of the city Bond had never visited before, so his arrival was one of surprise and delight.

The park itself is a long, landscaped strip running between the houses. There were signs that in summer it would be an idyllic spot with trees, rock gardens, and paths. Now, in mid-winter, the Esplanade Park took on a new, original function. Artists of varied ages and ability had turned the place into an open-air gallery of snow sculpture. From the fresh snow of recent days there rose shapes and figures lovingly created earlier in winter: abstract masses; pieces so delicate you would imagine they could only be carved from wood, or worked at with patience in metal. Jagged aggression stood next to the contemplative curves of peace, while animals – naturalistic or only suggested in angular blocks – squared up to one another, or bared empty winter mouths towards hurrying passers-by, huddled and furred against the cold.

The cab pulled up almost opposite a life-sized work of a man and woman entwined in an embrace from which only the warmth of spring could separate them.

Around the park, the buildings were mainly old, with a few modern edifices looking like new buffer states bridging gaps in living history.

For no logical reason, Bond had imagined that Paula would live in a new and shining apartment block. Instead, he found her address to be a house four storeys high, with shuttered windows and fresh green paint, decorated by blossoms of snow hanging like window-box flowers, and frosted along the scrollwork and gutters, as though December vandals had taken spray cans to the most available parts.

Two curved, half-timbered gables divided the house, which had a single entrance, glass-panelled and unlocked. Just inside the door, a row of metal mailboxes signified who lived where, the personal cards in tiny frames. The hallway and stairs were bare of carpet, and the smell of good polish mingled now with tantalising cooking fragrances.

Paula lived on the third floor – 3A – and Bond, slipping the buttons on his British Warm, began to make his way up the stairs. At each landing he noted two doors, to left and right, solid and well-built, with bell-pushes and the twins of the framed cards on the mailboxes set below them.

At the third turning of the stairs he saw Paula Vacker's name elegantly engraved on a business card under the bell for 3A. Out of curiosity, Bond glanced at 3B. Its occupant was a Major A. Nyblin. He pictured a retired army man holed up with military paintings, books on strategy and the war novels – such a going concern in Finnish publishing – keeping memories alive of those three Wars of Independence in which the nation fought against Russia: first against the Revolution; then against invasion; and, finally, cheek by jowl with the Wehrmacht.

Bond pressed Paula's bell, hard and long, then stood square to the small spy-hole visible in the door's centre panel. From the inside came the rattle of a chain, then the door opened, and there she was, dressed in a long silk robe fastened loosely with a tie belt. The same Paula, inviting and as attractive as ever.

Bond saw her lips move, as though trying to speak words of welcome. In that instant he realised that this was not the same Paula. Her cheeks were drained white, one hand trembled on the door. Deep in the grey-flecked eyes was the unmistakable flicker of fear.

Intuition, they taught in Service training, is something you learn through experience: you are not born with it, like an extra sense.

Loudly Bond said, 'It's only me from over the sea', at the same time sticking one foot forward, the side of his shoe against the door. 'Glad I came?' As he spoke, Bond grabbed Paula by the shoulder with his left hand, spinning her, pulling her on to the landing. His right hand had already gone for the automatic. In less than three seconds, Paula was against the wall near Major Nyblin's door, while Bond had sidestepped into the apartment, the Heckler & Koch out and ready.

There were two of them. A small runt, with a thin, pock-marked face was to Bond's left, flat against the inside wall, where he had been covering Paula with a revolver which looked like a Charter Arms Undercover .38 Special. At the far side of the room – there was no hallway – a large man with oversized hands and the face of a failed boxer stood poised beside a beauti-ful chrome and leather chair-and-sofa suite. His distinguishing features included a nose which looked like a very advanced carbuncle. He carried no visible weapon.

The runt's gun came up to Bond's left, and the boxer began to move. Bond went for the gun. The big Heckler & Koch seemed to move only fractionally in Bond's hand as it clipped down, with force, on to the runt's wrist. The revolver spun away, and there was a yelp of pain above the sharp crack of bone.

Keeping the Heckler & Koch pointing towards the larger man, Bond used his left arm to spin the runt in front of him like a shield. At the same time, Bond brought his knee up hard. The little gunman crumpled, his good hand flailing ineffectually to protect his groin. He squeaked like a pig and squirmed at Bond's feet.

The larger of the two seemed undeterred by the gun, which indicated either great courage or mental deficiency. A Heckler & Koch could, at this range, blow away a high percentage of human being.

Bond stepped over the body of the runt, kicking back with his right heel. Raising the automatic, arms outstretched, Bond shouted at his advancing adversary, 'Stop, or you're a dead man.' It was more of a command than a warning; for Bond's finger was already tightening on the trigger.

The one with the carbuncle nose did not do as he was told. Instead he suggested, in bad Russian, that Bond commit incest with his female parent.

Bond hardly saw him swerve. The man was better than he had estimated, and very fast. As he slewed, Bond moved to follow him with the automatic. Only then did he feel the sharp, unnatural pain in his right shoulder.

For a second, the blossom of agony took Bond off balance. His arms dropped, and Carbuncle-nose's foot came up. Bond realised that you cannot be right about people all the time. This was a live one, the real thing – a killer, trained, accurate, and experienced.

Together with this knowledge, Bond was conscious of three things going on simultaneously: the pain in his shoulder; the gun being kicked from his hand – the weapon flying away to hit the wall – and, behind him, the whimpering of the runt, decreasing in volume as he made his escape down the stairs.

Carbuncle-nose was closing fast, one shoulder dropped, the body sideways.

Bond took a quick step back and to his right, against the wall. As he moved, he spotted what had caused the pain in his shoulder. Embedded in the door's lintel was an eight-inch knife with a horn grip and a blade curving away towards the point. It was a skinning knife, like those used to great effect by the Lapps when separating the carcase of a reindeer from its hide.

Grabbing upwards, Bond's fingers closed around the grip. His shoulder now felt numb with pain. He crabbed quickly to one side, with the knife firmly in his right hand, blade upwards, thumb and forefinger to the front of the grip in the fighting hold. Always, they taught, use the thrust position, never hold a knife with the thumb on the back. Never defend with a knife; always attack.

Bond turned, square on, toward Carbuncle-nose, knees bending, one foot forward for balance in the classic knife-fighting posture.

Carbuncle-nose was familiar with the rules, but it did slow him down. Bond figured him as a knifeman who did not know much about guns. He certainly had knives taped: there was a similar weapon now in the large right hand. Legerdemain.

'What was it you said about my mother?' Bond growled, in better Russian than his adversary.

Carbuncle-nose grinned, showing stained teeth. 'Now we see, Mr Bond.'

They circled one another, Bond kicking away a small stand chair, giving the pair a wider fighting arena. Carbuncle-nose began to toss his knife from hand to hand, light on his feet, moving all the time, tightening the circle. It was a well-known confusion tactic: keep your man guessing and lure him in close, then strike.

Come on, Bond thought, come on; in; closer; come to me. Carbuncle-nose was doing just that, oblivious of the danger of winding the spiral too tightly. Bond kept his eyes locked with those of the big man, his senses tuned to the enemy knife as it glinted, arcing from hand to hand, the grip slapping the palm with a firm thump on each exchange.

The end came suddenly and fast.

Carbuncle-nose inched nearer to Bond, continuing to toss the knife between his hands. Bond stepped in abruptly, his right leg lunging out in a fencing thrust, the foot midway between his antagonist's feet. At the same moment, Bond tossed his knife from right to left. Then he feinted, as though returning the knife to his right hand as his opponent would have expected.

The moment was there. Bond saw the big man's eyes move slightly in the direction in which the knife should be travelling. There was a split second when Carbuncle-nose was uncertain.

Bond's left hand rose two inches, then flashed out and down. There was the ringing clash of steel against steel.

Carbuncle-nose had been in the act of tossing his knife between hands. Bond's blade caught the weapon in mid-air, smashing it to the floor. In an automatic reflex, the big man went down, his hand reaching after his knife. Bond's knife drove upwards.

The big man straightened up very quickly, making a grunting noise. His hand went to his cheek, which Bond's knife had opened into an ugly red canyon from ear to jaw-line. With another fast, upward strike from Bond, the knife slit the protective hand. This time, Carbuncle-nose gave a roar of mingled pain and anger.

Bond did not want to kill – not in Finland, not in these circumstances. But he could not leave it like this. The big man's eyes went wide with disbelief and fear as Bond again moved in. The knife flicked up again, twice, leaving a jagged slash on the other cheek and removing an ear lobe.

Carbuncle-nose had obviously had enough. He stumbled to one side and made for the door, breath rasping. Bond decided the man had more intelligence than he had originally thought.

The pain returned to Bond's shoulder and with it a sensation of giddiness. He had no intention of following the would-be assailant, whose stumbling, falling footsteps could be heard on the wooden stairs.

'James?' Paula had come back into the room. 'What shall I do? Call the police, or . . . ?' She looked frightened, her face drained of colour. Bond thought he probably didn't look so hot either.

'No. No, we don't want the police, Paula.' He sank into the nearest chair. 'Close the door, put the chain on, and take a look out of the window.'

Everything seemed to withdraw around him. Surprisingly, he thought vaguely, Paula did as he asked. Usually she argued. You did not normally give orders to girls like Paula.

'See anything?' Bond's own voice sounded far away.

'There's a car leaving. Cars parked. I can't see any people . . .'

The room tilted, then came back into normal focus.

'. . . James, your shoulder.' He could smell her beside him. 'Just tell me what happened, Paula. It's important. How did they get in? What did they do?'

'Your shoulder, James.'

He looked at it. The thick material of his British Warm had saved him from serious injury. Even so, the knife had razored through the epaulette, and blood seeped up through the cloth, leaving a dark, wet stain.

'Tell me what happened,' Bond repeated.

'You're wounded. I have to look at it.'

They compromised and Bond stripped to the waist. A nasty gash ran diagonally across his shoulder where the knife had cut half an inch deep into the fleshy parts. Using disinfectant, hot water, tape, and gauze, Paula cleaned and dressed the wound, telling her story at the same time. Outwardly she was calm, though Bond noticed how her hands shook slightly as she recounted what had happened.

The two killers had arrived only a couple of minutes before he himself rang the doorbell. 'I was running a little late,' she made a vague gesture, indicating the silky robe. 'Stupid. I didn't have the chain on, and just thought it was you. Didn't even look through the spy-hole.' The intruders had simply forced their way in, pushing her back into the room telling her what to do. They also described, in some detail, what they would do to her if she did not carry out instructions.

Bond considered that under the circumstances she had done the only thing possible. As far as he was concerned, however, there were questions that could be answered only through Service channels, which meant that, much as he might like to stay on in Finland, he must get back to London. For one thing, the very fact that the two men were inside Paula's apartment only a few minutes before he arrived led him to think they had probably been waiting for his cab to stop in Esplanade Park.

'Well, thanks for tipping me off at the door,' Bond said, easing his now taped and dressed shoulder.

Paula gave a little pout. 'I didn't mean to tip you off. I was just plain frightened.'

'Ah, you only acted frightened.' Bond smiled at her, 'I can tell when people are really frightened.'

She bent down, kissed him, then gave a little frown. 'James, I'm *still* frightened. Scared stiff, if you really want to know. What about that gun, and the way you reacted? I thought you were just a senior civil servant.'

'I am. Senior and very civil.' He paused, ready to ask the important questions, but Paula moved across the room to retrieve the automatic pistol, which she nervously handed to him.

'Will they come back?' Paula asked. 'Am I likely to be attacked again?'

'Look,' Bond said, spreading his hands, 'for some reason a couple of hoodlums were after me. I really don't know why. Yes, sometimes I do slightly dangerous jobs – hence the weaponry. But there's no reason I can think of for those two having a go at me here, in Helsinki.'

He went on to say that he might find out the real answer in London and felt that Paula would be quite safe once he was out of the way. It was too late to catch the British Airways flight home that night, which meant waiting for the regular Finnair service, just after nine the next morning.

'Bang goes our dinner.' His smile was meant to look apologetic.

Paula said she had food in the house. They could eat there. Her voice had begun to quaver. Bond decided quickly that it would be best to start his questioning on the positive side before he tackled the really big problem: how did the would-be assassins know he was in Helsinki, and – particularly – how did they know he was visiting Paula?

'Have you got a car near here, Paula?' he began.

She had a car and a parking space outside.

'I may well ask a favour of you later.'

'I hope so.' She gave him a brave, come-on smile.

'Okay. Before we get down to that, there are more important things.' Bond fired the obvious questions at her – rapid shooting, pressing her for fast return answers, not giving her time to avoid anything or think about replies.

Had she ever talked about him to friends, or colleagues, in Finland, since they had first met? Of course. Had she done the same in any other country? Yes. Could she remember the number of people to whom she had talked? She gave some names, obvious ones – close friends and people with whom she worked. Did she have any memory of other people being around when she had spoken about Bond? People she did not know? That was quite possible, but Paula could give no details.

Bond moved on to the most recent events. Had anyone been with her in the office when he had telephoned from the Inter-Continental? No. Was there any way the call could have been overhead? Possibly; someone could have been listening in at the switchboard. Had she spoken to anyone after the call – told anyone that he was in Helsinki, and picking her up at six-thirty? Only one person. 'I was meeting a girl – a colleague from another department. We'd arranged to discuss some work over dinner.'

This woman's name was Anni Tudeer, and Bond spent quite a long time getting facts about her. At last he lapsed into silence, stood up, crossed to the window and peered out, holding back the curtain.

Below, it looked bleak and a little sinister, the white frozen sculptures throwing shadows across the layer of frost on the ground. Two small fur bundles scuffed their way along the pavement opposite. There were several cars parked in the street. Two of them would have been ideal for surveillance: the angle at which they were parked gave good sight-lines to the front door. Bond thought he could detect movement in one of them but decided to put it out of his mind until the time came. He returned to his chair.

'Is the interrogation over?' Paula asked.

'That wasn't an interrogation.' Bond took out the familiar gunmetal case, offering her one of his Simmons specials. 'One day, maybe, I'll show you an interrogation. Remember I said I may have to ask a favour?'

'Ask, and it'll be given.'

There was luggage at the hotel, Bond told her, and he had to get to the airport. Could he stay in her flat until about four in the morning, then drive himself to the hotel in her car, pay the bill and get out 'clean', before going on to the airport? 'I can arrange for your car to be brought back here.'

'You're not driving anywhere, James.' She sounded stubbornly serious. 'You've got a nasty wound in your shoulder. It's going to need treatment, sooner or later. Yes, you stay here until four in the morning; then I'll drive you to the hotel and the airport. But why so early? The flight doesn't leave until after nine. You could make a booking from here.'

Once more, Bond reiterated that she wouldn't really be safe until he was out of her company. 'If I get to the airport in the early hours you'll be rid of me. Also, I'll have the advantage. There are ways of positioning yourself in a place like an airport concourse so that nobody can give you nasty surprises. And I'm not using your telephone for obvious reasons.'

She agreed, but remained adamant that she would do the driving. Paula being Paula, Bond conceded.

'You're looking better.' She gave him a peck on the cheek. 'Drink?'

'You know what I fancy.'

She went off into the kitchen and mixed a jug of his favourite martini. It was over three years ago, in London, that he had taught her the recipe – one which, because of certain publications, had become a standard with many people. After the first drink, the throbbing in his shoulder seemed less intense.

With the second, Bond felt he was almost back to normal. 'I love that robe.' His mind began saying things to his body, and, wound or not, his body answered back.

'Well,' she gave a shy smile, 'to tell you the truth, I've already got dinner organised here. I had no intention of going out. I *was* ready for you when those . . . when those brutes turned up. How's the shoulder?'

'Wouldn't stop me playing chess, or any other indoor sport you might name.'

With a single movement she pulled the tie belt, and her robe fell open. 'You said I knew what you fancy,' she said lightly, then, 'that is, if you feel up to it.'

'Up to it is the way I feel,' Bond replied.

It was almost midnight when they ate. Paula set a table with candles and produced a truly memorable meal: ptarmigan in aspic, glowfried salmon, and a delicious chocolate mousse. Then, at four in the morning, now dressed for the fierce cold of dawn, she allowed Bond to lead the way downstairs.

With the P7 unholstered, Bond used the shadows to creep into the street and make his way across the road, slick with ice, first to a Volvo, then an Audi. There was a man in the Volvo, asleep, his head back and mouth open, far away in whatever dreams bad surveillance men fall prey to during the night. The Audi was empty.

Bond signalled to Paula, who came, very sure-footed, across the pavement to her car. It started first time, the exhaust sending out thick clouds in the freezing air, and Paula drove with the skill of one used to taking a car through snow and ice for long periods each year. At the hotel, the pick-up and check-out went without a hitch; and there was no tail on them as Paula headed north towards Vantaa.

Officially Vantaa Airport is not open until seven in the morning, but there are always people about. At five o'clock it had that look you associate with the sour taste of too many cigarettes, constant coffee, and the, tiredness of waiting for night trains, or planes, anywhere in the world.

Bond would not let Paula linger. He assured her that he would ring from London as soon as possible and they kissed goodbye affectionately.

There were people sweeping the main departure concourse where Bond chose his spot. His shoulder was starting to throb again. Several stranded passengers tried to sleep in the deep, comfortable chairs and quite a number of police walked around in pairs, looking for trouble that never materialised.

Promptly at seven the place became alive. Already, Bond had taken up a stance at the Finnair desk, so as to be first in line. There was plenty of room on Finnair's 831, due out at 9.10.

The snow began to fall around eight o'clock. It had become quite heavy by the time the big DC9–50 growled off the runway at 9.12. Helsinki quickly disappeared in a storm of white confetti, which soon gave way to a towering cloudscape below a brilliant blue sky.

At exactly 10.10, London time, the same aircraft flared out over the threshold of Heathrow's runway 28 Left. The spoilers came in as they dumped lift, the whining Pratt & Whitney turbofans wailed into reverse thrust, and the aircraft's speed was gradually killed off as the landing was completed.

An hour later, James Bond arrived at the tall building overlooking Regent's Park which is the Headquarters of the Service. By this time his shoulder throbbed like a misplaced toothache, sweat dripped from his forehead, and he felt sick.

# 4

# MADEIRA CAKE

'They were definitely professionals?' M had already asked the question three times.

'No doubt on that score,' Bond answered, just as he had done before, 'And I stress again, sir, that I was the target.'

M grunted.

They were seated in M's office on the ninth floor of the building: M, Bond, and M's Chief-of-Staff, Bill Tanner.

Immediately on entering the building Bond had taken the lift straight up to the ninth floor, where he lurched into the outer office, the domain of M's neatly efficient PA, Miss Moneypenny.

She looked up and at first smiled with pleasure. 'James . . .' she began, then saw Bond totter, and ran from her desk to help him into a chair.

'That's wonderful, Penny,' Bond said, dizzy from pain and fatigue. 'You smell great. All woman.'

'No, James, all Chanel; while you're a mixture of sweat, antiseptic and a hint of something, I think, by Patou.'

M was out, at a Joint Intelligence Committee briefing, so within ten minutes, with Miss Moneypenny's help, Bond was down in the sick bay, being tended by the two permanent nurses. The duty doctor was already on the way.

Paula had been right: the wound needed attention, antibiotics as well as stitches. By three in the afternoon, Bond was feeling a good deal better, well enough to be taken back for an interrogation by M and the Chief-of-Staff.

M never used strong language, but his look now was of a man ready to give way to the temptation. 'Tell me about the girl again. This Vacker woman.' He leaned across the desk, loading his pipe by feel alone, the grey eyes hard – as though Bond was not to be trusted.

Bond painstakingly went through everything he knew about Paula.

'And the friend? The one she mentioned?'

'Anni Tudeer. Works for the same agency; similar grade to Paula. They're apparently co-operating on a special account at the moment, promoting a chemical research organisation based up in Kemi. In the North, but this side of the Circle.'

'I know where Kemi is,' M almost snarled. 'You have to land there en route to Rovaniemi and all places north.' He inclined his head towards Tanner. 'Chief-of-Staff, would you run the names through the computers for me? See if we have anything. You can even go hat in hand to Five: ask them if there's anything on their books.'

Bill Tanner gave a deferential nod and left the office.

Once the door was closed, M leaned back in his chair. 'So, what's your personal assessment, 007?' The grey eyes glittered, and Bond thought to himself that M probably had the truth already locked away in his head, together with a thousand other secrets.

Bond chose his words carefully. 'I think I was marked – fingered – either during the exercise in the Arctic, or when I got back to Helsinki. Somehow they got a wire on to my hotel phone. It's either that, or Paula – which I would find hard to believe – or someone she spoke to. It was certainly a random operation, because even I didn't know I was going to stay until we landed in Helsinki. But they moved fast, and undoubtedly they were out to put me away.'

M took the pipe from his mouth, stabbing it towards Bond like a baton, 'Who are *they*?'

Bond shrugged, and his shoulder gave a twinge at the

movement. 'Paula said they spoke to her in good Finnish. They tried Russian on me – terrible accents. Paula thought they were Scandinavian, but not Finnish.'

'Not the answer, 007. I asked who are *they*?'

'People able to hire local non-Finnish talent – professional blackout merchants.'

'But why the hiring, then?' M sat quite still, his voice calm.

'I don't make friends easily.'

'Without the frivolity, 007.'

'Well.' Bond sighed. 'I suppose it could have been a contract. Remnants of SPECTRE. Certainly not KGB – or unlikely. Could be one of a dozen half-baked groups.'

'Would you call the National Socialist Action Army a half-baked group?'

'Not their style, sir. They go for Communist targets – the big bang, complete with publicity handouts.'

M allowed himself a thin smile. 'They could be using an agency, couldn't they, 007? An advertising agency, like the one your Ms Vacker works for.'

'Sir.' Flat, as though M had become crazed.

'No, Bond. Not their style, unless they wanted the quick termination of someone they saw as a threat.'

'But I'm not . . .'

'They weren't to know that. They weren't to know you had stopped off in Helsinki for some playboy nonsense – a role which becomes increasing tiresome, 007. You were instructed to get straight back to London when the exercise in the Arctic was completed, were you not?'

'Nobody was insisting on it. I thought . . .'

'Don't care a jot what you thought, 007. We wanted you back here. Instead you go gadding around Helsinki. May have compromised the Service, and yourself.'

'I . . .'

'You weren't to know.' M appeared to have softened a little. 'After all, I simply sent you off to do a cold weather exercise, an acclimatisation. I take the responsibility. Should've been more explicit.'

'Explicit?'

M remained silent for a full minute. Above him, Robert Taylor's original 'Trafalgar' set the whole tone of M's determination and character. That painting had lasted two years. Before, there had been Cooper's 'Cape St Vincent', on loan from the National Maritime Museum, and before that . . . Bond could not recall, but they were always paintings of Britain's naval victories. M was the possessor of that essential arrogance which put allegiance to country first, and a firm belief in the invincibility of Britain's fighting forces, no matter what the odds, or how long it took.

At last M spoke. 'We have an operation of some importance going on in the Arctic Circle at this moment, 007. The exercise was a warm-up – if I dare use that expression. A warm-up for *you*. To put it in a nutshell, you are to join that operation.'

'Against?' Bond expected the answer.

'The National Socialist Action Army.'

'In Finland?'

'Close to the Russian border.' M hunched himself even further forward, like a man anxious not to be overheard. 'We already have a man there – or I should say we *had* a man there. He's on his way back. No need to go into details just now. Personality clashes with our allies, mainly. The whole team's coming out to regroup, and meet you, put you in the picture. You get a briefing from me first, of course.'

'The whole team being?'

'Being strange bedfellows, 007. Strange bedfellows. And now we may have lost some tactical surprise, I fear, by your dalliance in Helsinki. We had hoped you'd go in unnoticed. Join the team without tipping off these neo-Fascists.'

'The team?' Bond repeated.

M coughed, playing for time. 'A joint operation, 007; an unusual operation, set up at the request of the Soviet Union.'

Bond frowned. 'We're playing with Moscow Centre?'

M gave a curt nod. 'Yes' – as though he also disapproved. 'And not only Moscow Centre. We're also involved with Langley and Tel Aviv.'

Bond gave a low whistle, which brought raised eyebrows and a tightening of M's lips. 'I said strange bedfellows, 007.'

Bond muttered, as though he could hardly believe it, 'Ourselves, the KGB, CIA, and Mossad – the Israelis.'

'Precisely.' Now that the cat was out of the bag, M warmed to his subject. 'Operation Icebreaker. The Americans named it, of course. The Soviets went along with it because they were the supplicants . . .'

'The KGB *asked* for co-operation?' Bond still sounded incredulous.

'Through secret channels, yes. When we first heard the news, the few of us in the know were dubious. Then I had an invitation to step over to Grosvenor Square.'

'And they'd been asked?'

'Yes, and naturally, being the Company, they knew Mossad had been asked too. Within a day we had arranged a tripartite conference.'

Bond gestured, asking wordlessly if he could smoke. M went on speaking, giving a tiny motion of his hand as permission, pausing only now and again to light and relight his pipe. 'We looked at it from all sides. Searched for the traps – and there are some, of course – examined the options if it went sour, then decided to nominate field officers. We wanted at least three each. Soviets heel-tapped on three: too many, the need to contain, and all that kind of thing. Finally we met the KGB's negotiator, Anatoli Pavlovich Grinev . . .'

Bond nodded, knowingly. 'Colonel of the First Directorate, Third Department. With cover as First Secretary, Trade, in KPG.'

'Got him,' said M. KPG meant Kensington Palace Gardens and, more specifically, Number 13 – the Russian Embassy. The Third Department of the KGB's First Directorate dealt entirely with intelligence operations concerning the United Kingdom, Australia, New Zealand and Scandinavia. 'Got him. Little fellow, Toby jug ears.' That was a good description of the wily Colonel Grinev. Bond had dealt with the gentleman before and trusted him as he would trust a faulty land mine.

'And he explained?' Bond was not really asking. 'Explained why the KGB would want ourselves, the CIA and Mossad, to combine in a covert op. on Finnish territory? Surely they're on good enough terms with SUPO to deal direct?' SUPO was Finnish Intelligence.

'Not quite,' M replied. 'You've read everything we have on the NSAA, 007?'

Bond nodded, adding, 'What precious little there is – the detailed reports of their thirty-odd assassination successes. There's not much more than that . . .'

'There's the Joint Intelligence Analysis. You've studied those fifty pages, I trust?'

Bond said he had read them. 'They elevate the National Socialist Action Army from a small fanatical terrorist organisation to something more sinister. I'm not certain the conclusions are correct.'

'Really?' M sniffed. 'Well, I am certain, 007. The NSAA are fanatics, but the leading intelligence communities, and security arms, are in agreement: the NSAA are led, and nurtured, on old Nazi principles. They mean what they say; and it seems as though they're pulling more people into the net every day. The indications are that their leaders see themselves as the architects of the Fourth Reich. The target, at present, is organised Communism. But two other elements have recently appeared.'

'Which are?'

'Recent outbreaks of anti-semitism throughout Europe and the United States . . .'

'There's no proved connection . . .'

M silenced him with a hand raised. '. . . And, secondly, we have one of them in the bag.'

'A member of the NSAA? Nobody's . . .'

'Announced it, or spoken, no. Under wraps tighter than a mummy's shroud.'

Bond asked if M's statement that 'we' had one meant literally the United Kingdom.

'Oh yes. He's here, in this very building. In the guest wing.' M made a single stabbing downward motion, to indicate the large interrogation centre in the basement. The Headquarters had been redesigned when government defence cuts had denied the Service its 'place in the country', where interrogations used to take place.

M continued, saying they had taken the man concerned 'after the last bit of business in London', which referred to the slaughter six months ago, in broad daylight, of three British Civil Servants who had just left the Soviet Embassy after some trade discussions. One of the assassins had tried to shoot himself as members of the SPG closed in.

'His aim was off.' M smiled without humour. 'We saw to it that he lived. Most of what we know is built around what he's told us.'

'He's talked?'

'Precious little.' M shrugged. 'But what he has said allows us to read between the lines. Very few people know about any of it, 007. I'm only telling you this much so that you won't doubt we're on the right track. We are 80 per cent certain that the NSAA is global, growing and, if not stopped at this stage, will eventually lead to an open movement, one which might become tempting to the electorates of many democracies. The Soviets have a vested interest, of course.'

'Why go along with them, then?'

'Because no intelligence service, from the Bundesnachrichten-dienst to the SDECE, has come up with any other clues . . .'

'So . . . ?'

'Nobody, that is, except the KGB.'

Bond did not move a muscle.

'They don't know what we've got, naturally,' M continued. 'But they've provided a clue of some magnitude. The NSAA armourer.'

Bond inclined his head. 'They've always used Russian stuff, so I presume . . .'

'Presume nothing, 007, that's one of the first rules of strategy. The KGB have persuasive evidence that the NSAA's equipment is cunningly stolen within the Soviet Union and shipped out, probably by a Finnish national, to various pick-up points. That's the reason they wanted it clandestine: without knowledge of the Finnish government.'

'And why us?' Bond was beginning to see light.

'They say', M began, 'it's because there has to be back-up from countries other than the Eastern bloc. The Israelis are pretty obvious, because Israel could be the next target. Britain and America would present a formidable front to the world if they were seen to be involved. They also say that it is in our common interest to share.'

'You believe them, sir?'

M gave a bland, unsmiling look. 'No. Not altogether; but I don't think it's meant to be anything sinister, like some complicated entrapment of three intelligence services.'

'And how long's Operation Icebreaker been running?'

'Six weeks. They asked for you particularly at the outset, but I wanted to test the ice, if you see what I mean.'

'And it's firm?'

'It'll carry your weight, 007. Or I think it will. After what happened in Helsinki, of course, there is a new danger.'

There was silence for a full minute. Far away, behind the heavy door, a telephone rang.

'The man you put in . . . ?' Bond broke the silence.

'Two men, really. Each organisation has a resident director holed up in Helsinki. It's the field man we're pulling out. Dudley. Clifford Arthur Dudley. Resident in Stockholm for some time.'

'Good man.' Bond lit another cigarette. 'I've worked with him.' Indeed, they had done a complicated surveillance and character assassination on a Romanian diplomat in Paris a couple of years before. 'Very nimble,' Bond added. 'Good all-rounder. You say there was a personality clash . . . ?'

M did not look at Bond directly. He rose and walked over to the window, clasping his hands behind his back as he gazed down across Regent's Park. 'Yes,' he said slowly. 'Yes. Punched our American ally in the mouth.'

'Cliff Dudley?'

M turned. He wore his sly look. 'Oh, he did it on my instructions. Playing for time, like I said, testing the ice – and waiting for you to get acclimatised, if you follow.'

Again a silence, broken by Bond. 'And I'm to join the team.'

'Yes.' M seemed to have gone a little absent-minded. 'Yes, yes. They've all pulled out. You're to meet them as soon as possible. I've chosen the rendezvous, incidentally. How do you fancy Reid's Hotel in Funchal, Madeira?'

'Better than a Lapp *kota* in the Arctic Circle, sir.'

'Good. Then we'll give you a full briefing here, and if you're up to it, we'll speed you on your way tomorrow night. I'm afraid the Arctic'll be your next stop after Madeira, though. Now, there's a lot of work to be done. You must realise this thing's not going to be a piece of cake, as they used to say in World War Two.'

'Not even Madeira cake?' asked Bond.

M actually gave a short laugh.

# 5

# RENDEZVOUS AT REID'S

In the event, Bond did not get away from London as quickly as expected. There was much to be prepared, and the doctors also insisted on a complete check-up. Then, too, Bill Tanner appeared with the trace results on Paula Vacker and her friend, Anni Tudeer.

There were a couple of interesting, and troubling, pieces of information. As it turned out, Paula was of Swedish birth, though she had assumed Finnish citizenship. Apparently her father had at one time been with the Swedish Diplomatic Corps, though a note listed him as having 'militant right-wing tendencies'.

'Probably means the man's a Nazi,' M grunted.

The thought worried Bond, but Bill Tanner's next words disturbed him even more.

'Maybe,' the Chief-of-Staff said, 'but her girlfriend's father certainly is, or was, a Nazi.'

What Tanner had to say made Bond yearn for an opportunity to see Paula again quickly, and, more particularly, to meet Anni Tudeer.

The computers had little on the girl, but they disgorged a great deal about her father, a former high-ranking officer in the Finnish Army. Colonel Aarne Tudeer had been, in fact, a member of Finland's C-in-C's – the great Marshal Mannerheim's – staff in 1943, and, in the same year, when the Finns fought side by side with the German Army against the Russians, Tudeer had accepted a post with the Waffen SS. Though Tudeer was a soldier first, it remained clear that his admiration for Nazi Germany, and, in particular, for Adolf Hitler, knew no bounds. By the end of 1943 Aarne Tudeer had been promoted to the rank of SS-Oberführer and moved to a post within the Nazi fatherland.

When the war ended, Tudeer disappeared, but there were definite indications that he remained alive. The Nazi-catchers still had him on the wanted list, for among the many operations in which he played a prominent part was the 'execution' of fifty prisoners of war, recaptured after the famous 'Great Escape' from Stalag Luft III, at Sagan in March 1944.

Later, Tudeer fought bravely during the historic, bloody march of the 2nd SS Panzer Division ('Das Reich') from Montauban to Normandy. It is well-known that, during those two weeks in June 1944, acts of unbridled horror were committed which defied the normal rules of war. One was the burning of 642 men, women, and children in the village of Oradour-sur-Glane. Aarne Tudeer had more than a hand in that particular episode.

'A soldier first, yes,' Tanner explained, 'but the man is a war criminal and as such, even though he's an old-age pensioner now, the Nazi-hunters are still after him. There were confirmed sightings in South America during the 1950s, but it's pretty certain he came back to Europe in the 1960s after a successful identity change.'

Bond filed the information in his head, asking for the chance to study any existing documents and photographs.

'There's no chance of me slipping back into Helsinki, seeing Paula and meeting the Tudeer woman, I suppose?' Bond looked hard at M, who shook his head.

'Sorry, 007. Time is of the essence. The whole team's come out of its operational zone for two reasons – first, to meet and brief you; second, to plan what they reckon's going to be the final stage in their mission. You see, they think they know where the arms are coming from, how they're being passed on to the

NSAA, and – most important – who is directing all NSAA ops, and from where.'

M refilled his pipe, settled back in his chair and began to talk. In many ways, what he revealed was enough to make Bond's hair stand on end.

They stayed at HQ until late that night, after which Bond was driven back to his Chelsea flat and the tender mercies of May, his redoubtable housekeeper, who took one look at him and ordered him straight to bed in the tones of an old-fashioned nanny. 'You look washed out, Mr James. To bed with you. I'll bring you a nice light supper on a tray. Now, away to your bed.'

Bond did not feel like arguing. May appeared soon afterwards with a dish of smoked salmon and scrambled eggs, which Bond ate while he looked through the pile of mail that had been waiting for him. He had scarcely finished the meal before fatigue took over and, without a struggle, he dropped into a deep refreshing sleep.

When he woke, Bond knew that May had allowed him to sleep late. The numbers on his digital bedside clock showed that it was almost ten. Within seconds he was calling for May to get breakfast. A few minutes later the telephone rang.

M was shouting for him.

The extra time spent in London paid dividends. Not only was Bond given a thorough rundown on his partners for Operation Icebreaker but he also had an opportunity to talk at length with Cliff Dudley, the officer from whom he was taking over.

Dudley was a short, hard, pugnacious Scot, a man whom Bond both liked and respected. 'If I'd had more time,' Dudley told him, 'likely I'd have sniffed out the whole truth. But it was really you they wanted. M made that clear to me before I went. Mind you, James, you'll have to keep your back to the wall. None of the others'll look out for you. Moscow Centre are definitely on to something, but it all stinks of duplicity. Maybe I'm just suspicious by nature, but their boy's holding something back.

He's got a dozen aces up his sleeve, and all in the same suit, I'll bet you.'

'Their boy', as Dudley called him, was not unknown to Bond, at least by reputation. Nicolai Mosolov had plenty of reputation, none of it particularly appetising. Known to his friends within the KGB as Kolya, Mosolov spoke English, American-English, German, Dutch, Swedish, Italian, Spanish and Finnish fluently. Now in his late thirties, the man had been a star pupil at the basic training school near Novosibirsk, and worked for some time with the expert Technical Support Group of his Service's Second Chief Directorate, which is, in effect, a professional burglary unit.

In the building overlooking Regent's Park they also knew Mosolov under a number of aliases. In the United States he was Nicholas S. Mosterlane, Sven Flanders in Sweden and other Scandinavian countries. They knew, but had never nailed him – not even as Nicholas Mortin-Smith in London.

'Invisible man type,' M said. 'Chameleon. Merges with his background and disappears just when you think he's bottled up.'

Bond was no happier about his American counterpart on Ice-breaker. Brad Tirpitz, known in intelligence circles as 'Bad' Brad, was a veteran of the old-school CIA and had survived the multi-tude of purges in his organisation's headquarters at Langley, Virginia. To some, Tirpitz was a kind of swashbuckling, do-or-die, hero: a legend. There were others, however, who saw him in a different light – as the sort of field officer capable of using highly questionable methods, a man who considered that the end always justified the means. And the means could be, as one of his colleagues put it, 'Pretty mean. He has the instinct of a hungry wolf, and the heart of a scorpion.'

So, Bond thought, his future lay with a Moscow Centre heavy and a Langley sharp-shooter who tended to shoot first and ask questions later.

The rest of the briefing, and the medical, took the remainder of that day, and some of the following morning. So it was not until the afternoon of this third day that Bond boarded the two o'clock TAP flight to Lisbon, connecting with one of the Boeing 727 shuttles to Funchal.

The sun was low, almost touching the water, throwing great warm red blotches of colour against the rocks, when Bond's aircraft – now down to around 600 feet – crossed the Ponta de São Lourenço headland to make that exhilarating low-level turn which is the only way to get into the precarious little runway – perched, like an aircraft carrier's flight deck, among the rocks – at Funchal.

Within the hour a taxi deposited him at Reid's Hotel, and the following morning found him searching for either Mosolov, Tirpitz, or the third member of the Icebreaker group – the Mossad agent whom Dudley had described as, 'An absolutely deadly young lady, around five-six, clear skin, the figure's copied from the Venus de Milo, only this one's got both arms, and the head's different.'

'How different?' Bond had asked.

'Stunning. Late twenties, I'd say. Very, very good. I'd hate to be up against her . . .'

'In the professional sense, of course.' Bond could not resist the quip.

As far as M was concerned, the Israeli agent was an unknown quantity. The name was Rivke Ingber. The file said 'Nothing known'.

So now James Bond looked out over the hotel's twin swimming pools, his eyes shaded by sunglasses, as he searched faces and bodies.

For a moment his gaze fell on a tall, arresting blonde, in a Cardin bikini, whose body defied normal description. Well, Bond thought as the girl plunged into the warm water, there's no law against looking. He shifted his body on the sun lounger, wincing slightly at the ache in his now rapidly healing shoulder, and continued to watch the girl swimming, her lovely long legs opening and closing while her arms moved lazily in an act of almost conscious sensuality.

Bond smiled once more at M's choice for the rendezvous. Reid's remains one of the few hotels, among the package tour traps which run from Gran Canaria to Corfu, which has maintained standards – of cuisine and service – dating back to the 1930s. The hotel shop sells reminders of the old days – photographs of Sir Winston and Lady Churchill taken in the lush gardens. Lath-straight elderly men, with clipped moustaches, sit reading in the airy public rooms; young couples, dressed by YSL and Kenzo, rub shoulders with elderly titled ladies on the famous tea terrace. He was, Bond considered, in 'the Butler Did It' territory; undoubtedly M's cronies came to this idyllic time warp with the regularity of a Patek Philippe wristwatch.

As he lay there, Bond covered the pool and sunbathing area with carefully regulated sweeps of the eye. No sign of Mosolov. No sign of Tirpitz. He could recognise those two easily enough from the photographs studied in London. There had been no photograph of Rivke Ingber, and Cliff Dudley had merely smiled knowingly, telling Bond he would find out what she looked like soon enough.

People were now drifting towards the pool restaurant, open on two sides and protected by pink stone arches. Tables were laid, waiters hovered, a bar beckoned, and a long buffet had been set up to provide every conceivable kind of salad and cold meats, or – if the client so fancied – hot soup, quiche, lasagne or cannelloni.

Lunch. Bond's old habits followed him faithfully to Madeira. The warm air and sun of the morning watch now produced that pleasant need for something light at lunch-time. Putting on a towelling robe, Bond padded to the buffet, selected some thin slices of ham, and began to choose from the array of colourful salads.

'Don't you fancy a drink, Mr Bond? To break the ice?' Her voice was soft and unaccented.

'Miss Ingber?' Bond did not turn to look at her.

'Yes, I've been watching you for some time – and I think you me. Shall we have lunch together? The others have also arrived.'

Bond turned. It was the spectacular blonde he had seen in the pool. She had changed into a dry black bikini, and the visible flesh glowed bronze, the colour of autumn beech leaves. The contrast of colours – skin, the thin black material and the striking, gold curls cut close – made Rivke Ingber look not only acutely desirable, but also an object lesson in health and body care. Her face shone with fitness, unblemished, classical, almost Nordic – with a strong mouth and dark eyes in which a spirit of humour seemed to dance almost seductively.

'Well,' Bond admitted, 'you've outflanked me, Ms Ingber. *Shalom.*'

'*Shalom*, Mr Bond . . .' The pink mouth curved into a smile which appeared open, inviting and completely genuine.

'Call me James.' Bond made a small mental note of the smile.

She was already holding a plate carrying a small portion of chicken breast, some sliced tomatoes, and a salad of rice and apples. Bond gestured towards one of the nearby tables. She walked ahead of him, her body supple, the slight swing of her hips almost wanton. Carefully placing her plate on the table, Rivke Ingber automatically gave her bikini pants a tiny hitch, then ran her thumbs inside the rear of the legs, setting them over her high, neat buttocks. It was a gesture, performed naturally and without thought countless times each day by women on beaches and around swimming pools; but, executed by Rivke Ingber, the movement became a tantalising, overtly sexual invitation.

Now, sitting opposite Bond, she gave her smile again, running the tip of her small tongue across her upper lip. 'Welcome aboard, James. I've wanted to work with you for a long time –' a slight pause – 'which is more than I can say about our colleagues.'

Bond looked at her, trying to penetrate the dark eyes – an

unusual feature in a woman of Rivke's colouring. His fork was poised between plate and mouth as he asked, 'That bad?'

'Worse than that,' she said. 'I suppose you were told why your predecessor left us?'

'No.' Bond gazed at her innocently. 'All I know is that I was suddenly whisked on to this, with little time for briefings. They said the team – which seems a pretty odd mix to me – would give me the detailed story.'

She laughed again. 'There was what you might call a personality clash. Brad Tirpitz was being his usual boorish self, at my expense. Your man belted him in the mouth. I was a little put out. I mean, I could have dealt with Tirpitz myself.'

Bond took the mouthful of food, chewed and swallowed, then asked about the operation.

Rivke gave him a little flirtatious look, from under slightly lowered eyelids. 'Oh,' a finger mockingly to her lips, 'that's a no-no. Bait – that's what I am. I'm to lure you in to the pair of experts. We *all* have to be present at your briefing. To tell you the truth, I don't think they take me very seriously.'

Bond smiled grimly. 'Then they've never heard the most important saying about your service . . .'

'We are good at our task because the alternative is too horrifying to contemplate.' She spoke the words on a flat note, almost parrot-like.

'And are *you* good, Rivke Ingber?' Bond chewed another mouthful.

'Can a bird fly?'

'Our colleagues must be very stupid, then.'

She sighed. 'Not stupid, James. Chauvinists. They're not noted for their confidence in working with women, that's all.'

'Never had that trouble myself.' Bond's face remained blank.

'No. So I've heard.' Rivke suddenly sounded prim. Maybe it was even a 'keep off' sign.

'So. We don't talk about Icebreaker.'

She shook her head. 'Don't worry, you'll get enough of that when we go up to see the boys.'

Bond detected a hint of warning even in the way she looked at him. It was as though the possibility of friendship had been offered, then suddenly withdrawn. Just as quickly, Rivke became her old self, the dark eyes locking on to Bond's.

They finished their light meal without Bond attempting to touch on the subject of Icebreaker again. He talked about her country – which he knew well – and of its many problems, but did not try to advance the conversation into her private life.

'Time to meet the big boys, James.' She dabbed at her lips with a napkin, her eyes darting up towards the hotel.

Mosolov and Tirpitz had probably been watching them from their balcony, Rivke said. They had rooms next to each other on the fourth floor, with both balconies giving good views of the gardens, and sight-lines which allowed constant surveillance of the swimming pool area.

They went off to separate changing rooms, emerging in suitable clothes: Rivke in a dark pleated skirt and white shirt; Bond in his favourite navy slacks, a Sea Island cotton shirt, and moccasins. Together, they entered the hotel and took the elevator to the fourth floor.

'Ah, Mr James Bond.'

Mosolov was as nondescript as the experts maintained. He could have been any age – from mid-twenties to late forties.

'Kolya Mosolov,' he said, taking Bond's hand. The handshake was neither one thing nor the other, and the eyes – a clouded grey – looked dull, not meeting Bond's gaze with any certainty.

'Glad to be working with you.' Bond gave his most charming smile, while taking in what he could of the man – on the short side, blond hair cut with no style, but paradoxically neat. No character – or so it would seem – in either the man or his clothes: a short-sleeved brown check shirt, and slacks that looked as though they had been run up by an apprentice tailor on a particularly bad day, a face that appeared to change with moods, and in different lights, aging or shedding years.

Kolya indicated a chair, though Bond did not quite see how he did it – without gestures, or moving his body. 'Do you know Brad Tirpitz?' His English seemed flawless, even colloquial, with the slight hint of a London suburban accent.

The chair contained Tirpitz – a sprawled, large man with big, rough hands and a face chiselled, it appeared, out of granite. His hair was grey and cut short, almost to the scalp, and Bond was pleased to note the traces of bruising and a slight cut around the left side of the man's unusually small mouth.

Tirpitz lazily lifted a hand in a kind of salutation. 'Hi,' he grunted, the voice harsh, as though he had spent a lot of time getting his accent from tough-guy movies. 'Welcome to the club, Jim.'

Bond could detect no glimmer of welcome or pleasure in the man.

'Glad to meet you, *Mr* Tirpitz.' Bond paused on the *Mister*.

'Brad,' Tirpitz growled back. This time there was the hint of a smile around the corners of his mouth. Bond nodded.

'You know what this is all about?' Kolya Mosolov seemed to assume an almost apologetic mood.

'Only a little . . .'

Rivke stepped in, smiling at Bond. 'James tells me he was sent out here on short notice. No briefing from his people.'

Mosolov shrugged, sat down and indicated one of the other chairs. Rivke dropped on to the bed, curling her legs under her as though settling in.

Bond took the proffered chair, pushing it back against the wall into a position from which he could see the other three. It also gave him a good view of the window and balcony.

Mosolov took a deep breath. 'We haven't much time,' he began. 'We need to be out of here within forty-eight hours and back into the operational area.'

Bond gestured at the room. 'Is it quite safe to talk in here?'

Tirpitz gave a gruff laugh. 'Don't worry about it. We checked the place over. My room's next door; this one's on the corner of the building; and I sweep the place all the time.'

Bond turned back to Mosolov, who had waited patiently, almost subserviently, during the slight interruption. The Russian waited a second more before speaking: 'Do you think this strange? The CIA, Mossad, my people, and your people all working together?'

'Initially.' Bond appeared to relax. This was the moment M had warned him about. There was a possibility that Mosolov would hold certain matters back. If so, then he needed every ounce of extra caution. 'Initially I thought it strange, but, on reflection . . . well, we're all in the same business. Different outlooks, possibly, but no reason why we shouldn't work together for the common good.'

'Correct,' Mosolov said curtly. 'Then I'll give you the information in outline.' He paused, looked around him, giving a credible imitation of a near-sighted and somewhat vague academic. 'Rivke. Brad. Please add any points that you think I have omitted.'

Rivke nodded and Tirpitz laughed unpleasantly.

'All right.' The transmogrification trick again: Kolya changed from the slow professor into the sharp executive; decisive, in control. He was a joy to watch, Bond thought. 'All right. I'll give it to you quickly and straight. This – as you probably *do* know, Mr Bond – concerns the National Socialist Action Army: a proven threat to my country and to your countries too. Fascists in the old mould.'

Tirpitz gave his unpleasant laugh again. 'Mouldy old Fascists.'

Mosolov ignored him. It appeared to be the only way to deal with Brad Tirpitz's wisecracks. 'I am not a fanatic.' Mosolov dropped his voice. 'Nor am I obsessed by the NSAA. However, like your governments, I believe this organisation to be large and growing every day. It is a threat . . .'

'You can say that again.' Brad Tirpitz took out a pack of

Camels, thumped the end against his thumb, extracted a cigarette and lit it, using a book match. 'Let's cut through it, Kolya. The National Socialist Action Army's got you Soviets scared shitless.'

'A threat', Kolya continued, 'to the world. Not just to Soviet Russia and the Eastern bloc.'

'You're their main target,' Tirpitz grunted.

'And we're implicated, Brad, as you know. That's why my government approached your people. And Rivke's and Mr Bond's governments.' He turned back to Bond. 'As you may, or may not, know, all the arms used in operations carried out by the NSAA come from a Soviet source. The Central Committee were informed of this only after the fifth incident. Other governments and agencies suspected we were supplying arms to some organisation – possibly Middle Eastern – which was, in turn, passing them on. This was not so. The information solved a problem for us.'

'Someone had his fingers in the till,' Brad Tirpitz interjected.

'True,' Mosolov snapped. 'Last spring, during a spot inspection of stores – the first for two years – a senior officer of the Red Army discovered a huge discrepancy: an inexplicable loss of armaments. All from one source.' He rose, walked across the room to a briefcase and took out a large map, which he spread on the carpet.

'Here.' His finger pointed at the paper. 'Here, near Alakurtii, we have a large ordnance depot . . .'

Alakurtii lay some sixty kilometres east of the Finnish border, well into the Arctic Circle – about two hundred-plus kilometres north-east of Rovaniemi, where Bond had based himself during his recent expedition.

Kolya continued. 'During last winter that particular ordnance depot was raided. We were able to identify all the serial numbers of weapons used by the NSAA. They definitely came from Alakurtii.'

Bond asked what was missing.

Kolya's face went deadpan as he rattled off a list: 'Kalashni-kovs; RPKs; AKs; AKMs; Makarov and Stetchkin pistols; RDG–5 and RG–42 grenades . . . A large number, with ammunition.'

'Nothing heavier than that?' Bond made it sound casual, an off-the-cuff response.

Mosolov shook his head. 'It's enough. They disappeared in great quantities.'

First black mark, Bond thought. He already knew from M – who had his own sources – that Kolya Mosolov had omitted the most significant weapons: a large number of RPG – 7V Anti-Tank launchers, complete with rockets that carried several different kinds of warheads – conventional, chemical, and tactical nuclear – large enough to wreck a small town and devastate a fifty-mile radius from point of impact.

'This equipment disappeared during the winter, when we keep a small garrison at Base Blue Hare, as we call the depot. The Colonel who made the discovery used his common sense. He told nobody at Blue Hare, but reported straight back to the GRU.'

Bond nodded. That figured: the Glavnoye Razvedy-vatelnoye Upravleniye – Soviet Military Intelligence, an organisation linked umbilically with the KGB – would be the natural source to be informed.

'The GRU put in a pair of monks – that's what they like to call undercover men working in government offices, or army units.'

'And they lived up to their holy orders?' Bond asked without a smile.

'More than that. They've located the ringleaders – greedy NCOs being paid off by some outside source.'

'So,' Bond interrupted, 'you know how the stuff was stolen . . .'

Kolya smiled. 'How, and the direction in which it was moved. We're fairly certain that, last winter, the consignment was taken over the Finnish border. It's a difficult frontier to cover, though parts are mined, and we've cut away miles of trees. People still come in and go out every day. That's the way we believe the stuff went.'

'You don't know the first destination, then?' It was Bond's second testing question.

Mosolov hesitated. 'We're not certain. Our satellites are trying to pinpoint a possible location, and our people have their eyes open for the prime suspect. But the facts are still unclear.'

James Bond turned to the others. 'And is it just as uncertain to you two?'

'We only know what Kolya's told us,' Rivke said calmly. 'This is a friendly operation of trust.'

'Langley have given me a name nobody's mentioned yet, that's all.' Brad Tirpitz was obviously not going to say more, so Bond asked Mosolov if he had a name to say aloud.

There was a long pause. Bond waited for the name which M had given him on the last night, in that office high on the ninth floor of the building overlooking Regent's Park.

'It's so uncertain . . .' Mosolov did not wish to be drawn.

Bond opened his mouth to speak again, but Kolya quickly added: 'Next week. By this time next week we may well have it all sewn up. Our GRU monks report that another consignment is to be stolen. That's why we have little time. As a team, our job is to gain evidence of the theft, then follow the route by which the arms are removed – right up to their final destination.'

'And you think the man who'll receive them will be Count Konrad von Glöda?' Bond gave a broad smile.

Kolya Mosolov did not show any signs of emotion or surprise.

Brad Tirpitz chuckled. 'London has the same information as Langley, then.'

'Who's von Glöda?' Rivke asked, not attempting to disguise her shock. 'Nobody's mentioned any Count von Glöda to me.'

Bond removed the gunmetal cigarette case from his hip pocket, placed a slim white H. Simmons cigarette between his lips, lit it, inhaled smoke, then let it out in a long thin stream. 'My people – and the CIA too, it would appear – have information that the principal acting on behalf of the NSAA, in Finland, is a Count Konrad von Glöda. That true, Kolya?'

Mosolov's eyes still remained cloudy. 'It's a code name. A cryptonym, that's all. There was no point giving you that information yet.'

'Why not? Are you hiding anything else, Kolya?' Bond did not smile this time.

'Only that I would hope to lead you to von Glöda's retreat in Finland next week when we carry out our surveillance on Blue Hare, Mr Bond. I had also hoped you would accompany me into Russia to see it all for yourself.'

James Bond could hardly believe it. A KGB man was actually inviting him into the spider's web, under the pretext of witnessing the theft of a large quantity of arms. And there was no way, now, in which he could tell whether Kolya Mosolov meant it to be a genuine part of Operation Icebreaker, or whether Icebreaker was merely some carefully dreamed-up device to trap Bond on Soviet soil.

It was the latter possibility that M had warned Bond about, before 007 had left for Madeira.

# 6

# YELLOW vs SILVER

The four members of the Icebreaker team had arranged to meet for dinner, but Bond had other ideas. M's warnings of duplicity among the uneasy quartet had been made all too apparent at the short briefing in Kolya's room.

If it had not been for the nudge from Brad Tirpitz, the name of Count Konrad von Glöda would not have been mentioned; and, according to M, this mystery man was a key figure in any combined security investigation. Nor had Kolya bothered to give him full details of the more dangerous items missing from the Russian Blue Hare Ordnance Depot.

While Brad Tirpitz was obviously as well-informed as Bond, it seemed that Rivke remained very much in the dark. The whole projected operation – including the business of surveying a second large theft from the Russian side of the border – did not bode well.

Although the dinner meeting was agreed, Kolya had been insistent that all four members of Icebreaker should be off the island, heading back into the operational area in Finland, within the next forty-eight hours. A rendezvous had even been given, and accepted by all.

Bond knew there were things he had to do before joining the others in the bitter climate of the Arctic Circle. There were several flights out of Madeira on the Sunday morning, so doubtless Kolya would make suggestions – at dinner – as to how they should split up and travel separately. But James Bond was certainly not going to wait on Kolya Mosolov's instructions.

On leaving the room, he made his excuses to Rivke – who wanted him to have a drink with her in the bar – and made for his own quarters. Within fifteen minutes, James Bond was on his way in a cab to Funchal Airport.

There followed a long wait. It was Saturday, and he had missed the three o'clock flight. He didn't get away until the last aircraft of the night – the ten o'clock, which, at that time of year, runs only on Wednesdays, Fridays and Saturdays.

During the flight, Bond reflected on his next move, knowing that his colleagues would almost certainly begin arriving in Lisbon after the first aircraft out on Sunday. Bond preferred to be away, heading towards Helsinki, long before any of them reached the mainland.

His luck held. Technically there were no flights out of Lisbon after the final aircraft from Funchal. But the afternoon KLM service to Amsterdam had been badly delayed because of weather conditions in Holland, and there was a spare seat.

Bond finally made Schiphol Airport, Amsterdam, at four in the morning. He took a cab straight to the Hilton International, where even at that early hour, he was able to book a seat on the Finnair 846, leaving for Helsinki at five-thirty that evening.

In his room, Bond quickly checked his overnight bag and the customised briefcase, with its hidden compartments for the two Sykes Fairburn commando knives, and the Heckler & Koch P7 automatic, all screened so that they would not show up on airport X-ray machines or during security examinations – a device which the Armourer's assistant in Q Branch, Ann Reilly – known to all as Q'ute – had perfected to such a degree that she was loath to give even members of her own department the technical details.

After some argument, mainly from Bond, the Armourer had agreed on Heckler & Koch's P7, 'squeeze cocking', 9mm automatic in preference to the rather cumbersome VP70, with its long 'double action' pull for each shot. The weapon was lighter and more like his old beloved Walther PPK, now banned by the security services.

Before taking a shower and going to bed, Bond sent a fast-rate cable to Erik Carlsson, in Rovaniemi, with instructions about his Saab; then he ordered a call for eleven-fifteen, with breakfast.

He slept peacefully, even though, in the back of his mind, the problems regarding Mosolov, Tirpitz and Ingber – particularly Mosolov – nagged away. He woke, refreshed, but with those thoughts uppermost.

Adhering to his usual scrambled eggs, bacon, toast, marmalade and coffee, Bond finished breakfast before dialling the London number where he knew M would be found on a Sunday morning. There followed a conversation using a double-talk, which was standard, so far as Bond and his chief were concerned, when it came to open telephone calls in the field.

Once contact had been established, Bond gave M the outline details: 'I talked to the three customers, sir. They're interested, but I cannot be altogether certain they'll buy.'

'They tell you everything about their plans?' M sounded uncommonly young on the telephone.

'No. Mr East was decidedly cagey about the Principal we spoke of. I must say Virginia seemed to know most of the details, but Abrahams appeared to be completely in the dark.'

'Ah.' M waited.

'East is keen for me to go and see the source of the last shipment. He says there's another due out any time.'

'That's quite possible.'

'But I have to tell you he did *not* give me the full details of that last consignment.'

'I suggested he might hold back.' You could almost see M smile with the satisfaction of having been right.

'Anyway, I'm moving north again late this afternoon.'

'You have any figures?' M asked, giving Bond the opportunity to provide a map reference of the proposed meeting point.

He had already worked out the reference, so rattled off the figures, repeating them to give M the opportunity to jot down the numbers, which were purposely jumbled, each pair being reversed.

'Right,' M answered. 'Going by air?'

'Air and road. I've arranged for the car to be waiting.' Bond hesitated. 'There's one more thing, sir.'

'Yes?'

'You remember the lady? The one we had the problem with – sharp as a knife?'

'Yes.'

'Well, her girlfriend. The one with the funny father.' His reference was to Anni Tudeer.

M grunted an affirmative.

'I'll need a photograph for recognition.'

'I don't know. Could be difficult. Difficult for you as well as us.'

'I'd appreciate it, sir. I really think it's vital.'

'See what I can do.' M did not sound convinced.

'Just send it if you can. Please, sir.'

'Well . . .'

'If you can. I'll be in touch when there's more.' Bond rang off abruptly. There it was again – a reluctance in M: something he had not experienced before. It had been there when Rivke Ingber was mentioned during the London briefing. Now it was back at the first hint of positive ID on Anni Tudeer who, to Bond, was simply a name mentioned by Paula Vacker.

The Finnair DC9–50 that was Flight 846 from Amsterdam to Helsinki began its final approach at 9.45 that evening. Looking down on the lights, diffused by the cold and snow, Bond wondered if the other three had already reached Finland. In the short time since his last visit more snow had fallen, and the aircraft put down on an ice-cleared runway which was, in reality, a cutting through snow banks rising on either side, higher than the DC9–50 itself.

From the moment Bond walked into the terminal building, his senses went into high gear. Not only did he watch for signs of his three partners, but also for any other possible tail. He had good reason to remember his last brush, with the two killers, in this beautiful city.

Bond now took a cab to the Hesperia Hotel – a calculated choice. He wanted to do the journey to their RV on his own, and it was quite possible that Mosolov, Tirpitz and Rivke Ingber were, separately, already en route and in the Finnish capital. If any member of the group were looking for Bond, the Inter-Continental would almost certainly be watched.

With these thoughts in mind, Bond took great care about the way in which he moved – giving himself time to look around as he paid off the cab; waiting, for a moment, outside the main doors of the hotel; checking the foyer the moment he stepped inside.

Even now, while asking the girl at Reception about the Saab Turbo, Bond managed to place himself at a vantage point.

'You have a car here, I believe. A Saab 900 Turbo. Silver. Delivered in the name of Bond. James Bond.'

The girl at the long reception desk gave an irritated frown, as though she had better things to do than check on cars delivered to the hotel on behalf of foreign guests.

Bond registered for one night and paid in advance, but he had no intention of spending the night in Helsinki if the car had arrived. The journey from Rovaniemi to Helsinki at this time of the year took around twenty-four hours: that was providing there were no blizzards, and the roads did not become blocked. Erik Carlsson should make it easily, with his great skill and experience as a former rally driver.

He had made it, in staggering time. Bond had expected a wait, but the girl at the desk said the car was here, waving the keys as if to prove the point.

In his room, Bond took a one hour nap and then began to prepare for the work ahead. He changed into Arctic clothing – a track suit over Damart underwear, quilted ski pants, Mukluk boots, a heavy rollneck sweater and the blue padded cold-weather jacket, produced by *tol-ma oy* in Finland for Saab. Before slipping into the jacket, he strapped on the holster – especially designed by Q Branch – for the Heckler & Koch P7. This adjustable holster could be fitted in a variety of positions, from the hip to shoulder. This time, Bond tightened the straps so that it lay centrally across his chest. He checked the P7, loaded it, and slid several spare magazines – each with ten rounds – into the pockets of his jacket.

The briefcase contained everything else he might need – apart from the clothes in his overnight bag – and any other necessary armament, tools, flares, and various pyrotechnic devices were in the car.

While dressing, Bond dialled Paula Vacker's number. It rang twenty-four times without answer, so he tried the office number, knowing in his heart of hearts that there would be nobody there, not on a Sunday night at this late hour.

Cursing silently – for Paula's absence meant an extra chore before he left – Bond completed dressing: he slid a Damart hood over his head, topped it with a comfortable woolly hat, and protected his hands with thermal driving gloves. He also slipped a woollen scarf around his neck and pocketed a pair of goggles, knowing that, if he had to leave the car in sub-zero temperatures, it was essential to cover all areas of his face and hands.

Finally Bond rang reception to say he was checking out, then went straight to the parking area, where the silver 900 Turbo gleamed under the lights.

The main case went into the hatchback boot, where Bond checked that everything was loaded as he had asked: the spade; two boxes of field rations; extra flares; and a large Pains-Wessex 'Speedline' line-throwing pack, which would deliver 275 metres of cable over a distance of 230 metres with speed and accuracy.

Already Bond had opened the front of the car, in order to turn off the anti-intruder and tamper alarm switches. He now went forward again to go through the rest of the equipment: the secret compartments which contained maps, more flares and the big new Ruger Redhawk .44 Magnum revolver which was now his additional armament – a man-stopper, and, also, if handled correctly, a car-stopper.

At the press of one of the innocent-looking buttons on the dashboard, a drawer slid back, revealing half a dozen egg-shaped, so-called 'practice grenades', which are, in reality, stun grenades used by British Special Forces. At the rear of this 'egg box' there lay four more lethal hand bombs – the L2A2s that are standard British Army equipment, derived from the American M26s.

Opening the glove compartment, Bond saw that his compass was in place, together with a little note from Erik: *Good luck whatever you're doing*, to which he had added, *Remember what I've taught you about the left foot! Erik.*

Bond smiled, recalling the hours he had spent with Carlsson learning left foot braking techniques, to spin and control the car on thick ice.

Lastly he walked around the Saab to be certain all the tyres were correctly studded. It was a long drive to Salla – something like a thousand kilometres: easy enough in good weather, but a slog in the ice and snow of winter.

Running through the control check like a pilot before take-off, Bond switched on the head-up display unit, modified and fitted from the Saab Viggen fighter aircraft. The illuminated display gave digital speed and fuel readings, as well as showing the graded converging lines which would help a driver to steer safely – tiny radar sensors indicating any snowdrifts, or piles, to left and right, thereby eliminating the possibility of ploughing into any deep or irregular snow.

Before leaving for Salla, he had one personal call to make. He started the engine, reversed, then took the car up the ramp into the main street, turning down the Mannerheimintie, and heading towards Esplanade Park.

The snow statues were still decorating the park; the man and woman remained clamped in their embrace; and, as he locked the car, Bond thought he could hear, far away across the city, a cry like an animal in pain.

Paula's door was closed, but there was something odd. Bond was aware of it immediately: that extra sense which comes from long experience. He quickly unclipped two of the centre studs on his jacket, giving access to the Heckler & Koch. Placing the ungainly rubber toe of his right Mukluk boot against the outer edge of the door, he applied pressure. The door swung back, loose on its hinges.

The automatic pistol was in Bond's hand in a reflex action the moment he saw the lock and chain had been torn away. From a quick glance, it looked like brute force – certainly not a sophisticated entrance. Stepping to one side, he stood holding his breath, listening. Not a sound, either from inside Paula's flat or from the rest of the building.

Slowly Bond moved forward. The flat was a shambles: furniture and ornaments broken and strewn everywhere. Still walking softly, and with the P7 firmly in his grip, he went towards the bedroom. The same thing. Drawers and cupboards had been opened, and clothes were scattered everywhere; even the duvet had been slashed to pieces with a knife. Going from room to room, Bond found the same wreckage, and there was no sign of Paula.

All Bond's senses told him to get out: leave it alone, maybe telephone the police once he was clear of Helsinki. It could be a straight robbery, or a kidnapping disguised to look like a burglary. A third possibility, though, was the most probable, for there was a paradoxical order among the chaos, the signs of a determined search. Somebody had been after a particular item.

Bond quickly went through the rooms a second time. Now

there were two clues – three if you counted the fact that the lights were all on when he arrived.

On the dressing table, which had been swept clear of Paula's rows of unguents and make-up, lay one item. Carefully Bond picked it up, turning it over and weighing it in his hand. A valuable piece of Second World War memorabilia? No, this was something more personal, more significant: a German Knight's Cross, hanging on the distinctive black, white and red ribbon, with an oak leaves and swords clasp. A high honour indeed. As he turned it, the engraving was clearly visible on the reverse side of the medal: 'SS-Oberführer Aarne Tudeer. 1944.'

Bond slipped the medal into one of the pockets of his jacket, and, as he turned away, heard a tinkling noise, as though he had kicked something metallic on the floor. He scanned the carpet and spotted the dull glow near the chrome leg of a bedside table. Another decoration? No, this was a campaign shield, again German: a dark bronze, surmounted by an eagle, the shield stamped with a rough map of the far north of Finland and Russia. At the top, one word: LAPLAND. The Wehrmacht shield for service in the far north, also engraved on the back, but dated 1943.

Bond put it in his pocket with the Knight's Cross and headed for the main door. There were no bloodstains anywhere and he could only hope that Paula was simply away on one of her many business, or pleasure, jaunts.

Back in the Saab, he turned up the heating and swung the car out of Esplanade Park. Going back up the Mannerheimintie he headed for Route 5, which would take him on the long trek north, skirting the cities of Lahti, Mikkeli, Varkaus and on into Lapland, the Arctic Circle, Kuusamo and then, just short of Salla, to the Hotel Revontuli, the RV arranged with the three other members of Icebreaker.

It had been bitterly cold when he left Paula's apartment building. There was the smell of snow in the air, and frost was almost visibly rising around the buildings of Helsinki.

Once clear of the city, Bond placed all his concentration on driving, pushing the car to its limits within the road and visibility conditions. The main Finnish roads are exceptional, even when you get far north; and there, in the depths of the winter, snow ploughs keep the main arteries open, though for most of the time as a solid surface of ice.

There was no moon, and for the next eight or nine hours Bond was conscious only of the glaring white, thrown back as his headlights hit the snow, suddenly dulling as great acres of fir trees, sheltered from snow, loomed ahead.

The others would be travelling by air, of that he was sure, but Bond wanted his own mobility, even though he knew it would have to be abandoned at Salla. If he was to cross the border with Kolya, they would have to move with great stealth through the forests, across lakes, and over the hills and valleys of the winter wasteland of the Circle.

The Saab's head-up display was invaluable – almost a complete guidance system, showing Bond the way the snow was banked on either side of the road. The farther north he travelled, the more sparse the villages, and, at this time of year, there were only a few hours that could be called daylight. The rest was either dusk, a seemingly perpetual dusk, or utter darkness.

He stopped twice, for petrol and a snack meal. By four in the afternoon – though it could well have been midnight – the Saab had taken him to within some forty kilometres of Suomussalmi. Now he was relatively close to the Russo-Finnish border, and within a few hours of the Arctic Circle. There was still a lot of driving to be done, though, and so far the weather conditions had not proved especially hostile.

Twice the Saab had run into patches of heavy snow, whipped into white and blinding whirlpools by strong winds. But each time Bond had pressed on, outrunning the blizzards, and praying they were isolated. They were; yet so strange was the weather that he had also encountered sudden rises in temperature which set up misty conditions, slowing him even more than the snow.

There were times when the Saab travelled on long flat stretches of iced road, through small communities going about their daily round – lights bright in shops, muffled figures stomping along pavements, women pulling tiny plastic sledges behind them, piled high with groceries bought at small supermarkets. Then, once out of the town or village, there seemed to be nothing but the endless landscape of snow and trees, the occasional heavy lorry, or car heading back towards the last town; or great monster log-bearing trucks, lumbering in either direction.

Fatigue came in small waves. Bond occasionally pulled over, allowing the bitter cold to enter the car for a few moments, then resting for a very short period. Occasionally he sucked a glucose tablet, blessing the comfort of the Saab's adjustable seating.

After some seventeen hours on the road, Bond found himself around thirty kilometres from the junction between Route 5 and the fork which would take him farther east, on the direct road running east-west between Rovaniemi and the border area of Salla. The fork itself is 150 kilometres east of Rovaniemi, and just over forty kilometres west of Salla.

The landscape picked up in his headlights remained unchanged – snow, blank to an unseen horizon; great forests, frosted with ice, suddenly turning to brown and a matt green, as though camouflaged, in sections which had escaped the full force of blizzards, or remained unaffected by the heavy frost. Occasionally, he glimpsed a clearing with the shape of a snow-covered *kota* – the Lapp wigwam, made of poles and skin, very similar to that of some North American Indians – or the wreckage of a log cabin, collapsed by the weight of snow.

Bond relaxed, fighting the wheel, correcting, alert to any sudden shift in control as he sent the Saab screaming on at a safe rate across the ice and packed snow. He could already smell success – arrival at the hotel without needing to use air transport. He might just get to their RV first, which would be a bonus.

He was on a lonely stretch now, with nothing but the fork in the road about ten kilometres ahead, and little between this point and Salla except for the odd Lapp camp or deserted summer log cottages. He slackened speed to take a long curve in the road and, as he rounded the bend, was conscious of a turning to his right, and some lights ahead. Bond flicked down the headlight beams, then up again, for a second, to see what was ahead. In the dazzle he caught sight of a giant yellow snow plough, its lights on full and the great bow of the plough like that of a warship.

This was not a modern snow-blower, but the more sturdy kind of monster. The snow plough they used mainly in this part of the world had a great high body, with a thick glass cabin on top, giving maximum view. The body was driven by wide caterpillar tracks, like those on self-propelled field artillery; while the actual plough was operated, ahead of the vehicle, by a series of hydraulic pistons which could alter angle or height in a matter of seconds.

As for the ploughs on these massive machines, they were sharp steel, V-shaped bows, some ten feet high, curving back from the cutting edge so that the snow and ice were forced to each side, then tossed away by the sheer momentum of the blade's attack.

Though they appeared cumbersome, the machines could reverse, traverse and turn with the ability of a heavy tank. What was more, they were specifically designed to remain mobile in the worst possible winter conditions.

The Finns had long since conquered the problems of snow and ice on their main arterial roads, and these brutes were often followed by the big snow-blowers to clean up after the first devastating assault on deep snow and ice.

Damn, Bond thought. Where there were snow ploughs there would almost certainly be the remnants of a blizzard. Silently he cursed, for it would be bad luck, having already outrun two blizzards, to be caught in the aftermath of a third.

Changing down, he glanced into his mirror. Behind him, with

its lights also full on, a second plough appeared – presumably from the turning he had just passed.

He allowed the car to coast, then picked up the engine again, edging gently forward. If there were bad falls of snow ahead, and even off to the east, he wanted to pull over as far as possible and allow the great juggernaut complete right of passage.

As he pulled over, Bond realised the plough ahead was holding the centre of the road. Another glance in the mirror told him the plough behind was doing the same thing. In that instant, Bond felt the hair on the nape of his neck prickle with the sensed danger. He passed a crossroads and one glance to the right told him the road was relatively clear. These ploughs, therefore, were not out on their normal job: their purpose was more sinister.

Bond was only three seconds past the crossroads when he acted, wrenching the wheel to the right, slamming his left foot hard on to the brake, feeling the back begin to swing into the inevitable skid, then gunning the accelerator and spinning the Saab in a controlled turn. In that instant, Bond had changed direction. Gently he increased the revs, correcting the back swing which would send him into a second spin across the coating of ice below him.

The plough which had been behind was considerably closer than he had judged, and, as he increased his own speed, concentrating on the feel of the car, ready to correct at the first hint of a developing swing, the solid metal hulk grew larger, bearing down on him as they closed.

He would be lucky to make the crossroads before the plough, and, though there was no time to look, Bond knew the other snow plough had also increased speed. If he did not reach the crossroads in time, either he would hit the snowbank at the side of the road – burying the Saab's nose deep so that the car would be at anyone's mercy – or the two ploughs would catch him, front and rear, crushing the car between their knife-like curved blades.

One hand left the wheel for a second, to punch at two of the buttons on the dashboard. There was a quiet hiss as the hydraulic system opened two of the hidden compartments. Now the grenades and his Ruger Super Redhawk were within reach. So were the crossroads. Straight ahead.

The snow plough in front of him, burning yellow and steel in Bond's headlights, was about twelve metres from the intersection. Feinting like a boxer, Bond started to turn right. He saw the plough grind to its left, pounding out speed in an attempt to cut into the Saab as it took the right-angled turn.

Then, at almost the last moment, when he had all but committed himself to the turn, Bond swung the wheel even harder right, left-footed on to the brake again, and once more increased the revs, tramping down on the accelerator.

The car spun like an aircraft, Bond's feet coming off both brake and accelerator at the same moment, just as the vehicle was halfway through the spin and starting to move, broadside on, lining up with the road opposite – the road that would have been his left turn.

Correcting the steering, and slowly increasing the revs, Bond felt the car react, like a perfectly controlled animal, the rear sliding slightly. Correct. Slide. Correct. Accelerator. Then he was on line, moving comfortably forward with the huge bulk of the two snow ploughs rising to his right and left.

As he cleared the blade of the more dangerous plough – now on his right – Bond snatched at the grenades, doing the unforgivable and ripping the pin from an L2A2 with his teeth as he part-opened the driving door to drop it clear, and in his wake. The bitter air blasted into the car as Bond struggled to slam the door shut. Then he felt the shudder as the Saab's rear grazed the steel blade of the plough to his right.

For a second, he thought the touch would throw him right off track and into the heavily piled snow on either side of the secondary road into which he was heading. But the car steadied and he regained control, hearing the snow piled at the side of the road spume upwards as his mudguards hit it. There was just enough room to take the car up the smaller road between the high white mounds. Then, from behind, came the crump of the grenade. A quick glance into the mirror – for he hardly dared take his eyes from the road and the head-up display – showed a dark red flower of flame coming from directly beneath one of the high yellow ploughs. With luck, the grenade would be enough to bog down that plough for ten minutes or so, while the other pushed it, incapacitated, out of the way.

In any case, Bond figured, even along this narrow, dangerous, snow-flanked gulley of a road, he could outrun any snow plough. That was, any snow plough behind him. He had not counted for yet another – dead ahead, spotlights splitting the darkness, dazzling him as it came, seemingly from nowhere. This time there was no place to hide.

Behind, with good fortune, one plough would be out of action and another ready to follow up as soon as the way was clear. Ahead, yet a third yellow monster came on, snow pluming from its bows. Presumably, Bond thought, there would be a fourth lying silent, with lights dowsed, along the other road of the cross.

Like some classic military armoured operation, someone had laid an ambush, strictly for Bond. Just at the right place, and the right time.

But he did not stop to work out the logic, or the intelligence, which might have led someone to set the trap. The yellow plough had locked lights with the Saab, but even through the dazzle, Bond could see the curved blade move downwards until it was just clipping the ice at the centre of the road, its bows still distributing the gathered snowdrifts away and behind it with the ease of a motorboat throwing off water at speed.

Mind racing, Bond pulled over as far as he dared and stopped the car. Staying inside now would be lunacy. Think of it as a military assault. He was cornered, and there was only one thing to be done – stop the snow plough bearing down on him.

The Redhawk, with its .44 Magnum punch – and fast double

action – was the handgun needed now. Bond grabbed it, stuffed two L2A2s into his jacket pockets, opened the door gently and, just before rolling low out of the car, grabbed at one of the stun grenades – 'flash-bangs' as the Special Air Service dubbed them.

The ground was hard, and the biting cold hit Bond like iced water as he rolled to the rear of the car and launched himself into the high snowdrift to the left. The snow was powdery and soft. In a second he was waist-deep and sinking. Bond kicked backwards, getting his legs into a kneeling position, still sinking until he was buried almost to the shoulders.

But this was a new and very different vantage point from which to fight. The dazzle of the snow plough's lights and the big spot above the cab was gone. Through his goggles, Bond could see two men at the controls, and the cumbersome vehicle shifting, aiming itself towards him. There was no doubt. They were going in for the kill prepared to slice the Silver Beast in half. Silver versus yellow, thought Bond, and raised his right arm, the left hand still clutching the stun grenade, wrist under right wrist to steady his aim.

His first shot took out the spotlight; the second shattered the glass screen of the plough's cabin. Bond had aimed high. He wanted no killing if it could be avoided.

One of the doors opened and a figure began to climb out. At that moment Bond lowered the Redhawk, switched it to his left hand in exchange for the stun grenade, pulled the pin and lobbed the hard green egg with all the force he could muster towards the shattered screen of the cab.

The grenade must have gone off right inside the cab. Bond heard the thunderclap, but averted his eyes. The flash would certainly cause temporary blindness, and the explosion might rupture the occupants' eardrums.

Holding the revolver high, Bond rolled himself out of the snowdrift, almost swimming his way out through the thick, heavy powder, until he could stand and move – with some caution – towards the plough.

One of the crew was lying unconscious beside the big machine: the man who had tried to jump clear, Bond reckoned. The other, in the driver's seat, had both arms over his face and rocked to and fro, moaning in harmony with the wind which screamed down the funnel of the road.

Bond found a grip, pulled himself up on to the driver's side, and tugged the cab door open. Some instinct must have told the driver of danger near by, for he cringed away. Bond clipped the man sharply on the back of the neck with the Ruger's barrel, and he went to sleep with no further argument.

Oblivious to the cold, Bond hauled the man down, dragging him around the front of the plough and dumping him next to his partner before returning to the cab. The snow plough's engine was running, and Bond felt as though he was sitting a mile above the wicked hydraulics and the great blade. The array of levers was daunting, but the engine still chugged away. All that concerned Bond was getting the brute off the road, or at least past the Saab and into a position in which it would block the remaining plough at the crossroads.

In the end it was simple. The normal mechanism worked with a wheel, clutch and throttle. It took Bond about three minutes to edge the giant down, past the Saab, and then across the road. He turned off the engine, removed the key and threw it out over the smooth snow dunes. The crew were both still unconscious, and would probably suffer from frostbite as well as the damage to their ears. That was little enough to pay, Bond thought, for having tried to carve him into a series of frozen joints.

Back in the car, he turned the heating full up to dry out, returned the Redhawk – after reloading – and the grenades to their respective hiding places, reset the buttons and consulted the map.

If the snow plough had come down the entire track, it should be clear right up to the main Salla road. Two hours' more driving and he would make it. In the end, it took almost three full hours, for the track twisted and doubled back on itself before reaching the direct road.

At ten past midnight, Bond finally spotted the big illuminated sign proclaiming the Hotel Revontuli. A few minutes later there was the turn-off and the large crescent building, with a great ski jump, chair lift and ski run, brightly lit, climbing up behind the structure.

Bond parked the car, surprised that within a few moments of turning off the engine, the screen and bonnet began to frost over. Even so it was difficult to believe the cold. In the open air Bond slipped the goggles into place, made certain his scarf covered his face, then, taking the briefcase and his overnight bag from the car, set the sensors and alarms and operated the central locking device.

The hotel was all modern carved wood and marble. A large foyer with a bar leading off. People talked, laughed and drank at the bar. As Bond trudged towards Reception, a familiar voice greeted him.

'Hi, James,' called Brad Tirpitz. 'What kept you? You ski the whole way?'

Bond nodded, pushing up the goggles and unwinding his scarf. 'Seemed a nice night for a walk,' he replied, straight-faced.

They were expecting him at Reception, so checking in took only a couple of minutes. Tirpitz had returned to the bar – where, Bond noted, he drank alone – and neither of the others was in view. Bond needed sleep. The plan was to meet up at breakfast each day until the whole team arrived.

A porter took his case, and he was just turning towards the lifts when the girl on duty at Reception said there was an express airmail package for him. It was a slim manila envelope with a stiff card backing.

Once the porter had left his room, Bond locked the door and slit open the envelope. Inside was a small plain sheet of paper and a photograph. M had written in his own hand: *This is the only available photograph of the subject. Please destroy.* Well, Bond thought, at least he would know what Anni Tudeer looked like. He dropped on to the bed and held up the photograph.

Bond's stomach turned over, then his muscles tensed. The face that stared back at him from the matt print was that of Rivke Ingber, his Mossad colleague. Anni Tudeer, Paula's friend, daughter of the Finnish Nazi SS officer still wanted for war crimes, was Rivke Ingber.

With painful slowness, James Bond took a book of matches from the ashtray by the bed, struck one and set both photograph and note on fire.

# 7

# RIVKE

For years Bond had nurtured the habit of taking cat naps and being able to control his sleep – even under stress. He had also acquired the knack of feeding problems into the computer of his mind, allowing the subconscious to work away while he slept. Usually he woke with a clear mind, sometimes with a new slant on difficulties, inevitably refreshed.

After the exceptionally long and hard drive from Helsinki, Bond felt natural fatigue, though his mind was active with a maze of conflicting puzzles.

There was nothing he could do immediately about the break-in, and wrecking, of Paula's Helsinki apartment. His main concern was for the girl's safety. In the morning, a couple of telephone calls should establish that.

Much more worrying was the attack on him by the snow ploughs. Since he had left Madeira quickly, dog-legging his way to Helsinki via Amsterdam, this attempt on his life meant only one thing. Someone was watching all points of entry into Finland. They must have picked him up at the airport and, later, had knowledge of his departure by car.

Someone obviously wanted him out of the game, just as they had wanted him out before he had even been briefed: hence the knife assault in Paula's apartment.

Dudley, who had filled in while M was waiting for Bond's return, had indicated his mistrust of Kolya Mosolov. Bond himself had other ideas, and the latest development – the discovery that Mossad's agent, Rivke Ingber, appeared to be the daughter of a wanted Finnish SS officer – was much more alarming.

Bond allowed these problems to penetrate his thoughts, as he showered and prepared for bed. Momentarily he considered food, then opted against it. Better fast until morning, when he would breakfast with the others – providing they had all arrived at the hotel.

He seemed to have been asleep for only a few minutes when the tapping broke through his consciousness. His eyes snapped open. The tapping continued – soft double raps at the door.

Without making a noise, Bond slipped the P7 from under his pillow and crossed the room. The tapping was insistent. The double rap, then a long pause followed by another double rap.

Keeping to the left of the door, his back against the wall, he whispered, 'Who's there?'

'Rivke. It's Rivke Ingber, James. I have to talk to you. Please. Please let me in.'

His mind cleared. There were several answers to the questions facing Bond when he went to sleep. One was so obvious that he had already taken it into account. If Rivke was, in fact, the daughter of Aarne Tudeer, there could easily be a link between her and the National Socialist Action Army. She must be only thirty years old, thirty-one at the most, which meant that her formative years had probably been spent in some hiding place with her father. If this was so then it was quite possible that Anni Tudeer was a neo-Fascist deep penetration agent working inside Mossad and that she may have been tipped off that the British were close to her true identity. It was also possible that she suspected Bond's colleagues would not be averse to withholding the information from the CIA and KGB. It had been done before, and Icebreaker was already proving to be an uneasy alliance.

Bond glanced at the illuminated dial of his Rolex Oyster Perpetual. It was four-thirty in the morning. Psychologically, Rivke could not have chosen a better moment.

'Hang on,' Bond whispered, recrossing the room to shrug himself into a towelling robe and replace the Heckler & Koch automatic under his pillow.

When he opened the door, Bond quickly decided she had come unarmed. There were very few places she could manage to hide anything in the outfit she wore: an opalescent white négligé hanging loose over a sheer, clinging matching nightdress. She would have been enough to make any man drop his guard, with her tanned body quite visible through the soft material, and the dazzling contrast of colour, underlined by the blonde shimmer of hair, and the eyes pleading in a hint of fear.

Bond allowed her into the room, locked the door, and stood back. Well, he thought, his gaze quickly travelling down her body, she is either an ultra-professional or a very natural blonde.

'Didn't even know you'd got to the hotel,' he said calmly. 'Welcome.'

'Thank you.' She spoke quietly. 'May I sit down, James? I'm terribly sorry to . . .'

'My pleasure. Please . . .' He indicated a chair. 'Can I send for anything? Or do you want a drink from the fridge?'

Rivke shook her head. 'This is so silly.' She looked around as though disorientated. 'So stupid.'

'You want to talk about it?'

A quick nod. 'Don't think me a complete fool, James, please. I'm really quite good with men, but Tirpitz . . . well . . .'

'You told me you could handle him, that you could have dealt with him before, when my predecessor thumped him.'

She was quiet for a moment, then, when she spoke it was a snap, a small explosion: 'Well, I was wrong, wasn't I? That's all there is to it.' She paused. 'Oh, I'm sorry, James. I'm supposed to be highly trained and self-reliant. Yet . . .'

'Yet Brad Tirpitz you can't handle?'

She smiled at Bond's mocking timbre replying in kind: 'He knows nothing of women.' Then her face tightened, the smile disappearing from the eyes. 'He really has been most unpleasant.

Tried to force his way into my room. Very drunk. Gave the impression he wasn't going to let up easily.'

'So, you didn't even hit him with your handbag?'

'He was really scary, James.'

Bond went over to the bedside table, picked up his cigarette case and lighter, offering the open case to Rivke, who shook her head as Bond lit up, blowing a stream of smoke towards the ceiling.

'It's out of character, Rivke.' He sat on the end of the bed, facing her, searching the attractive face for some hint of truth.

'I know.' She spoke very quickly. 'I know. But I couldn't stay alone in my room. You've no idea what he was like . . .'

'You're not a wilting flower, Rivke. You don't normally come running to the nearest male for protection. That's back-to-the-cave-dwellers stuff – everything people like you hate, and despise.'

'I'm sorry.' She made to get up, her anger almost tangible for a second. 'I'll go, and leave you in peace. I just needed company. The rest of this so-called team doesn't give anyone company.'

Bond put out a hand, touching her shoulder, quietly pushing her back into the chair. 'Stay, by all means, Rivke. But please don't take me for an idiot. You could handle Brad Tirpitz, drunk or sober, with a flick of your eyelashes . . .'

'That's not quite true.'

The ploy, Bond thought, dated back to the Garden of Eden, the oldest in the book. But who was he to argue? If a beautiful girl comes to your room in the middle of the night asking for protection – even though she is quite capable of looking after herself – she does so for one reason. But that was in the real world, not this maze of secrets and duplicity in which both Bond and Rivke lived and worked.

Taking another long pull on his cigarette, he made the vital decision. Rivke Ingber was alone in his room, and he knew who she really was. Before she made any other move it would, perhaps, be best for him to put the cards firmly on the table.

'A couple of weeks ago, Rivke, maybe even less – I seem to have lost all sense of time – did you do anything when Paula Vacker told you I was in Helsinki?'

'Paula?' She looked genuinely perplexed. 'James, I don't know . . .'

'Look, Rivke,' he leaned forward, taking her hands in his, 'our business breeds odd friends; and, sometimes, strange enemies. I don't want to become your enemy. But you need friends, my dear. You see, I know who you are.'

Her brow creased, the eyes becoming wary. 'Of course. I'm Rivke Ingber. I work for Mossad; and I'm an Israeli citizen.'

'You don't know Paula Vacker?'

There was no hesitation. 'I've met her. Yes, a long time ago I knew her quite well. But I haven't seen her for . . . Oh, it must be three, four years.'

'And you haven't been in touch with her lately?' Bond heard his own voice, slightly supercilious. 'You don't work with her in Helsinki? You didn't have a dinner date – which Paula cancelled – just before leaving for the Madeira meeting?'

'No.' Plain; open; straightforward.

'Not even under your real name? Anni Tudeer?'

She took a deep breath, then exhaled, as though trying to expel every ounce of air from her body. 'That's a name I like to forget.'

'I'll bet.'

She quickly pulled her hands away. 'Please James, I'll have that cigarette now.' Bond gave her one of his H. Simmons specials, lighting it for her. She inhaled deeply and allowed the smoke to trickle from her mouth. 'You seem to know so much; I should let you tell *me* the story.' Her voice was cold, all the friendly, even seductive, undertone gone.

He shrugged. 'I know only who you are. I also know Paula Vacker. She told me she'd confided in you that we were meeting in Helsinki. I went to Paula's apartment. There were a couple of knife experts keeping an eye on her and ready to treat me like a prime joint.'

'I've told you, Paula hasn't spoken to me in years. Apart from knowing my old name, and, presumably, the fact that I'm a former SS officer's daughter, what do you really know?'

Bond smiled. 'Only that you're very beautiful. I know nothing about you, except what you call your old name.'

She nodded, face set, mask-like. 'I thought so. All right, Mr James Bond, let me tell you the full story, so that you can set the record straight. After that, I think we'd both better try to find out what's going on – I mean what happened at Paula's . . . I'd like to know where Paula Vacker fits into all this.'

'Paula's flat was done over. I went there before leaving Helsinki yesterday. There was also a slight altercation with three – four – snow ploughs on my way here. The snow ploughs indicated they wanted to remodel my car, with me inside it. Somebody does not want me here, Anni Tudeer, or Rivke Ingber, whichever is your real name.'

Rivke frowned. 'My father was – is – Aarne Tudeer; that's true. You know his history?'

'That he was on Mannerheim's staff, and took the Nazis up on an offer to become an SS officer. Brave; ruthless; a wanted war criminal.'

She nodded. 'I didn't know about that part until I was around twelve years old.' She spoke very softly, but with a conviction Bond felt was genuine. 'When my father left Finland he took several of his brother officers, and some enlisted men, with him. In those days, as you know, there was a fair assortment of camp followers. On the day he left Lapland, my father proposed to a young widow. Good birth, had large holdings of land – forest mainly – in Lapland. My mother was part Lapp. She accepted, and volunteered to go with him, so becoming a kind of camp follower herself. She went through horrors you'd hardly believe.' She shook her head, as though still not crediting her own mother's actions. Tudeer had married on the day after leaving

Finland, and his wife stayed near him until the collapse of the Third Reich. Together they had escaped.

'My first home was in Paraguay,' Rivke told him. 'I knew nothing, of course. It wasn't until later I realised that I spoke four languages almost from the beginning – Finnish, Spanish, German and English. We lived in a compound in the jungle. Quite comfortable really, but the memories of my father are not pleasant.'

'Tell me,' Bond said. Little by little, he coaxed it out of her. It was, in fact, an old tale. Tudeer had been autocratic, drunken, brutal, and sadistic.

'I was ten years old before we escaped – my mother and I. To me it was a kind of game: dressed up as an Indian child. We got away by canoe, and then, with the help of some Guarani, made it to Asunción. My mother was a very unhappy lady. I don't know how it was managed, but she got passports for both of us, Swedish passports, and some kind of grant. We were flown to Stockholm, where we stayed for six months. Every day my mother would go to the Finnish Embassy, and, eventually, we were granted our Finnish passports. Mother spent the first year in Helsinki getting a divorce and compensation for her lost land – up here, in the Circle. We lived in Helsinki, and I got my first taste of schooling. That's where I met Paula. We became very good friends. That's about it.'

'*It?*' Bond repeated, raising his eyebrows.

'Well, the rest was predictable enough.'

It was while she was at school that Rivke began to learn the facts about her father. 'By the age of fourteen I knew it all, and was horrified; disgusted that my own father had left his country to become part of the SS. I suppose it was an obsession – a complex. By the time I was fifteen, I knew what had to be done as far as my life went.'

Bond had heard many confessions during interrogations. After years of experience you develop a sense about them. He would have put money on Rivke's being a true story – if only because it came out fast, with the minimum of detail. People operating under a deep cover often give you too much.

'Revenge?' he asked.

'A kind of revenge. No, that's the wrong word. My father had nothing to do with what Himmler called the Final Solution – the Jewish problem – but he was associated, he was a wanted criminal. I began to identify with the race that lost six million souls, in the gas chambers and the camps. Many people have told me I over-reacted, I wanted to do something concrete.'

'You became a Jew?'

'I went to Israel on my twentieth birthday. My mother died two years later. The last time I saw her was the day I left Helsinki. Within six months I made the first steps to conversion. Now I'm as Jewish as any Gentile-born can be. In Israel they tried every-thing in the book to put me off, but I stuck it out – even military service. It was that which finally clinched it.' Her smile was one of pride this time. 'Zamir himself sent for me, interviewed me. I couldn't believe it when they told me who he was – Colonel Zwicka Zamir, the head of Mossad. He arranged everything, I was an Israeli citizen already. Now I went for special training, for Mossad. I had a new name . . .'

'And the revenge part, Rivke? You had atoned, but what about the revenge?'

'Revenge?' Her eyes opened wide. Then she frowned, anxiety crossing her face. 'James, you *do* believe me, don't you?'

In the couple of seconds which passed before he replied, Bond's mind ran through the facts. Either Rivke was the best deception artist he had ever met, or, as he had earlier decided, completely honest. These feelings had to be put next to his long and intimate knowledge of Paula Vacker. From their first meet-ing, Bond had never suspected Paula of being anything but a charming, intelligent, hard-working girl. Now, if Rivke was tell-ing the truth, Paula became a liar and possibly an accessory to attempted murder. The knife artists had cornered him in Paula's flat, yet she had taken care of him, had driven him to the airport.

Someone obviously had fingered him on the road to Salla. That could only have been done from Helsinki. Paula?

Bond switched back to the Paula connection. 'There're reasons why I shouldn't believe you, Rivke,' he began. 'I've known Paula for a long time. When I last saw her, when she told me she'd confided in you, Anni Tudeer, she was very specific. She said Anni Tudeer worked with her in Helsinki.'

Rivke slowly shook her head. 'Unless someone else is using my name . . .'

'You've never worked in her world? In advertising?'

'You're joking. I've said no already. I've told you the story of my life. I knew Paula at school.'

'And did she know who you were? Who your father was?'

'Yes.' Softly. 'James, you can easily settle it. Call her office, check with them; ask if they have an Anni Tudeer working for them. If so, then there are two Anni Tudeers – or Paula's lying.' She leaned closer, speaking very distinctly, 'I'm telling you, James, there are *not* two Anni Tudeers. Paula's lying, and I would like to know why.'

'Yes.' Bond nodded. 'Yes, so would I.'

'Then you believe me?'

'There's no point in you lying to me, when all the facts can be checked. I thought I knew Paula very well, but now . . . well, my instincts tell me to believe you. We can run traces, even from here, certainly from London. London already says that you're Anni Tudeer.' He smiled at her. She was, at close proximity, a very lovely young woman. 'I believe you, Rivke Ingber. You're straight Mossad, and you've only left one thing out – the question of vengeance. I can't believe you simply want to atone for your father's actions. You either want him in the bag or dead. Which is it?'

She gave a provocative little shrug. 'It doesn't really matter, does it? Whichever way it goes, Aarne Tudeer will die.' The musical voice altered for a second, steel hard, then back once more to its softness, and a small laugh. 'I'm sorry, James. I shouldn't have tried to play games with you. Brad Tirpitz *was* a nuisance tonight, but, yes, I could've taken care of him. Maybe I'm not the professional I thought I was. I was naive enough to imagine I could con you. Lure you.'

'Lure? Into what web?' Bond, 99 per cent sure of Rivke's motives and claims, still kept that tiny 1 per cent of wariness in reserve.

'Not a web, exactly.' She put out a hand, fingers resting in Bond's palm. 'To be honest, I don't feel safe with either Tirpitz or Kolya. I wanted to be sure you'd be on my side.'

Bond let go of her hand, placing his own fingers lightly on her shoulders. 'We're in the business of trust, Rivke; and we both need it from someone, because I'm not happy with this set-up any more than you are. First things first, though. I have to ask you this, simply because I suspect it: do you know, for certain, that your father's mixed up with the NSAA?'

She did not pause to think. 'Yes. For certain.'

'How do you know?'

'That's why I'm here; it's why I was put on this job. Back in Israel the people on the ground began computer analysis immediately after the first National Socialist Action Army incident. It was natural they should look at the old leaders – the former Party members, the SS, and those who'd escaped from Germany. Several names came up. My father was high on the list. You'll have to take my word for the rest, but Mossad has evidence that he is tied in very closely. It's not coincidence that the arms are coming out of Russia through Finland. He's here, James – new name, almost a new face, the whole business of a new identity. There's a new mistress as well. He's spry and tough enough, even at his age. I know he's here.'

'A game bird.' Bond gave a wry smile.

'And game is in season, James. My dear father's well in season. Mother used to say that he saw himself as a new Führer, a Nazi Moses, there to lead his children back to their promised land. Well, the children are growing in strength, and the world's in such a mess that the young, or the pliable, will lap up any half-baked ideology. You only have to look at your own country . . .'

Bond bridled. 'Which has yet to elect, or allow, a madman into power. There's a stiff backbone there that will eventually – sometimes a little late, I admit – get matters straight.'

She gave a friendly pout. 'Okay, I'm sorry. All countries have their faults.' Rivke bit her lip, her mind drifting off-course for a few seconds. 'Please, James. I *do* have an edge, privileged information if you like. I need you on my side.'

Go along with it, Bond thought. Even though you are almost sure, take every bit of the bait, but hold back the 1 per cent and remain alert. Aloud he said, 'All right. But what about the others? Brad and Kolya?'

'Brad and Kolya are both playing death and glory games, and I'm not certain if they're doing it together or against each other. They're serious enough yet not serious enough. Does that sound stupid? A paradox? It's true. Watch them.' She looked straight into his eyes, as though trying to hypnotise him. 'Look, I get the feeling – and it's only intuition – that either the CIA or the KGB has something it wants to bury. Something to do with the NSAA.'

'I'd put my money on it being Kolya,' Bond replied lightly. 'The KGB asked us in, after all. The KGB came to *us* – to the USA, Israel and the UK. I suppose it's possible they've found more than a simple arms leak to the National Socialist Action Army. That may be part of it, but what if there's more? Something hideous?'

Rivke shifted her chair closer to the end of the bed where Bond sat. 'You mean if they've found themselves with an arms leak, and some other funny business that's going to look very bad? Something they can't contain?'

'It's a theory. Plausible enough.' She was so close that Bond could smell her: the traces of her scent, plus the natural odour of an attractive woman. 'Only a theory,' he repeated. 'But it's possible. This is all out of character for the KGB. They're usually so closed up. Now they come and ask for help. Could they be pulling us in? Having us for suckers? So that, when the truth – whatever it is – comes spewing out, we'll be implicated. Israel, America and Britain will all take the blame. It's devious enough for them.'

'Fall guys.' Rivke spoke softly again.

'Yes. Fall guys.' Bond wondered what his old and ultra-conservative-minded chief would make of the expression. M hated slang in any form.

Rivke said if there was even a possibility of a KGB plot to discredit them, it would be wise to make a pact now to stick together. 'We really do have to watch each other's backs, even if the theory doesn't hold.'

Bond gave Rivke his most charming smile, leaning close, his lips only inches from her mouth. 'You're quite right, Rivke. Though I'd be much happier watching your front.'

Her lips, in return, seemed to be examining his mouth. Then: 'I don't frighten easily, James, but this has got me twitchy . . .' Her arms came up, winding around his neck, and their lips brushed, first in a light caress. Bond's conscience nagged at him to take care. But the warnings were cauterised in the conflagration as their lips touched.

It seemed an eternity before their mouths parted, and Rivke, panting, clung on to Bond, her breath warm near his ear as she murmured endearments. Slowly, he drew her from the chair on to the bed where they lay close, body to body, then mouth to mouth once more, until together, as though at some inaudible signal, their hands groped for one another.

What began as a kind of lust, or an act of need – two people alone, and responding to a natural desire for comfort and trust – slowly became tender, gentle, even truly loving.

Bond, still vaguely aware of the tiny remaining doubt in the back of his head, was quickly lost in this lovely creature, whose limbs and body seemed to respond to his own in an almost telepathic way. They were as two perfectly attuned dancers, able to predict each other's moves.

Only later, with Rivke curled up under the covers, like a child in his arms, did they speak again of work. For them, the brief hours they had spent together had been but a short retreat from the harsh reality of their profession. Now it was after eight in the morning. Another day, another scramble through the dangers of the secret world.

'For the sake of this operation, then, we work together.' Bond's mouth was unusually dry. 'That'll cover both of us . . .'

'Yes, and . . .'

'And I'll help you see SS-Oberführer Tudeer in hell.'

'Oh please, James darling. Please.' She looked up at him, her face puckered in a smile that spoke only of pleasure – no malice, or horror, even though she was already pleading for the death of her hated father. Then the mood changed again: a serenity, the laugh in her eyes, and at the corners of her mouth. 'You know, this is the last thing I thought would happen . . .'

'Come on, Rivke. You don't arrive in a man's room at four in the morning, dressed in practically nothing, without the thought crossing your mind.'

'Oh,' she laughed aloud, 'the thought was there. It's just that I didn't really believe it would happen. I imagined you were much too professional, and I thought I too was so determined and well-trained that I could resist anything.' Her voice went small. 'I did go for you, the moment I saw you, but don't let it go to your head.'

'It didn't.' Bond laughed.

The laugh had hardly died when he reached over for the telephone. 'Time to see if we can get something out of our so-called friend Paula.' He began to dial the apartment in Helsinki, while casting an admiring eye over Rivke as she put on the film of silk which passed as a nightdress.

At the other end of the line, the telephone rang. Nobody answered.

'What do you make of it, Rivke?' Bond put down the telephone. 'She's not there.'

Rivke shook her head. 'You'll ring her office, of course – but I don't understand any of it. I used to know her well enough, but why lie about me? It doesn't make sense; and you say she was a good friend . . .'

'For a long time. I certainly didn't spot anything sinister about her. None of it makes sense.' Bond was on his feet now, walking towards the sliding louvred doors of the wardrobe. His quilted jacket hung inside, and he took the two medals from the pocket, tossing them across the room so that they jangled on to the bed. This would be the last throw in any present round of suspicion. 'What d'you think about those, darling?'

Rivke's hand went out and she held the medals for a moment, then let out a tiny cry, dropping them back on to the bed as though they were red hot.

'Where?' The one word was enough: delivered fast, like a shot.

'In Paula Vacker's flat. Lying on the dressing table.'

All humour had gone from Rivke. 'I haven't seen these since I was a child.' Her hand went out to the Knight's Cross and she picked it up again, turning it over. 'You see? His name is engraved on the back. My father's Knight's Cross with Oak Leaves and Swords. In Paula's apartment?' The last with complete bewilderment and disbelief.

'Right there on the dressing table, for anyone to see.'

She dropped the medal back on to the bed and came towards him, throwing her arms around his neck. 'I thought I knew it all, James; but what's it really about? Why Paula? Why the lies? Why my father's Knight's Cross and the Northern Campaign Shield – he was particularly proud of that one, by the way – but why?'

Bond held her close. 'We'll find out. Don't worry. I'm as concerned as you. Paula always seemed so . . . well, level. Straight.'

After a minute or so, Rivke drew away. 'I have to clear my head, James. Will you come down the ski run with me?'

He made a negative gesture. 'I've got to see Brad and Kolya; and I thought we were going to watch out for each other . . .'

'I just have to get out there in the open for a while.' She hesitated before adding, 'Darling James, I'll be okay. Back in time for breakfast. Make my apologies if I'm a bit late.'

'For heaven's sake be careful.'

Rivke gave a little nod. Then shyly, 'That was all quite something, Mr Bond. It could become a habit.'

'I hope so.' Bond pulled her to him, and they kissed by the door.

When she had gone, he turned back to the bed, bending down to retrieve Aarne Tudeer's medals. The scent of her was everywhere, and she still seemed very close.

# 8

# TIRPITZ

James Bond was profoundly disturbed. All but one tiny doubt told him that Rivke Ingber was absolutely trustworthy, just who she said she was: the daughter of Aarne Tudeer; the girl who had taken to the Jewish faith, and was now – even according to London – a Mossad agent. There was a sense of shock, however, at the mystery of Paula Vacker. She had been close to Bond over the years, never giving him the least cause to think of her as anything but an intelligent, fun-loving, hard-working girl who excelled in her job. But set against Rivke, and recent events, Paula appeared suddenly to have feet of melting wax.

Rather more slowly than usual, Bond showered, shaved and dressed – in heavy cavalry twill slacks, a cable-knit black rollneck and short leather jacket, to hide the P7, which, after checking the mechanism, he strapped in place. He added a pair of spare magazines, clipping them into the specially sewn-in pocket at the back of his slacks.

This gear, with soft leather moccasins on his feet, would be warm enough inside the hotel and, as he left the room, Bond made a vow that from now on he would go nowhere without the weapon.

In the corridor, he paused, glancing at his Rolex. It was already nearly nine-thirty. Paula's office would be open. He returned to the room to dial Helsinki – this time the office number. The same operator who had greeted him on the day of that fateful call, which seemed so long ago now, answered in Finnish.

Bond spoke in English, and the operator complied, just as she had done previously. He asked for Paula Vacker and the reply came back – sharp, final, and, surprisingly to Bond, not entirely unexpected.

'I'm sorry. Miss Vacker is on holiday.'

'Oh?' he feigned disappointment. 'I promised to get in touch with her. I suppose you've no idea where she's gone?'

The operator asked him to wait a moment. 'We're not sure of the exact location,' she told him at last, 'but she said something about going to get some skiing up north – too cold for me. It's bad enough here.'

'Yes. Well, thank you. Has she gone for long?'

'She left on Thursday, sir. Would you like me to take a message?'

'No. No, I'll catch her next time I'm in Finland.' Bond hung up quickly.

So Paula had moved north, just like the rest of them. He glanced out of the window. You could almost see the cold – as though you could cut it with a knife – in spite of the clear blue sky and bright sunshine. Those incredible skies, blue as they were, held no warmth; and the sun shone like dazzling light reflected from an iceberg. The signs, from the safety of an hotel room, could be treacherously deceptive in this part of the world, as Bond well knew. Within an hour or so the sun could be gone, replaced by slanting, stinging snow, or hard, visible frost, blotting out the light.

His room was at the rear of the building, and from it he had a clear view of the chair lift, with the ski run, and the curve of the jump. Tiny figures, taking advantage of the short spell of daylight and the clear atmosphere, were boarding the endlessly moving lift, while high above, outlined like black speeding insects against the snow, others made the long descent, curving in speed-checking traverses, or racing straight on the fall line, with bodies crouched forward, knees bent.

Rivke, Bond thought, could well be one of those dots schussing down over the pure sparkling white landscape. He could almost feel the exhilaration of a straight downhill run and, for a second, wished he had gone with her. Then, with one last glance at the snowscape, relieved only by the skiers, the movement of the chair lift, and the great banks of fir trees sweeping away on either side, green and brown, decorated like Christmas trees by the heavy frozen snow, he rose, left the room and headed down to the main dining room.

Brad Tirpitz sat alone at a corner table near the windows, looking out on the same view Bond had just observed from higher in the building. He spotted Bond's arrival and nonchalantly raised an arm in a combination of greeting and identification.

'Hi, Bond.' The rock-like face cracked slightly. 'Kolya sends his apologies. Been delayed organising some snow scooters.' He leaned closer. 'It's tonight apparently – or in the early hours of tomorrow, if you want to be accurate.'

'What's tonight?' Bond responded stiffly, the perfect caricature of the reserved Englishman.

'What's tonight?' Tirpitz raised his eyes to heaven. 'Tonight, friend Bond, Kolya says a load of arms is coming out of Blue Hare – you remember Blue Hare? Their ordnance depot near Alakurtii?'

'Oh that.' Bond gave the impression that the theft of arms from Blue Hare was the last thing to interest him. Picking up the menu, he immersed himself in the long list of dishes available. When the waiter appeared, he merely rattled off his usual order, underlining his need for a very large cup of coffee.

'Mind if I smoke?' Tirpitz was laconic to the point of speaking like an Indian sign.

'As long as you don't mind me eating.' Bond did not smile. Perhaps it was his background in the Royal Navy, and working all those years close to M, but he considered smoking while someone else ate to be only a fraction above smoking before the Loyal Toast.

'Look, Bond.' Tirpitz moved his chair closer. 'I'm glad Kolya's not here. Wanted a word with you alone.'

'Yes?'

'Got a message for you. Felix Leiter sends his best. And Cedar sends her love.'

Bond felt a slight twinge of surprise, but he showed no reaction. His best friend in the USA, Felix Leiter, had once been a top CIA man; while Felix's daughter, Cedar, was also Company-trained. In fact, Cedar had worked gallantly with him on a recent assignment.

I know you don't trust me,' Tirpitz continued, 'but you'd better think again, brother. Think again, because maybe I'm the only friend you have around here.'

Bond nodded. 'Maybe.'

'Your chief gave you a good solid briefing. I was briefed at Langley. We both probably had the same information, and Kolya wasn't letting it all out of the bag. What I'm saying is that we need to work together. Close as we can. That Russian bastard isn't coming up with all the goodies, and I figure he has some surprises ready for us.'

'I thought we were all working together?' Bond made it sound bland, urbane.

'Don't trust anyone – except me.' Tirpitz, though he had taken out a packet of cigarettes, made no attempt to light up. There was a pause while the waiter brought Bond's scrambled eggs, bacon and coffee. When he had gone, Tirpitz continued. 'Look, if I hadn't spoken up in Madeira, the biggest threat wouldn't even have been mentioned – this phony Count. You've had the dope on him, same as me. Konrad von Glöda. Kolya wasn't going to give him to us. D'you know why?'

'Tell me.'

'Because Kolya's working two sides of the street. Some

elements of the KGB are mixed up in this business of arms thefts. Our people in Moscow gave us that weeks ago. It's only just been cleared for consumption by London. You'll probably get some kind of signal in due course.'

'What's the story, then?' It was Bond who played it laconically now. Brad Tirpitz appeared to be confirming the theory already discussed with Rivke.

'Like a fairy tale.' Tirpitz gave a growling laugh. 'The word from Moscow is that a dissatisfied faction of senior KGB people – a very small cell – have got themselves mixed up with a similarly dissatisfied Red Army splinter group.' These two bodies, Tirpitz maintained, made contact with the nucleus of what was later to emerge as the National Socialist Action Army.

'They're idealists, of course,' said Tirpitz, chuckling. 'Fanatics. Men working within the USSR to subvert the Communist ideal by Fascist terrorism. They were behind the first arms theft from Blue Hare, and they got caught, up to a point . . .'

'What point?'

'They got caught, but the full facts never came out. They're like the Mafia – or ourselves, come to that. Your people look after their own, don't they?'

'Only when they can get away with it.' Bond forked some egg into his mouth, reaching for the toast.

'Well, the boys in Dzerzhinsky Square have so far managed to keep the army man who caught them out at Blue Hare as sweet as a nut. What's more, they're conducting this combined clandestine operation with one of their own in the driving seat – Kolya Mosolov.'

'What you're saying is that Kolya's going to fail?' Bond turned, looking Tirpitz full in the face.

'He's not only going to fail, he's going to make sure the next shipment gets out. After that, it'll look as though Comrade Mosolov got himself killed among all this snow and ice. Then guess who's going to be left holding the bucket?'

'Us?' Bond suggested.

'Technically us, yes. In fact, the plan is for it to be you, friend Bond. Kolya's body'll never be found. I suspect yours will. Of course Kolya'll eventually rise from the grave. Another name, another face, another part of the forest.'

Bond nodded energetically. 'That's more or less what I thought. I didn't think Kolya was taking me into the Soviet Union to watch arms being lifted just for the fun of it.'

Tirpitz gave a humourless smile. 'Like you, buddy, I really have seen it all: Berlin, the Cold War, Nam, Laos, Cambodia. This is the triple cross of all time. You *need* me, brother . . .'

'And I suspect you need me too . . . er, brother.'

'Right. If you play it my way, do it the way I ask – as the Company asks – while you're playing snowman on the other side of the border; if you do that, I'll watch your back, and make sure we both end up in one piece.'

'Before I ask what I'm supposed to do, there's one important question.' Bond had ceased to be bemused by the conversation. First Rivke had wanted a favour from him, now Tirpitz: it added a new dimension to Operation Icebreaker. Nobody trusted the next person. All wanted at least one ally, who, Bond suspected, would be ditched or stabbed in the back at the first hint of trouble.

'Yeah?' Tirpitz prodded, and Bond realised he had been distracted by some newly arrived guests who were being treated like royalty by the waiters.

'What about Rivke? That's what I wanted to ask. Are we leaving her in the cold with Kolya?'

Brad Tirpitz looked astounded. 'Bond,' he said quietly, 'Rivke Ingber may well be a Mossad agent, but you do know *who* she is, I take it. I mean, your Service must have told you . . .'

'The estranged daughter of a Finnish officer who went along with the Nazis, and is still on the wanted war criminals list? Yes.'

'Yes and no.' Tirpitz's voice rose. 'Sure, we all know about that bastard of a father. But nobody has any real idea about which side of the line the girl stands – not even Mossad. The likes of us haven't been told that part, but I've seen her Mossad PF. I'm telling you, even they don't know.'

Bond spoke calmly. 'I'm afraid I believe she's genuine – completely loyal to Mossad.'

Tirpitz made an irritated little noise. 'Okay, believe away, Bond; but what about the man?'

'The man?'

'The so-called Count Konrad von Glöda. The guy who's behind the arms shipments and is probably running the whole NSAA operation – correction, almost certainly running the whole NSAA Reichführer-SS von Glöda.'

'What about him?'

'You mean nobody at your end gave you the full picture?'

Bond shrugged. M had been precise and detailed in his briefing, but stressed that there were certain matters about the mysterious Count von Glöda which could not be proved. M, being the stickler he was, refused to take mere probability as fact.

'Brother, you're in trouble. Rivke Ingber's deranged and estranged Papa, SS-Oberführer Aarne Tudeer, is also the Ice King of this little saga. Aarne Tudeer *is* the Count von Glöda: an apt name.'

Bond moistened his lips with coffee, his brain racing. If Tirpitz was giving him correct information, London had not even suggested it. All M had provided was the name, the possibility that he was behind at least the arms running, and the fact that the Count almost certainly arranged staging posts, between the Soviet border and the final jumping-off point, for the arms supplies. There had been no mention of von Glöda being Tudeer.

'You're certain of this?' Bond refused to show anything but nonchalant calm.

'Sure as night follows day – which is pretty fast around here . . .' Tirpitz stopped abruptly as he looked across the dining room, his gaze resting on the couple who had come in to such an enthusiastic welcome.

'Well, what do you know?' The corners of Tirpitz's mouth turned down even further. 'Take a look, Bond. That's the man himself. The Count Konrad von Glöda, and his lady, known simply as the Countess.' He gulped some coffee. 'I said it was an apt name. In Swedish, Glöda means Glow. At Langley we gave him the cryptonym Glow-worm. He glows with gold from old Nazi pickings, and all he must be raking in now as Commander of the NSAA; and he's also a worm. I am personally going to bottle that specimen.'

The couple certainly looked distinguished. Bond had seen the heavy and expensive fur coats borne away when they had arrived. Now they even sat as though they owned Lapland, looking almost like a Renaissance prince and his lady.

Konrad von Glöda was tall and well-muscled. He held himself straight as a lath. He was also one of those men whom age does not weary. He could be an old-looking fifty or a very young seventy, for it was impossible to calculate the age of a man whose face and bone structure were so fine and bronzed. He sported a full head of iron-grey hair, and as he talked to the Countess he leaned back in his chair, using one hand for gestures while the other was draped over the chair arm. The brown face, glowing with health, had about it an animation which would not have been out of place in that of a thrusting young executive, and there was no doubt, from the glittering grey eyes to the aristrocratic sharp chin and arrogant tilt of the head, that this was a man to be reckoned with. Glow was the word.

'Star quality?' Tirpitz whispered.

Bond gave a small nod. You had only to see the man to know he possessed that sought-for quality: charisma.

The Countess also carried herself with the air of one who had the means, and ability, to buy or take anything she wanted. She was, despite the impossibility of guessing the Count's age, obviously much younger than her partner. She too had the look of a person who prized her body and its physical condition. She gave the impression of one to whom all sport, and exercise, came as second nature. Bond observed the woman's smooth-skinned beauty, the svelte grooming of her dark hair, and the classic features and reflected that this would certainly include the oldest of indoor sports.

Bond was still covertly watching the couple when a waiter came hurrying over to the table. 'Mr Bond?' he asked.

Bond nodded.

'There's a telephone call for you, sir. In the box by the reception desk. A Miss Paula Vacker wishes to speak to you.'

Bond was on his feet quickly, catching the slightly quizzical look in Brad Tirpitz's eye.

'Problems?' Tirpitz's voice appeared to have softened, but Bond refused to react. 'Bad' Brad, he decided, should be treated with a caution reserved for rattlesnakes.

'Just a call from Helsinki.' He began to move, inwardly bewildered that Paula could have found him here.

As he passed the von Glödas' table, Bond allowed himself a straight, seemingly disinterested, glance at the couple. The Count himself raised his head, catching Bond's eye. The look was one of near tangible malice: a hatred which Bond could feel long after he had passed the table, as though the Count's glittering grey eyes were boring into the back of his head.

The receptionist indicated a small, half-open booth containing a telephone. Bond was there in two strides, lifting the receiver and speaking immediately.

'Paula?'

'One moment,' from the operator. There was a click on the line, and the sense that someone was on the other end.

'Paula?' he repeated.

If questioned then, Bond could not have sworn on oath that it was Paula's voice, though he would have claimed a 90 per cent certainty. Unusually for the Finnish telephone system, the line was not good, the voice seeming hollow, as though from an echo chamber.

'James,' the voice said. 'Any minute now, I should imagine. Say goodbye to Anni.' There followed a long and eerie laugh, which trailed away, as though Paula were deliberately moving the receiver from her lips, then slowly returning it to its cradle.

Bond's brow creased, a concern building quickly inside him. 'Paula? Is that you . . . ?' He stopped, knowing there was no point in talking into a dead instrument. Say goodbye to Anni . . . What on earth? Then it struck him. Rivke was on the ski run. Or maybe she hadn't even reached it. Bond raced for the main doors of the hotel.

His hand was already outstretched when a voice behind him snapped, 'Don't even think of it, Bond. Not dressed like that.' Brad Tirpitz was at his shoulder. 'You'd last less than five minutes out there. It's well below freezing.'

'Get me some gear, and fast, Brad.'

'Get your own. What in hell's the matter?' Tirpitz took a step towards the cloakroom near Reception.

'I'll explain later. Rivke's out on the ski run, and I've a hunch she's in danger.' It crossed his mind that Rivke Ingber might not, after all, be on the slopes. Paula had said, 'Any minute now, I should imagine,' Whatever was planned could have already happened.

Tirpitz was back, his own outdoor clothes grasped in his arms – boots, scarf, goggles, gloves and padded jacket. 'Just tell me', the voice commanding, 'and I'll do what I can. Go get your own stuff. I always play safe and keep the winter gear close at hand.' Already he was kicking off his shoes and pulling boots on. There was obviously no arguing with Tirpitz.

Bond turned towards the row of lifts. 'If Rivke's on the slopes, just get her down fast, and in one piece,' he shouted, banging at the button. On reaching his room, Bond took less than three minutes to get into outdoor clothes. As he made the change, he glanced constantly out of the window, towards the chair lift and ski slopes. Everything appeared normal, as it did when he finally reached the bottom of the chair lift outside, just six minutes after leaving Reception.

Most people had already made their way back into the hotel: the best time for skiing was over. Bond recognised the figure of Brad Tirpitz standing near the hut at the bottom of the lift, with a couple of others.

'Well?' Bond asked.

'I got them to telephone the top. Her name's on the list. She's on her way down now. She's wearing a crimson ski suit. Give me the full dope on this, Bond. Is it to do with the op?'

'Later.' Bond craned, narrowing his eyes behind the goggles, searching the upward sheen of snow for a sight of Rivke.

The shallow mountain ridge formed a series of steps, covering some one and a half kilometres. The top of the run was hidden from view, but the marked piste was curving and intricate: sliding between fir trees at points, some of it so gentle that it appeared almost flat, while there were sections, following easy downhill runs, that steepened to awesome angles.

The last half kilometre was a nursery slope, no more than a long, straight, gentle run out. Two young men, in black ski suits with white striped woollen hats, were expertly completing what had obviously been a fast run down from the top. They executed showy finishes on the run out, laughing and making a lot of noise.

'Here she comes.' Brad handed over his binoculars, with which he had been scanning the top of the final fall line. 'Crimson suit.'

Bond raised the glasses. Rivke was obviously very good, side-slipping and traversing the steep slope, coming out of it into a straight run, slowing as the snow flattened, then gathering a little speed as she breasted the rise and began to follow the fall line down the long final slope. She had just touched the run out, less than half a kilometre away from them, when the snow seemed to boil on either side of her, and a great white mist rose

behind. In the centre of the blossom of fine snow, a sudden fire –
red, then white – flashed upwards.

The sound of the muffled crump reached them a second after
Bond saw Rivke's body turning over in mid air, thrown up with
the exploding snow.

# 9

# SPEEDLINE

Bond felt the gut-twist of impotent horror as he watched, peering through the goggles into the rising haze of snow. The crimson figure, twirling like a rag doll, disappeared into the fine white spray, while the few people near Tirpitz and Bond flattened themselves on the ground, as though under mortar fire. Brad Tirpitz, like Bond, remained upright. His only action was to grab back the binoculars and lift them to his eyes.

'She's there. Unconscious, I think.' Tirpitz spoke like a spotter on the battlefield calling in an air strike, or ranging artillery. 'Yes, face up, half buried in snow. About one hundred yards down from where it happened.'

Bond took back the glasses to look for himself. The snow was settling, and he could make out the figure quite clearly, spread-eagled in a drift.

Another voice came from behind them. 'The hotel's called the police and an ambulance. It's not far, but no rescue team's going to get up there quickly. The snow's too soft. They'll have to bring in a helicopter.'

Bond turned. Kolya Mosolov stood near them, also with raised binoculars.

In the few seconds following the explosion, Bond's mind had gone into overdrive. Paula's telephone call – if it was Paula – bore out most of what Rivke had said, hardening his earlier conclusions. Paula Vacker was certainly not what she had seemed. She had set up Bond at the apartment during the first visit to

Helsinki. Somehow she knew about the night games with Rivke and had set her up as well. Even more, Paula had arranged this present ski slope incident with incredible timing. She knew where Bond had been; she knew where Rivke was; she knew what had been arranged. It could add up to one thing only: Paula had some kind of access to the four members of Icebreaker.

Bond pulled himself from his thoughts. 'What do you reckon?' He turned to Kolya for a second, before looking back up the slope.

'I said. A helicopter. The centre of the run out is hard, but Rivke's bogged-down in the soft snow. If we want action fast, it has to be a helicopter.'

'That's not what I meant,' Bond snapped. 'What do you reckon happened?'

Kolya shrugged, under the layers of winter clothing. 'Land mine, I guess. They still get them around here. From the Russo–Finnish Winter War, or World War Two. Even after all this time. They move, too – in early winter with the first blizzards. Yes, I'd guess a land mine.'

'What if I told you I was warned?'

'That's right,' Brad said, his binoculars still glued to the flash of red that was Rivke. 'Bond had some kind of message. A phone call.'

Kolya seemed uninterested. 'Ah, we'll have to talk about it. But where the hell are the police and the helicopter?'

As if on cue, a police Saab Finlandia came skidding into the main hotel car park, pulling up a few paces short of where Kolya, Tirpitz, and Bond stood. Two officers got out. Kolya was immediately beside them, speaking Finnish like a native born. There was some uncharacteristic gesticulating, then Kolya turned back to Bond, muttering an obscene Russian oath. 'They can't get a chopper here for another half hour.' He looked very angry. 'And the rescue team'll take as long.'

'Then we have . . .'

Bond was cut short by Brad Tirpitz. 'She's moving. Conscious. Trying to get up. No, she's down again. Legs, I think.'

Bond quickly asked Kolya if the police car carried such a thing as a loud-hailer. There was another fast exchange. Then Kolya shouted back to Bond, 'Yes, they've got one.'

Bond was off, running as best he could over the frozen ground, his gloved hand unclipping a jacket pocket to reach for his car keys. 'Get it ready,' he shouted back. 'I'll bring her down myself. Get the loud-hailer ready.'

The locks on the Saab were well-oiled and treated with anti-freeze, so Bond had no difficulty in opening up. He switched off the alarm sensors, then went to the rear, pulling up the big hatchback, and removing a pair of toggle ropes and the large drum that was the Pains-Wessex Speedline. He locked up again, resetting the alarms, and hurried back to the foot of the ski run where one of the policemen – looking a little self-conscious – held a Graviner loud-hailer.

'She's sitting up. Waved once, and indicated she couldn't move any more.' Tirpitz passed on the information as Bond approached.

'Right.' Bond held out his hand and took the loud-hailer from the policeman, flicking the switch and raising it in Rivke's direction. He was careful not to let the metal touch his lips.

'If you can hear me, Rivke, raise one arm. This is James.' The voice, magnified by the amplifier to a volume ten times that of his normal speech, echoed around them.

He saw the movement, and Tirpitz, with the binoculars up, reported it: 'She's lifted an arm.'

Bond checked that the loud-hailer was aimed directly towards Rivke. 'I'm going to fire a line to you, Rivke. Don't be scared. It's propelled by a rocket that should pass quite close to you. Signify if you understand.'

Again the arm was raised.

'When the line reaches you, do you think you can secure it around your body, under the arms?'

Another affirmative.

'Do you think we could then slowly pull you down?'

Affirmative.

'If this proves to be impossible, if you are in any pain as we drag you down, signify by raising both hands. Do you read me?'

Once more the affirmative sign.

'All right.' Bond turned back to the others, giving them directions.

The Pains-Wessex Speedline is a complete, self-contained, line-throwing unit which looks like a heavy cylinder with a carrying handle and trigger mechanism at the top. It is arguably the best line-throwing unit in the world. Bond removed the protective plastic covering at the front of the cylinder, exposing the rocket, well-shielded, in the centre, and the 275 metres of packed, ready-flaked line which took up the bulk of the space. He removed the free end of the line, instructing the others to make it fast around the Finlandia's rear bumper, and placed himself almost directly below the crimson figure in the snow.

When the line was secure, Bond removed the safety pin at the rear of the carrying handle, then shifted his hand to the moulded grip behind the trigger guard. He dug the heels of his Mukluk boots into the snow and advanced four paces up the slope. The snow was soft and very deep to the right of the broad ski slope fall line – where it was packed rock hard and only negotiable with the aid of ice climbing equipment.

Four steps and Bond was sinking almost to his waist, but the position was reasonable for a good shot with the line – the far end of which trailed out behind him to the bumper of the Finlandia. Bracing himself, Bond held the cylinder away from his body, allowing it to find the correct point of balance. When he was certain the rocket would clear Rivke, he pressed the trigger.

There was a dull thud as the firing pin struck the igniter. Then, with spectacular speed and a plume of smoke, the rocket leaped into the clear air, its line threading out after it, seeming to gain speed as it went, a single-strand bow of rope curling high above the snow.

The rocket passed well clear of Rivke's body, but right on course, taking the line directly above her, to land with a dull plop. For a second, the line appeared to hang in its arc, quivering in the still air. Then, with an almost controlled neatness, it began to fall – a long brown snake running from a point high above where Rivke lay.

Bond fought his way through the thick snow, back to the others, taking the loud-hailer from one of the policemen. 'Raise your arm if you can pull the rope above you down to your body.' Bond's voice once more echoed off the slopes.

In spite of the freezing weather, several people had come out to watch. Others could be seen peering through the hotel windows. The sound of an ambulance's klaxon was increasing as it approached.

'Binoculars, please.' Bond was commanding, not asking. Tirpitz handed over the glasses, and Bond adjusted the knurled wheel, bringing Rivke into sharp focus.

She appeared to be lying at an odd angle, waist deep in snow, though there were traces of cracked, hard snow and ice around the area in which she lay. From what little he could see of the girl's face, Bond had the impression that she was in pain. Laboriously she hauled back on the line, pulling the far end towards her from above. The process seemed to take a very long time. Rivke – obviously in distress, and suffering from cold as well as pain – kept stopping to rest. The simple job of hauling the line down had turned into a major battle. From his view through the binoculars, it seemed to Bond as though she were pulling a heavy dead weight on the line.

From time to time, when he could see she was flagging, he urged her on, his loud voice throwing great bouncing echoes around them. Finally she pulled the whole line in and began the struggle of getting it around her body.

'Under the arms, Rivke,' Bond instructed. 'Knot it and slide the knot to your back. Then raise your hands when you're ready.'

After an age, the hands lifted.

'All right. Now we're going to bring you down as gently as we can. We will be dragging you through the soft snow, but don't forget, if it becomes too painful, raise both arms. Stand by, Rivke.'

Bond turned to the others, who had already unknotted the line from the Finlandia's bumper, and slowly pulled in the slack from Rivke to the bottom of the slope.

Bond had been aware of the ambulance arriving but now registered its presence for the first time. There was a full medical team on board, complete with a young, bearded doctor. Bond asked where they would take her, and the doctor – whose name turned out to be Simonen – said they were from the small hospital at Salla. 'After that,' he raised his hands in an uncertain gesture, 'it depends on her injuries.'

It took the best part of three-quarters of an hour to pull Rivke to within reaching distance. She was only half conscious when Bond, pushing through the snow, came near her. He guided those who pulled on the line to bring her gently right down to the edge of the run out.

She moaned, opening her eyes as the doctor got to her, immediately recognising Bond. 'James, what happened?' The voice was small and weak.

'Don't know, love. You had a fall.' Under the goggles and scarf muffling his face, Bond felt the anxiety etched into his own features, just as the telltale white blotches of frostbite were visible on the exposed parts of Rivke's face.

After a few moments the doctor touched Bond's shoulder, pulling him away. Tirpitz and Kolya Mosolov knelt by the girl as the doctor muttered, 'Both legs fractured, by the look of it.' He spoke excellent English, as Bond had discovered during their earlier exchange. 'Frostbite, as you can see, and advanced hypothermia. We have to get her in fast.'

'As quick as you can.' Bond caught hold of the doctor's sleeve. 'Can I come to the hospital later?'

'By all means.'

She was unconscious again, and Bond could do nothing but stand back and watch, his mind in confusion, as they gently strapped Rivke on to a stretcher and slid her into the ambulance. Pictures seemed to overlap in his head: the present cold, the ice and snow, and the ambulance, crunching off towards the main hotel car park exit, flashed between visions which came, unwanted, from his memory bank: another ambulance; a different road; heat; blood all over the car; and an Austrian policeman asking endless questions about Tracy's death. That nightmare – the death of his only wife – always lurked in the far reaches of Bond's mind.

As though the two pictures had suddenly merged, he heard Kolya saying, 'We have to talk, James Bond. I have to ask questions. We must also be ready for tonight. It's all fixed, but now we're one short. Arrangements will have to be made.'

Bond nodded, slowly trudging back towards the hotel. In the foyer, they agreed to meet in Kolya's room at three.

In his own room, Bond unlocked his briefcase, and operated the internal security devices which released the false bottom and sides – all covered by Q'ute's ingenious screening device. From one of the side compartments he took out an oblong unit, red in colour, and no larger than a packet of cigarettes – the VL34, so-called 'Privacy Protector', possibly one of the smallest and most advanced electronic 'bug' detecting devices. On his arrival the previous night, Bond had already swept the room and found it clean, but he was not going to take chances now.

Drawing out the retractable antennae, he switched on the small machine and began to sweep the room. In a matter of seconds, a series of lights began to glow along the front panel. Then, as the antennae pointed towards the telephone, a yellow light came on, verifying that a transmitter and microphone were somewhere in the telephone area.

Having located one listening bug, Bond carefully went over the entire room. There were a couple of small alarms, near the radio and television sets, but the failsafe yellow signal light did not lock on. Within a short time, he had established that the only bug in the room was the first one signalled – in the telephone. Examining the instrument, he soon discovered it contained an updated version of the old and familiar 'infinity bug', which turns a telephone into a transmitter, giving a twenty-four hour service. Even at the other end of the world, an operator can pick up not only telephone calls, but also anything said within the room in which the telephone is located.

Bond removed the bug, carried it to the bathroom and ground it under the heel of his Mukluk before flushing it down the lavatory. 'So perish all enemies of the state,' he muttered with a wry smile.

The others would almost certainly be covered by this – or similar – bugs. The questions remained: how, and when, had the bug been planted, and how had they so neatly timed the attempt on Rivke's life? Paula would have had to move with great speed to act against Rivke – or any of them. Unless, Bond thought, the Hotel Revontuli was so well-penetrated that things had been fixed up well in advance of their arrival.

But to do that, Paula, or whoever was organising these counter-moves, would have had to be in on the Madeira briefing. Since Rivke had become a victim, she was already in the clear. But what of Brad Tirpitz and Kolya? He would soon discover the truth about those two. If the operation connected with the Russian Ordnance Depot, Blue Hare, was really 'on' tonight, perhaps the whole deck of cards would be laid out.

He stripped, showered and changed into comfortable clothes, then stretched out on the bed, lighting one of his Simmons cigarettes. After two or three puffs Bond crushed the butt into the ashtray and closed his eyes, drifting into a doze.

Waking with a start, Bond glanced at his watch. It was almost three o'clock. He crossed to the window and looked out. The snowscape appeared to change as he stood there, the sudden sharp white altering as the sun went down. Then came the magic of what in the Arctic Circle they call 'the blue moment', when the glaring white of snow and ice on ground, rocks, buildings, and trees, turns a greenish-blue shade for a minute or two before the dusk sets in.

He would be late for the meeting with Kolya and Tirpitz, but that could not be helped. Bond quickly went to his now bug-free telephone, and asked the operator for the hospital number at Salla. She came back quite quickly. Bond got the dialling tone and picked out the number. His first thought on waking had been Rivke.

The hospital receptionist spoke an easy English. He enquired about Rivke and was asked to wait.

Finally the woman came back on the line. 'We have no patient of that name, I'm afraid.'

'She was admitted a short time ago,' Bond said. 'After an accident at the Hotel Revontuli. On the ski slopes. Hypothermia, frostbite, and both legs fractured. You sent an ambulance and doctor . . .' he paused, trying to remember the name, '. . . Doctor Simonen.'

'I'm sorry, sir. This is a small hospital and I know all the doctors. There are only five, and none is called Simonen . . .'

'Bearded. Young. He told me I could call.'

'I'm sorry, sir, but there must be some mistake. There have been no ambulance calls from the Revontuli today, I've just checked. No female admissions either; and we have no Doctor Simonen. In fact we have no young bearded doctors at all. I only wish we had.'

Bond asked if there were any other hospitals near by. No. The nearest hospital was at Kemijärvi, and they would not operate an emergency service in this area any more than the hospital at Pelkosenniemi. Bond asked for the numbers of both those hospitals, and the local police, then thanked the girl and began to dial again.

Within five minutes he knew the bad news. Neither of the hospitals had attended an accident at the hotel. What was more, the local police did not have a Saab Finlandia operating on the roads that day. In fact, no police patrol had been sent to the hotel. It was not a mistake; the police knew the hotel very well. So well that they did their ski training there.

They were very sorry.

So was Bond. Sorry, and decidedly shaken.

# 10

# KOLYA

James Bond was furious. 'You mean we aren't going to do anything about Rivke?' He did not shout, but his voice was cold, brittle as the ice decorating the trees outside Kolya's window.

'We'll inform her organisation.' Kolya appeared unconcerned. 'But later, after this is over. She could've turned up by then anyway. We haven't got time to go snow-shoeing around the countryside after her now. If she doesn't surface, Mossad will have to look for her. What does it say in the Bible? Let the dead bury the dead?'

Bond's temper was frayed. Already he had been within an ace of losing it a couple of times since joining the remnants of the Icebreaker team in Kolya's room. Kolya had opened up at his knock, and Bond had pushed past him, a finger to his lips, the other hand holding up the VL34 detector like a talisman.

Brad Tirpitz gave a sarcastic grin, which changed to a withering look of displeasure as Bond unearthed another infinity device from Kolya's phone, plus some additional electronics from under the carpet and in the toilet roll holder.

'Thought you dealt with the sweeping,' Bond snapped, looking suspiciously at Tirpitz.

'I did all our rooms when we first got here. Checked yours out as well, buddy.'

'You also claimed the rooms were clean in Madeira.'

'So they were.'

'Well, how come they – whoever *they* are – were able to pinpoint us here?'

Unruffled, Tirpitz repeated he had swept the rooms for electronics. 'Everything was hygienic. In Madeira, and here.'

'Then we've got a leak. One of us – and I know it's not me,' Bond said acidly.

'One of us? Of *us*?' Now Kolya's voice turned nasty.

As yet Bond had not been able to give Kolya the full details of the warning telephone call that he supposed came from Paula. He did so now, watching the Russian's face alter. Mosolov's features were like the sea, he thought. This time the change was from anger to placidity, then concern, as Bond outlined how the trick could have been managed. Whoever was operating against them knew a great deal about their private lives.

'That was no ageing land mine out there,' he stated bleakly. 'Rivke is good on skis. I'm not bad myself, and I should imagine you're not exactly a novice, Kolya. Don't know about Tirpitz . . .'

'I can hold my own.' Tirpitz had assumed the expression of a surly schoolboy.

The explosion on the slopes, Bond continued, could have been operated by a remote control system. 'They could also have used a sniper, in the hotel. It's been done before – a bullet activating an explosive charge. Personally, I go for the remote control because it ties in with everything else: the fact that Rivke was on the slopes, that I got a telephone call which must have coincided with her leaving the top of the run.' He spread his hands. 'They have us bottled up here; they've taken one of us out already, which makes it easier for them to close in on the rest . . .'

'And Count von Glöda was here for breakfast, with his woman.' Tirpitz came out of his sullen mood. He pointed at Kolya Mosolov. 'Do you know anything about that?'

Mosolov gave a half nod. 'I saw them. Before the business on the slopes. Saw them when I got back to the hotel.'

Bond followed up what Tirpitz had started. 'Don't you think it's time, Kolya? Time you came clean about von Glöda?'

Mosolov made a gesture meant to convey that he was at a loss about all the fuss. 'The so-called Count von Glöda is a prime suspect . . .'

'He's the *only* suspect,' Tirpitz snapped.

'The probable power behind the people we're all trying to nail,' added Bond.

Kolya sighed. 'He was not mentioned in previous meetings because I've been waiting for positive proof – identification of his command headquarters.'

'And you have that proof now?' Bond moved close to Kolya, almost menacing him,

'Yes.' Clear and unshakable. 'All we need. It's part of the briefing for tonight,' Kolya paused, as though pondering the wisdom of going any further with the information. 'I suppose you both know who von Glöda really is?' It was as though he intended to deliver some *coup de grâce*.

Bond nodded. 'Yes.'

'And the relationship with our missing colleague,' added Tirpitz.

'Good,' said Kolya in a slightly peeved tone. 'Then we'll get on with the briefing.'

'And leave Rivke to the wolves.' The thought still stung Bond.

Very quietly Kolya turned his head, eyes clashing with Bond's. 'I suggest that Rivke will be okay. That we leave her in – what's your expression – leave her in baulk? I predict that Rivke Ingber will reappear when she's ready. In the meantime, if we are to collect the evidence that will eventually smash the National Socialist Action Army – which is our sole reason for being here – we must go into tonight's operation with some care.'

'So be it,' Bond said, masking his anger.

The object of the exercise, Kolya Mosolov had already put forward, was that they should view, and possibly photograph, the theft of arms from ordnance depot Blue Hare, located near

Alakurtii. Kolya spread a detailed survey map on the floor. It was covered in marks – crosses in red, various routings in black, blue and yellow.

Kolya's forefinger rested on a red cross just south of Alakurtii, about sixty kilometres inside the Russian border and some seventy-five kilometres from where they now sat.

'I understand', he said, 'that we're all fairly expert on snow scooters.' He looked first at Tirpitz, then at Bond. Both men nodded their assent. 'I'm glad to hear it, because we're all going to be under pressure. The weather forecast for tonight is not good. Sub-zero temperatures, rising a little after midnight when light snow is expected, then dropping to hard freezing conditions again.'

Kolya pointed out that they would be travelling through difficult country, by snow scooter, during much of the night.

'As soon as I realised Rivke would be in the hospital . . .' he began again.

'Where she is not,' interrupted Bond. Kolya ignored him.

'. . . I made other arrangements. We need at least four bodies on the ground for what we have to do. We must cross the Russian border without help from my people, following a route which I suspect will also be used by NSAA vehicles. The intention was to leave two of us as markers along the route while Bond and I went all the way to Alakurtii. My information is that the NSAA convoy will be arriving, by arrangement with the officer in command of Blue Hare and his subordinates, at about three in the morning.'

The loading of whatever vehicles were to be used would take only an hour or so. Kolya guessed that they would employ amphibious tracked APCs, probably one of the many variants of the Russian BTRs. 'They have everything ready, so my people tell me. Bond and I will take VTR and still pictures, using infra-red if necessary: though I presume there'll be a lot of light. Blue Hare is in the back of beyond and nobody's going to bother much during the loading. The care will be taken on the way in, and, more especially, during the transportation out. At Blue Hare itself, I expect all the floodlights to be on.'

'And where does von Glöda come into all this?' Bond had been examining the map and its pencilled hieroglyphics. He was not happy with it. The way across the border looked more than difficult – through heavily wooded areas, over frozen lakes and long stretches of open, snow-covered country which, in summer, would be flat tundra. Mainly, though, it was the heavily forested patches that worried him. He knew what it was like to navigate, and find a trail, with a snow scooter, through these great black blocks of fir and pine.

Kolya gave a kind of secret smile. 'Von Glöda', he said very slowly, 'will be here.' His finger hovered over the map, then stabbed down at a section marked out in oblongs and squares. The map reference showed it to be just inside the Finnish border, a little to the north of where they would expect to cross and return.

Both Bond and Tirpitz craned forward, Bond quickly memorising the co-ordinates on the map. Kolya continued talking.

'I am 99 per cent certain that the man your people, Brad, call Glow-worm, will be safely tucked away there tonight; just as I'm sure the convoy from Blue Hare will end up at the same point.'

'Ninety-nine per cent certain?' Bond raised an eyebrow quizzically, his hand lifting to brush the small comma of hair from his forehead. 'Why? How?'

'My country . . .' Kolya Mosolov's tone contained no jingoism, or especial pride, 'my country has a slight advantage, from a geographical viewpoint.' His finger circled the whole area around the red oblong marks on the map. 'We've been able to mount considerable surveillance over the past weeks. It's also to our advantage that agents on the ground have made exhaustive enquiries. There are of course still a large number of ruined old defensive points along this part of the frontier. You can see the remains of defences in many European countries – in France for instance, even in England. Most are intact but unusable, the bunker walls sound enough but the interiors crumbling. So you can imagine how many blockhouses and fortifications were constructed all along here during the Winter War, and, again, after the Nazi invasion of Russia.'

'I can vouch for that.' Bond smiled, as though trying to let Kolya know he was not entirely a stranger to this part of the world.

'My people know about them too.' Tirpitz was not to be outdone.

'Ah.' Kolya's face lit up in what might haved passed for a benign smile.

Silence, for a good half minute.

Then Kolya nodded, his strange trick of sudden facial change turning him sage-like. 'Once we were alerted to what was going on at Blue Hare, our Special Operations Departments were given precise orders. High flying aircraft and satellites were set on new routes. Eventually they came up with these.' He slid a small, clear plastic folder from under the map and began to pass around a series of photographs. There were a number of pictures, obviously taken from reconnaissance aircraft – probably the Russian Mandrake, Mangrove or Brewer-D, all ideal for the purpose. Even in black and white the photographs clearly showed large areas of disturbed ground. They had been taken during the late summer months or in early autumn before the snows, and on most of them some kind of large concrete bunker entrance was unmistakable.

The other photographs were also of a type with which both Bond and Brad Tirpitz were familiar: military reconnaissance satellite pictures, taken from miles above the earth, with varied cameras and lenses. The most interesting were those which showed, in vivid colour, changes in geological structure.

'We put one of our Cosmos military intelligence birds on the job. Good, eh?'

Bond's eyes flicked from the satellite pictures to the small drawings on the map. The pictures, mostly magnified and blown up, showed that considerable work had taken place under the earth's surface. The textures and colours made it plain that the building was well-executed, with a great deal of steel and concrete used. It was a highly symmetrical structure with all the signs of a complete and active underground complex.

'You see,' Kolya continued, 'I have more than just the photographs.' He produced yet another folder, containing both plan and elevation drawings of what could only be a very large bunker. 'We were alerted by the satellite findings. Then our field agents moved in. There were also one or two interesting maps of the area, used at the time of the Winter War, and later. Finnish military engineers built a large, underground arms dump on exactly this spot during the late 1930s. It was big enough to contain at least ten-tracked tanks, as well as ammunition and facilities for repair. The main bunker entrance was large – here,' he pointed directly to the photographs and the plan view drawing. 'From our people on the ground, and existing records, we know the bunker was, in fact, never used. However, about two years ago during the summer, much activity was reported in the general area – builders, bulldozers, the usual paraphernalia. It is, without much doubt, von Glöda's lair.' His finger started to trace along the drawings. 'There, you see, the original entrance has been rebuilt and sealed off – large enough to take vehicles, with plenty of room below for storage.'

It was a very clear, and convincing, batch of evidence. The complex seemed large, divided into two areas: one for vehicles and stores, the other a vast honeycomb of living quarters. At least three hundred people would be able to live underground in this place, year in and year out. The bigger entrance lay parallel to a smaller access and both sloped down similar gradients to a depth of some three hundred metres, which, as Tirpitz said, was 'deep enough to bury a lot of bodies'.

'We believe it is where *all* the bodies are buried.' Kolya showed no sign of humour. 'I personally think it constitutes the headquarters, and planning control command post, of the National

Socialist Action Army. The place has also become a major staging point for the arms and munitions stolen from Red Army bases. That refurbished bunker, in my opinion, is the heart of the NSAA.'

'So all we have to do', Tirpitz glanced at Kolya, the sarcasm practically tangible, 'is take some pretty pictures of your army people betraying their country, then follow the vehicles back to here,' finger on the map, 'to the bunker. Their cosy little Ice Palace.'

'Exactly.'

'Just like that. Three of us – with me, I presume, acting as a backstop on the frontier, where any hairbrained asshole could pick me off like a jack-rabbit.'

'Not if you're as good as they tell me,' Kolya said, returning like for like. 'For my part, I've taken the liberty of bringing in another of my people – simply because there are *two* crossing points.' He indicated another line, slightly farther north than the route he and Bond would be taking, explaining that both border crossings should be covered. 'Originally I wanted Rivke up there, just in case. We need a spare, so I've arranged it.'

There was a brief pause. Then Bond said, 'Kolya, I want to know something.'

'Go ahead.' The face lifted towards him, open and frank.

'If this runs to plan – if we get the evidence, and we follow the convoy back to the bunker you say is here,' Bond pointed at the map, 'when we've done all that, what's the next move?'

Kolya did not even stop to think. 'We make certain we have our proof. After that, we do one of two things. Either we report back to our respective agencies, or, if it looks feasible, we finish the job ourselves.'

Bond made no further comment. Kolya had signalled an interesting endgame. If he was, in fact, involved in any KGB-Red Army conspiracy, the action of 'finishing the job ourselves' would be as good a method as any to cover things up for ever. The more so, Bond calculated, if Kolya Mosolov saw to it that

Bond and Tirpitz did not return. Meanwhile, if the conspiracy theory held any water, the NSAA command headquarters could already be set to move out to another hiding place; another bunker.

They talked on, going over the minutiae: where the snow scooters were hidden, the kind of cameras they would be using, the exact point at which Tirpitz would take up his post and the position of Kolya's new agent, identified solely by the crypto-nym Mujik, a little joke of Kolya's, or so he maintained, a *mujik* being in old Russia a peasant, regarded by the law as a minor.

After an hour or so of this close briefing, Kolya handed out maps to both Tirpitz and Bond. They covered the entire area, were as near to Ordnance Survey standard of cartography as you could get, and had the routes over the frontier marked in thin pencil, together with the position of Blue Hare, and the same series of oblongs denoting the underground complex of what they had taken to calling the Ice Palace. Blue Hare and the Ice Palace, Kolya maintained, were drawn in to exact scale.

They synchronised their watches, and were to meet at mid-night at the RV point – which meant leaving the hotel, indi-vidually, between eleven-thirty and eleven-forty.

Bond re-entered his room silently, taking out the VL34 to check the entire suite again. Gone were the days, he thought in passing, when you could keep a watch on your room by leaving tiny slivers of matchstick in the door, or wedged into drawers. In the old days, a small piece of cotton would do wonders; but now, in the age of the micro-chip, life had become more sophis-ticated, and considerably more difficult.

They had been at it again during the briefing. Not just the automatic 'infinity' in the telephone this time, but a whole screen of listening devices as back-ups: one behind the mirror in the bathroom; another in the curtains, neatly sewn in place; a third disguised as a button in the small 'housewife' pack of needles and thread tucked into its pocket inside the hotel stationery folder, and another bug ingeniously fitted *within* a new lamp bulb by the bed.

Bond treble-swept the place. Whoever was doing the surveillance certainly knew the job. As he destroyed the various items, he even wondered if the new infinity bug in the telephone was merely a dummy, placed there in the hope he would not continue the search after finding it.

Once he was assured that the room was clean, Bond spread out his map. From the briefcase he had already removed a military pocket compass which he intended to carry that night. Using a small pad of flimsies and a credit card as a ruler, Bond started to make calculations and trace the routes on to the map – noting the exact compass bearings they would have to follow to get across the border and locate Blue Hare, then the bearings out from Blue Hare, following both the route in and its alternative.

He also took care to check angles and bearings that would lead them to the Ice Palace. All the time he worked, Bond felt uneasy – a sense he had experienced more than once since the Madeira meeting. He was aware of the basic cause: from time to time he had worked in conjunction with another member of either his own, or a sister, service. But Icebreaker was different. Now he had been forced to act with a team and Bond was not a team man – especially not a team that blatantly contained grave elements of mistrust.

His eyes searched the map, as though looking for a clue and, quite suddenly, without his really trying to find it, an answer stared back at him.

Ripping off one of the flimsies from his small pad, Bond carefully placed it over the Ice Palace markings and traced in the pencil lines showing the extent of the underground bunker. Then he added in the local topography. When this tracing was completed, Bond slid the flimsy in a northeasterly direction on the map, covering the equivalent of around fifteen kilometres.

The diagonal move carried the Ice Palace across the frontier zone into Russia. What was more, the local topography fitted exactly, down to the surrounding ground levels, wooded areas, and summer river-lines. The topography in general was all very similar, but this was quite extraordinary. Either the maps had been specially printed, or there really were two locations – one on either side of the frontier – exact in every topographical detail.

With the same concentration, Bond copied the possible secondary position of the Ice Palace on to his map. He then made one or two further compass bearings. It was possible that von Glöda's headquarters, and the first stage of the arms convoy, lay not in Finland, but still on the Russian side of the frontier. Even bearing in mind the similarity of the landscape at any point along this part of the border, it was a strange coincidence to find two exactly identical locations within fifteen kilometres of one another.

He now thought about the position of the main bunker entrances at the Ice Palace. Both faced towards the Russian side. If it was on the Russian side of the border, he had to remember that this section of the Soviet Union had once belonged to Finland – before the great clash of the Winter War of 1939–40. But either way, for the entrances of the original fortifications to face towards Russia was odd; particularly if the bunkers were built before the Russo-Finnish war of 1939; not so odd if they were erected after the peace, when large tracts of land, including much of this zone, were handed over to the Soviet Union, following the Finnish surrender of March 13th, 1940.

To Bond, it was a definite possibility that the Ice Palace was of Russian origin. If it truly was the headquarters of the Fascist National Socialist Action Army, then it showed two things: the leader of the NSAA was even more cunning than Bond had thought, and the coercion, and betrayal, within the Red Army, GRU and KGB, might be more widespread than anyone had first imagined.

Bond's next job was to get some form of message out to M. Technically, he could simply dial London on his room telephone. Certainly it was now free of listening devices, but who knew if calls were also being monitored via the hotel exchange?

Quickly, Bond committed the compass bearings, and co-ordinates, to memory, using his well-tried form of mnemonics. He then tore up the flimsies from his pad – removing several of the back sheets at the same time – and flushed them down the lavatory, waiting for a few moments to make certain they had all been carried away.

Climbing into his outdoor gear, Bond left the room and went down to his car. Among the many pieces of secret equipment he now carried in the Saab, there was one only recently fitted by Q Branch. In front of the gear lever there nestled what seemed to be a perfectly normal radio telephone, an instrument which was useless unless it had a base unit somewhere within about twenty-five miles radius. But twenty-five miles was no good to Bond, any more than a normal telephone was any good to him, in the present circumstances. The Saab car phone had two great advantages. The first of these was a small black box, from which hung a pair of terminals. The box was not much larger than a pair of cassettes stacked one on top of the other, and Bond took it from its hiding place, in a panel behind the glove compartment.

Reactivating the sensor alarms, he trudged through the hard, iced snow, back to the hotel and his room. Taking no chances, Bond did a quick sweep with the VL34, and was relieved to find the room still clean after his short absence. Quickly he unscrewed the underside plate on the telephone. He then connected the terminals of the small box and removed the receiver from its rests, placing it close at hand. The advanced electronics contained in that small box ensured that he now had an easily available base unit from which to operate the car telephone. Access to the outside world, illegally using the Finnish telephone service, was assured.

There was, moreover, the car phone's second advantage. On

returning to the Saab, Bond pressed one of the unmarked square black buttons on the dashboard. A panel slid down behind the telephone housing, revealing a small computer keyboard and a minute screen – a telephone scrambler of infinite complexity, which could be used to shield the voice or send messages which would be printed out on a compatible screen in the building overlooking Regent's Park.

Bond pressed the requisite keys to link the car phone with his base unit. Tapping the get-out code from Finland and the dial-in code for London, he followed on with the London code and the number for the Headquarters of his Service. He then fed in the required cipher of the day and began to tap out his message in clear language. It came up on his screen, as it would at the Headquarters building, in a jumble of grouped letters. It would be deciphered rapidly to read out on the HQ screen in clear language.

The whole transmission took around fifteen minutes, with Bond bent inside the dark car lit only by the glow from the tiny screen, very conscious of the ice build-up on the windows. Outside there was a light wind and the temperature continued to drop. When the whole message had been sent, Bond closed up, reactivated the sensors and returned to the hotel. Once more, playing it safe, he quickly swept the room, then removed the base unit from the hotel telephone.

He had only just packed away the base unit in his briefcase – intending to return it to the Saab before the real business of the night began – when there was a knock at the door. Now playing everything by the book, Bond picked up the P7 and went to the door, slipping the chain on before asking who was there.

'Brad,' the answer came back. 'Brad Tirpitz.'

'Bad' Brad Tirpitz looked a shade shaken as he came into the room. Bond noticed a distinct pallor, and a wariness around the big American's eyes.

'Bastard Kolya,' Tirpitz spat.

Bond gestured towards the armchair. 'Sit down, get it off your chest. The room's clean now. I had to delouse again after we had the meeting with Kolya.'

'Me too.' A slow smile spread over Tirpitz's face, stopping short, as always, at the eyes. It was as though a sculptor had worked slowly at the rocky features and suddenly given up. 'I caught Kolya in the act though. Did you figure out who's working for whom yet?'

'Not exactly. Why?'

'I left a small memento in Kolya's room after the briefing. Just stuffed it down behind the chair cushion. I've been listening in ever since.'

'And heard no good of yourself, I'll warrant.' Bond opened the fridge, asking if Tirpitz wanted a drink.

'Whatever you're having. Yeah, you're right. It's true what they say – you never hear good of yourself.'

Bond quickly mixed a brace of martinis, handing one to Tirpitz.

'Well.' Tirpitz took a sip, raising his eyebrows in a complimentary movement. 'Well, old buddy, Kolya made several telephone calls. Switched languages a lot and I couldn't figure most of it – double-talk on the whole. The last one I did understand, though. He talked to someone without beating about the bush. Straight Russian. Tonight's trip, friend, is taking us to the end of the line.'

'Oh?'

'Yep. Me they're giving the Rivke treatment – right on the border, to make it look like a land mine. I even know the exact spot.'

'The exact spot?' Bond queried.

'Not dead ground – if you'll excuse the expression – but right in the open. I'll show you.' Tirpitz held out his hand for Bond's map.

'Just give me the co-ordinates.' Nobody, trusted or not, was going to see Bond's map, particularly now that he had put in the possible true location of the Ice Palace.

'You're a suspicious bastard, Bond.' Tirpitz's face changed back to the hard granite, chipped, sharp, and dangerous.

'Just give me the co-ordinates.'

Tirpitz rattled off the figures, and, in his head, Bond worked out roughly where the point came in relation to the whole area of operations. It made sense – a remote-controlled land mine at a spot where they would be travelling a few metres away from real minefields anyway.

'As for you,' Tirpitz growled, 'you ain't heard nothing yet. They've got a spectacular exit organised for our Mr Bond.'

'I wonder what's in store for Kolya Mosolov?' Bond said, with an almost innocent look.

'Yeah, my own thoughts too. We think alike, friend. This is a dead-men-tell-no-tales job.'

Bond nodded, paused, took a sip of his martini and lit a cigarette. 'Then you'd better tell me what's in store for me. It looks as if it's going to be a long, cold night.'

# 11

# SNOW SAFARI

Every few minutes, James Bond had to reduce speed to wipe the rime of frost from his goggles. They could not have chosen a worse night. Even a blizzard, he thought, would have been preferable. 'A snow safari,' Kolya had laughingly called it.

The darkness seemed to cling to them, occasionally blowing free to give a glimmer of visibility, then descending again as though blindfolds had blown over their faces. It took every ounce of concentration to follow the man in front, and the only comfort was that Kolya, leading the column of three, had his small spotlight on, dipped low. Bond and Tirpitz followed without lights, chasing this rapid winter will o' the wisp with difficulty. The three big Yamaha snow scooters roared on through the night making enough noise, Bond thought, to draw any patrols within a ten mile radius.

After his lengthy talk with Brad Tirpitz, Bond had prepared himself with even greater care than usual. First there was the job of clearing up – packing away anything that would not be required and taking it out to the Saab, from which other items had to be collected. Having locked the briefcase and overnight bag in the boot, Bond slipped into the driving seat. Once there, he had reason to thank whatever saint watched over agents in the field.

He had just replaced the telephone base unit in its hiding place behind the glove compartment when the tiny pinprick of red light started to blink rapidly beside the car phone. Bond immediately pressed the chunky button which gave access to the scrambler computer and its screen. The winking pinhead light indicated that a message from London was stored within the system.

He ran quickly through all the activating procedures, then tapped out the incoming cipher code. Within seconds the small screen – no larger than the jacket of a paperback novel – was filled with groups of letters. Another few deft movements of Bond's fingers on the keys brought the groups into a further jumble, then removed them completely. The instrument whirred and clicked as its electronic brain started to solve the problem. A running line of clear print ribboned out on the screen. The message read:

FROM HEAD OF SERVICE TO 007 MESSAGE RECEIVED MUST WARN YOU TO APPROACH SUBJECT VON GLÖDA WITH UTMOST CAUTION REPEAT UTMOST CAUTION AS THERE IS NOW POSITIVE REPEAT POSITIVE ID VON GLÖDA IS CERTAINLY WANTED NAZI WAR CRIMINAL AARNE TUDEER STRONG POSSIBILITY THAT YOUR THEORY IS CORRECT SO IF CONTACT IS MADE ALERT ME IMMEDIATELY AND RETURN FROM FIELD THIS IS AN ORDER LUCK M

So, Bond thought, M was concerned enough to haul in the line if he went too close. The word 'line' brought other expressions to his mind – 'the end of the line'; 'line of fire'; being 'sold down the line'. All these could well be applicable now.

Having secured the car, Bond returned to the hotel, where he rang down for food and a fresh supply of vodka. The agreement was that all three would stay in their rooms until it was time to RV at the snow scooters.

An elderly waiter brought in a small trolley-table with Bond's dinner order – a simple meal of thick pea soup laced with lean chunks of meat, and excellent reindeer sausages.

As he ate, Bond slowly realised that his edginess over this assignment, Icebreaker, was not entirely due to the mental excuses he had made about his operational attitudes, working on his own, relying on his professionalism and intuition. There was another element – one that had appeared with the name Aarne Tudeer, and the linking of that name with the Count von Glöda.

Bond pondered on other powerful individuals with whom he had fought dangerous, often lonely, battles. At random he thought of people like Sir Hugo Drax, a liar and cheat, whom he had beaten, by exposing him as a card sharp, before taking the man on in another kind of battle. Auric Goldfinger was of the same breed, a Midas man, whom Bond had challenged on the field of sport as well as the deeper, dangerous zone of battle. Blofeld – well, there were many things about Blofeld which still chilled Bond's blood: thoughts about Blofeld, and his relative, with whom Bond had only recently come face to face.

But Konrad von Glöda – Aarne Tudeer as he really was – seemed to have cast a depressing gloom over this whole business. A massive question mark. 'Glöda equals Glow,' Bond said aloud.

He wondered if the man had a strange sense of humour, if this pseudonym contained a message. A key to his personality? Glöda was a cipher, a ghost, glimpsed once in the dining room of the Hotel Revontuli – a fit, elderly weather-bronzed, iron-haired, military-looking man. If Bond had met him in a London club he would not have given him a second thought – ex-army written all over him. There was no aura of evil around the person. No way of telling.

For a flitting second, Bond experienced the strange sensation of a clammy hand running down his spine. Because he had not really met von Glöda face to face, or even read a full dossier on the man, Bond felt an unusual unease. In that fraction of time, he even wondered if, at long last, he might have met his match.

He inhaled sharply, mentally shaking himself. No, Konrad von Glöda was not going to beat him. What was more, if contact came with the phony Count, 007 would turn a blind eye to M's instructions. James Bond could certainly not leave the field and run from von Glöda, or Tudeer, if he really was responsible for the terrorist activities of the NSAA. If there was any chance of wiping out that organisation, Bond would not let it slip through his fingers.

He felt confidence leap back into his system – a loner again, with no one to trust out here in the crushing cold of the Arctic. Rivke had vanished, and he cursed the fact there had been no time to search for her. Kolya Mosolov was about as credible as a starved and injured tiger. Brad Tirpitz? Well, even though they were allies on paper, Bond could not bring himself to a state of complete faith in the American. Certainly, in the emergency they had worked on a contingency plan to cover the attempt which, according to Tirpitz, was to be made on his life. But that was all. The chains of trust between them were not yet welded.

At that moment, before the night even got under way, Bond made a vow. He would play it alone, by his rules. He would bend his will to nobody.

So now they proceeded, at somewhere between sixty and seventy kph, swerving and bucketing along a rough track between the trees, about a kilometre from the Russian border and parallel to it.

Snow scooters – known by tourists as 'Skidoos' – can rip across snow and ice at a terrifying speed. They are to be handled with care. Unique in design, with their wicked-looking, blunt bonnets and long strutting skis protruding forward, the scooters have revolving tracks studded with great pointed spikes which thrust the machine along, giving initial momentum which builds up very quickly as the skis glide across the surface below. There is little protection for the driver – or any passenger – apart from short deflector windshields. On their first ride, people tend to handle snow scooters wrongly, like motorcycles. A motorcycle can turn at acute angles, while a snow scooter has a much wider turning circle. There is also a tendency for a tyro rider to stick out a leg on the turn. He does it once only and probably ends up in hospital with a fracture, for the leg merely buries itself in the snow, dragged back by the speed of the scooter.

Ecologists curse the arrival of this particular machine, claiming that the spikes have already rutted and destroyed the texture of land under the snow; but it has certainly altered the pattern of life in the Arctic – particularly for the nomadic natives of Lapland.

Bond kept his head down, and was quick in his reactions. A turn needed considerable energy, especially in deep, hard snow, as you had to pull the skis around with the handlebars, then hold them, juddering, as they tried to resume their normal forward direction. Following someone like Kolya presented other difficulties. You could easily get caught in the ruts made by the leader's scooter, which gave problems of manoeuvrability, for it was like being trapped on tram lines. Then, if the leader made an error, you could almost certainly end up by screaming into him.

Bond tried to weave behind Kolya, slewing from side to side, glancing up continually, trying to glimpse the way ahead from the tiny glow of Kolya's light. Occasionally he pulled out too far, sending the scooter rearing up like some fairground ride, producing a roll first to the right, then left, slipping upwards almost to the point of losing control, then sliding back again and up the other side until, wrestling with the handlebars, he recovered.

Even with face and head completely covered, the cold and wind sliced into Bond like razor cuts and he was constantly flexing his fingers in the fear that they would go numb on him.

In fact, Bond had done everything within his power to come prepared. The P7 automatic was in its holster across his chest, inside the quilted jacket. There was no chance of getting at it quickly, but at least it was there, with plenty of spare ammunition. The compass hung from a lanyard around his neck, the instrument tucked safely inside the jacket. Some of the smaller pieces of electronics were scattered about his person, and the maps were accessible in a thigh pocket of his quilted ski pants. One of the long Sykes Fairburn commando daggers lay strapped inside his left boot, and a shorter Lapp reindeer knife hung from his belt.

On his back, Bond carried a small pack containing other items – a white coverall, complete with hood, in case there should be need for snow camouflage, three of the stun grenades, and two L2A2 fragmentation bombs.

The trees seemed to be getting thicker, but Kolya twisted in and out with ease, obviously knowing the exact route. Palm of his hand stuff, Bond thought, holding position a couple of metres from the Russian's tail, and aware of Brad Tirpitz somewhere behind him.

They were turning. He could sense it even though the move was not immediately obvious. Kolya took them through gaps in the trees, twisting to left and right, but Bond could feel them pulling ever farther right – to the east. Soon now they would break cover. Then it would be a kilometre of open country, into the woods again, and the long dip into the valley, where a great swathe was cut through the forests to mark the frontier and deter people from attempting a crossing.

Quite suddenly they shot out of the trees, and even in the darkness the transition was unnerving. Within the forest there had been a kind of safety. Now the blackness lifted slightly as the open snow, showing grey around them, took over. Their speed increased – a straight run with no dodging or sudden swerving in a change of direction. Kolya seemed to have set his course, opened the throttle and given his machine its head. Bond followed, straying slightly to the right, dropping back a little now that they were in open country.

The cold became worse, either from lack of shelter or just

because they were making more speed across open country. Maybe it was also because they had been on the trail for the best part of an hour, and the cold had begun to penetrate their bones, even through the layers of warm clothing.

Ahead, Bond caught sight of the next belt of trees. If Kolya took them through that short line of forest at speed, they would be in the long open dip in a matter of ten minutes.

The valley of death, Bond thought; for it was down in the open valley floor, which made up the border protection zone, that the trap was to be sprung on Brad Tirpitz. They had worked out the theory in Bond's hotel room. Now the moment drew closer as the three scooters sent snow flying around them. When it came, there could be no stopping or turning back for Bond to see if their planned counter-measures worked. He simply had to trust Tirpitz's own timing, and ability to survive.

Into the trees again – like going from relative light into the instant darkness of a gloomy cathedral. Fir branches whipped around Bond's body, stinging his face, as he hauled on the handlebars: left; then right; straight; left again. There was a moment when he almost misjudged the wide turn, feeling the forward ski touch the base of a tree hidden by snow; another when he thought he would be thrown off as the scooter crunched over thick roots covered with ice, slewing the machine into the start of a skid. But Bond held on, heaving at the controls, straightening the machine.

This time, when they broke cover, the landscape ahead seemed clearer, even through the frost-grimed goggles. The white valley stretched away on either side, the slope angling gently downwards to flatten, then climbing up the far side into a regiment of trees lined up in battle order.

In the open again, their speed increased. Bond felt his scooter nose down as the strain came off the engine. Now the struggle was to prevent the machine from going into a slide.

As they descended, the feeling of vulnerability became more

intense. Kolya had told them this route was used constantly by border-crossers, for there were no frontier units within fifteen kilometres on either side, and they rarely made any night patrols. Bond hoped Kolya was right. Soon they would sweep into the bottom of the valley – half a kilometre of straight ice – before climbing up the far side and into the trees of Mother Russia. Before then, Brad Tirpitz would be dead – at least that was what had been planned.

Bond's mind flitted back to a drive he had made in winter, a fair time ago now, through the Eastern Zone to West Berlin. The ice and snow were not as raw or killing as this, but he recalled going through the checkpoint from the West at Helmstedt, where they cautioned him to follow the wide freeway through the Eastern Zone without deviation. For the first few kilometres the road had been flanked by woods, and he clearly saw the high wooden towers with their spotlights, and Red Army soldiers in white winter garb, crouching in the woods and by the side of the road. Was that what awaited them in the trees at the top of the slope?

They flattened out, beginning the straight run. If Brad had got it right, the whole thing would happen in a matter of minutes – two, three minutes at the most.

Kolya increased his speed, as though racing ahead to get well up front. Bond followed, allowing himself to drop back slightly, praying that Tirpitz was ready. Moving himself in the tough saddle, Bond glanced behind. To his relief, Brad's scooter had dropped far behind, just as they planned. He could not see if Tirpitz was still there: only the blur and black shape as the scooter slowed.

As Bond turned his head, it happened. It was as though he had been counting the seconds: working out the exact point. Maybe intuition?

The explosion came later. All he saw was the violent flash from where the dull black shape sped behind him – the crimson heart of flame and a great white phosphorescent outline, lighting the column of snow which soared into the night.

Then the noise, the heavy double clump, stunning the eardrums. The shock waves struck Bond's scooter, hammering him in the back, propelling him off course.

# 12

# BLUE HARE

At the moment of explosion, Bond's reflexes came automatically into play. He hauled on the controls, throttling back so that his scooter slewed sideways into a long skid, then slowed towards its inevitable halt. Almost before he knew it, Bond came alongside Kolya's scooter.

'Tirpitz!' Bond yelled, not really hearing his own voice, ears tingling from the cold and deadened by the passing shock waves. Strangely, he knew what Kolya was shouting back at him, though he was uncertain of Kolya's actual words.

'For God's sake don't come alongside!' Kolya shrieked, his voice rising like the wind within a blizzard. 'Tirpitz is finished. He must've strayed off course and hit a mine. We can't stop. Death to stop. Keep directly behind me, Bond. It's the only way.' He repeated, '*Directly* behind me!' and this time Bond knew he had heard the words clearly.

It was over. A glance back showed a faint glow as pieces of Tirpitz's scooter burned out in the snow. Then came the whine of Kolya's scooter, zipping away over the ice. Bond gunned his motor and followed, keeping close now and well in line behind the Russian.

If the plan had worked, Tirpitz would already be on the skis which he had smuggled out to the scooters a good hour before they were due to leave.

The idea had been to drop skis, sticks, and pack about three minutes from the point where Kolya had planned to have him taken out. A minute later, Tirpitz was to set and lock his handlebars; then make a slow roll-off, low into the snow, opening the throttle at the last moment. With good timing and luck, he could lie well clear of the explosion, then take to the skis almost at leisure. There was time enough for him to reach the point arranged with Bond.

Put him from your mind, Bond thought, in any event. Consider Tirpitz dead. It's yourself and nobody else.

The far slope was not easy, and Kolya maintained a cracking pace, as though anxious to reach the relative cover of the trees. Half-way up the first flurries of fresh, falling snow started to eddy around them.

At last they reached the trees and their blackness. Kolya pulled up, beckoning Bond alongside him and leaning over to speak. But for the gentle throb of the idling engines, it was very still among the tall firs and pines. Kolya did not appear to shout, and this time his words were perfectly clear.

'Sorry about Tirpitz,' he said. 'It could've been any of us. They may have rearranged the mine pattern. Now we're still one short.'

Bond nodded, saying nothing.

'Follow me like a leech.' Kolya went on. 'The first two kilometres are not easy, but after that we're more or less on wide tracks. A road, in fact. Any sign of the convoy and I'll switch off my light, then stop. So pull up if my light goes out. When we get near to Blue Hare we'll hide the scooters and go in on foot with the cameras.' He tapped the packs attached to the back of his machine. 'It'll be a short walk through trees. About five hundred metres.'

Around half a mile, Bond thought. That was going to be fun.

'If we take it steadily – roughly an hour and a half's ride from here,' Kolya continued. 'You fit?'

Bond nodded again.

Kolya slowly took his machine forward, and Bond, pretending to check his gear, yanked on the lanyard, pulling out the compass. He opened it, fumbling with his gloves, then laid it flat on his palm and lowered his head to see the luminous dial. He watched the needle settle and took a rough bearing. They were approximately where Kolya had said they should be. The real test, then, would come later, if they managed to follow the convoy from Blue Hare to the Ice Palace.

Bond slid the compass back inside his jacket, straightened himself and raised an arm to indicate his readiness to continue. Slowly they moved off, covering the difficult first two kilometres at almost a walking pace. It was obvious there would be a wider path leading into this protective stretch of woods, if the convoy were coming in from Finland.

As Kolya had predicted, however, once past the first stage they found themselves on a wide, snow-covered track – the snow hard and packed, frozen solid, but deeply rutted in places. Perhaps Kolya was playing straight after all. The ruts suggested a previous passage of tracked vehicles, though it was impossible to tell how recently they had been made. The cold was now so intense that anything heavy, breaking the surface of the frozen snow, would leave tracks frozen equally hard within minutes.

Kolya began to pile on the speed, and as Bond followed easily on the flat surface, numbed as his mind was by the chill and marrow-freezing temperature, he started to ask questions. Kolya had shown almost incredible expertise on the way over the border – particularly going through the forests. It was impossible for him not to have followed the same route before: many times. For Bond it had been a time of unrelieved concentration, while Tirpitz had stayed well to the rear for most of the trip. Now the impression came back to Bond that Brad Tirpitz had not even been close during the zig-zagging journey through the trees.

Had both of them crossed the frontier by this route before? It was certainly a possibility. On reflection, Bond was even more puzzled, for Kolya had kept up a rapid pace even in the most difficult areas, and had done so without reference to bearings by compass or map. It was as though he was being navigated through by external means. Radio? Perhaps. Neither he nor Tirpitz had seen Kolya out of his gear, when they met at the scooters. Had the Russian brought them through on some kind of beam? Earphones would be easy to hide under the thermal hood. Bond made a note to look for leads plugged into Kolya's scooter.

If not radio, was there a marked path? That was also a possibility, for Bond had been so busy keeping his own machine on Kolya's tail that it was doubtful whether he would have noticed any pinpoint lights or reflectors along the way.

Another thought struck him. Cliff Dudley, his predecessor on Icebreaker, had not been forthcoming about what kind of work the team had been doing, in the Arctic Circle, before the row with Tirpitz and the briefing in Madeira. Had not M suggested, or said outright, that they had wanted Bond on the team from the outset?

Indeed, what had those representatives of four different intelligence agencies been up to? Was it possible they had been into the Soviet Union already? Had they already reconnoitred Blue Hare? Yet almost all the hard information had come from Kolya – from Russia; from the hi-fly photographs, and the satellite pictures, not to mention the sniffing out of information on the ground.

There had been talk of the search for von Glöda, of identifying him as the Commander-in-Chief of the NSAA, even as Aarne Tudeer. Yet von Glöda was there, at breakfast in the hotel, large as life, recognised by all. And nobody had appeared to be in the least concerned.

If Bond had started by trusting nobody, the feeling had now grown into deep suspicion towards anybody connected with Icebreaker. And that even included M, who had also been like a clam when it came to detail.

Was it just possible, Bond wondered, that M had deliberately set him up in an untenable situation? As they racketed and slid through the snow, he saw the answer plainly enough. Yes: it was an old Service ploy. Send a very experienced officer into a situation almost blind, and let him discover the truth. The truth for 007, hammered home again, was that he was well and truly on his own. The conclusion to which he had privately come earlier was, in reality, the basis of M's own reasoning. There had never been a 'team' in the strict sense of the word: merely representatives of four agencies, working together, yet apart. Four singletons.

The thought nagged away at Bond's mind as he heaved and hauled the scooter at speed, following Kolya over the never-ending snow and jagged ice. He lost all track of time, conscious only of the cold, and the motor growl, and the endless ribbon of white behind Kolya's machine.

Then, slowly, Bond became aware of light somewhere ahead to his left – to the north-west – rising, bright, from among the trees. A few moments later, Kolya flicked off the small beam of his headlamp. He was slowing down, pulling into the trees to the left of the road. Bond brought his scooter to rest beside Kolya's machine.

'We'll haul them into the woods,' Kolya whispered. 'That's it over there – Blue Hare, with all the lights blazing like a May Day celebration.'

They parked the scooters, camouflaging them as best they could. Kolya suggested they get into the white snow suits. 'We'll be in deep snow, overlooking the depot. I have night glasses, so don't bother with anything special.'

Bond, however, was already bothering. Under cover of getting into the snow camouflage, he fumbled with numbed fingers at the clips of his quilted jacket. At least he could now get at the P7 automatic quickly. He also managed to transfer one stun grenade and one of the L2A2 fragmentation bombs from his pack to the copious pockets of the loose, hooded white garment that now covered him.

The Russian did not seem to have noticed. He carried a weapon of his own quite openly on his hip. The large night glasses were slung around his neck, and, in the gloom, Bond thought he could even detect a smile on that mobile face as Kolya handed over the automatic infra-red camera. The Russian was carrying a VTR pack clipped to his belt, the camera hanging by straps below the binoculars.

Kolya gestured towards the point where the light now seemed to blast straight up between the trees, behind a slope above them. He led the way, with Bond close on his heels – a pair of silent white ghosts passing into dead ground, moving from tree to tree.

Within a few paces they had reached the bottom of the uphill climb. The top of the rise was illuminated by the lights, which cast their beams up from the far side. There was no sign of guards or sentries, and Bond found the going difficult at first, his limbs still stiff with cold from the long scooter ride.

As they neared the crest, Kolya gave a 'get down' signal with the palm of his hand. Close together, the pair squirmed through the deep snow which buried the roots and trunk bases of the trees. Below them, in a blaze of light, lay the ordnance depot known as Blue Hare. Having strained to see through darkness and snow for over three hours, Bond was forced to close his eyes against the sudden shock of arc lights and big spots. It was not surprising, he thought fleetingly as he peered down, that the men and NCOs of Blue Hare had been so easily suborned into a treasonable act of selling military weapons, ammunition and equipment. To live the year round in this place – bleak and uninviting during the winter, mosquito-ridden through the short summer – would be enough to tempt any man, even just for the hell of it.

As his eyes adjusted, Bond thought about their dreary life. What was there to do in a camp like this? The nightly games of cards; drink? Yes, a perfect place to post alcoholics; crossing off the days to some short leave, which probably entailed a long journey; the occasional trip into Alakurtii which, by his reckoning, was six or seven kilometres away. And what would there be in Alakurtii? The odd café, the same food cooked by different hands; a bar where you could get drunk. Women? Possibly. Maybe some Russian-born Lapp girls, easy prey to disease and the brutal, licentious soldiery. All soldiers were, in the civilian mind, brutal and licentious, Bond thought. Syphilis and other venereal diseases would be rife. The occasional case of rape hushed up, paid off so that the soldiers of Blue Hare could remain untroubled.

Bond's eyes had cleared now. He studied Blue Hare without discomfort: a long, wide oblong cleared of trees, some of which had begun to grow again, encroaching on the tall wire fences with their barbed tops and angled lights. A pair of high gates had been hauled open immediately below them, and the road, snaking in through the trees, had been cleared of snow and ice, either by burners or hard sweat. Within the compound, the layout was neat and orderly. A guard room with wooden towers and search-lights on either side stood near the gate, and the metalled roadway ran straight through the centre of the base, around a quarter of a kilometre long. The storage dumps were placed on either side of this interior road: large Nissen hut-like structures with corrugated curved roofs and high sides, each with a jutting loading ramp.

It all made sense. Vehicles could drive straight in, load, or unload at the ramps, then follow the road to the far end of the camp at which there was a hard-standing turning circle. Any delivery or collection could be made at speed – the lorries, or armoured vehicles, coming in, taking off their cargo, and going on, to turn, drive back and out, the same way as they had come.

Behind the storage huts were long log cabins, certainly the troops' quarters, mess halls, and recreation centres. It was all very symmetrical. Take away the wire enclosure, and the long lines of ramps, add a wooden church and you had the makings of a village, built to support a small factory.

Bond's circulation had been restored slightly by the walk up to the ridge. Now the cold began to build in him again. He felt as though melting snow flowed through his veins and arteries, while his bones were made of the same ice that hung, sharp and glistening, Damoclean, from the branches above.

He glanced to his left. Kolya was already recording the scene for posterity, the VTR camera buzzing as he pressed the trigger, adjusted the lens, and pressed again. Bond held the small infrared camera loaded in front of him. Leaning on his elbows, he raised his goggles and pressed the rubber eyepiece to his right eye, bringing the lens into focus. In the next few minutes he took a full thirty-five still pictures of the armament transfer at Blue Hare.

Kolya's information was impeccable. The lights were on, heedless of any security. Drawn up beside the ramps were four big tracked armoured troop carriers. BTR–50s, just as Kolya had predicted. Give the man another crystal ball, Bond thought. Too good to be true.

The Russian BTRs came in various forms: the basic tracked amphibious troop carrier, for two crew and twenty men; the gun carrier; or the type now below them. These were strictly for transporting loads over difficult terrain. They had been stripped down to the bare essentials, with much of the support armour removed, and they sat on their well-chained tracks, each with a heavy bulldozer in front so that rubble, ice, deep snow, or fallen trees, could be swept from their paths. The BTRs were painted an identical grey, their flat tops unlocked and folded back down the sides, to reveal deep metal oblong holds into which crates and boxes were being stored quickly and efficiently.

The crews of the BTRs stood to one side, as if they were above the manual labour of dragging and lifting the heavy cargo, though one man from each BTR occasionally spoke to the chief loading NCO on the ramp, checking off items on a clip board.

The men doing the work were dressed in light grey fatigues, with rank badges and shoulder boards plainly visible. The fatigues were obviously worn over heavier winter gear, and their heads were encased in fur hats with enormous ear flaps which came almost to the chin. The caps were decorated in front with the familiar Red Army star.

The two-man crews, however, wore a different dress which brought a crease to Bond's brow and a sudden churning of the stomach. Under short leather coats, thick navy blue trousers could be seen, while their feet and calves were encased in heavy, serviceable jackboots. They wore ear muffs, but, above those, simple navy berets with glinting cap badges. The rig reminded Bond all too vividly of another era, a different world.

Kolya jogged his arm and handed over the night glasses, pointing to the foremost part of the first ramp. 'The Commanding Officer,' he whispered. Bond took the glasses, adjusted them, and saw a pair of men in conversation. One was from the BTR crews, the other a stocky, sallow-faced figure, muffled in a greatcoat which bore the shoulder boards of a Warrant Officer, the thick red stripe plainly visible through the glasses.

'Non-commissioned officers here,' commented Kolya, still in a whisper. 'Mainly disgruntled NCOs, or people other units want to get rid of. That's why they were such a pushover.'

Bond nodded, handing back the glasses.

The depot at Blue Hare appeared very close – a trick of the brilliant light, and the frost, which hung tendril-like in the air. Below, the working men seemed to be emitting steam from mouths and nostrils, like over-worked horses, while orders floated up, muffled by the atmosphere; sharp Russian growling, urging the labourers on. Bond even caught the sound of a voice saying, 'Faster then, you dolts. Just think of the nice bonus at the end of this, and the girls coming over from Alakurtii tomorrow. Get the job done and then you'll rest.'

One of the men turned towards the NCO, shouting, 'I'll need all the rest I can get if Fat Olga's coming over . . .' The sentence was lost on the air, but the raucous laughter suggested it ended with some lewd witticism.

Bond edged his compass out on its lanyard, surreptitiously taking a bearing, and doing some quick mental calculations. Then there was a roar below. The first BTR's motor had come to life. Men were swarming over the metal, folding up the thick flaps and locking them into place to form the flat top.

The other BTRs were almost fully loaded. Men worked in their holds, making final adjustments to straps and ropes. Then the second engine started.

'Time to be getting down,' Kolya whispered, and they saw the first carrier advance slowly towards the turning circle. It would take the whole convoy around fifteen minutes to lock up, turn, and form their line.

Slowly the pair edged back. Once below the skyline, they had to lie still for a few moments, allowing their eyes to readjust to darkness. Then the slippery descent – much quicker than the climb up – and, down among the trees, feeling their way through to where the snow scooters were hidden.

'We'll wait until they've passed.' Kolya spoke like a commander. 'Those BTRs have engines like angry lions. The crews won't hear a thing when we start up.' He put out a hand to retrieve the camera from Bond and stowed it with the VTR pack.

The lights still cut into the sky from Blue Hare, but now, in the stillness, the sound of the BTRs' motors assumed a loud; raucous, aggressive tone. Bond did another quick calculation, hoping he was right. Then the noise rose towards them and began to echo from the trees.

'They're on the move,' Kolya said, nudging him. Bond craned forward, trying to see the convoy up the road. The motor reverberations grew louder, and, even with the acoustics distorted by the ice and trees, they could be pinpointed, advancing from Bond's and Kolya's left.

'Ready?' muttered Kolya. He appeared suddenly nervous, half standing in the saddle of his scooter, head turning stiffly.

The grumble of engines reduced to a low growl. They've reached the road junction, Bond thought. Then, quite plainly, he heard one BTR's motor rise with the grind of gears. The sounds all took on new patterns, and Kolya raised himself even higher. The engine noise settled. All four BTRs were now on the same track, moving at a similar speed, in convoy. Yet something was wrong. It took Bond a second or two to realise that the echoes from the engines were decreasing.

Kolya swore in Russian. 'They're going north,' he said, spitting the words out. Then his voice appeared to mellow. 'Ah, good. It means they're taking the alternative route back. My agent will be covering them. Ready?'

Bond nodded, and they started up the scooters. Kolya wheeled out on to the snow, picking up speed immediately.

The rumble from the BTRs was audible even above the snow scooters' engines, and they were able to keep well back – with the last vehicle just visible – for a matter of ten or eleven kilometres. The small convoy stayed on the same main road until Bond thought they were getting dangerously near to Alakurtii. Then he saw Kolya signal him for a turn – a left angle into the woods again, though this time the track was of reasonable width, the snow deep and hard, newly rutted by the heavy armoured, and chained, tracks of the BTRs.

It seemed uphill all the way. Constant weaving, to stay clear of the BTRs' now dangerous tracks. The engine of Bond's scooter constantly protested at the strain, while Bond himself tried to get a fix on their direction.

If they really were heading back to the border, this was a cross-country run which should take them almost to the point at which they had entered the trees on the Russian side. For a long time that was where they appeared to be heading: south-west. Then, after an hour or so, the track forked. The BTRs moved right, taking them north-west.

There was a moment when Kolya considered they had got too close and motioned a halt. Bond just had time to haul out the compass and take a fix from the luminous dial. If the BTRs continued on their present course they would, without doubt, end up very near to the position Bond had pinpointed for the Ice Palace, if it was on the Russian side.

After another few kilometres Kolya stopped again, motioning Bond up to him. 'We'll be crossing in a few minutes.' He spoke loudly. The wind was in their faces now, cutting through the protective clothing and dragging the heavy noise of the BTR convoy back towards them. 'My replacement agent should be up ahead, so don't be surprised if another scooter joins us.'

'Shouldn't we cross an open patch this way?' Bond asked, with as much innocence as he could muster in the teeth of the biting wind.

'Not this way. Remember the map?'

Bond remembered the map vividly. He also saw his own marks, and the way the Ice Palace could, in reality, lie well to this, the Russian, side of the border. For a second he contemplated shooting Kolya out of hand, dodging his other agent, making certain that the loaded BTRs went into the bunker, and then high-tailing it out of the Soviet Union as fast as the scooter would carry him.

The thought lasted only for a moment. See it through, a voice said from deep inside him.

It was a good fifteen minutes later before they saw the other scooter. A slim figure, heavily muffled against the cold, sat upright in the seat, waiting to move forward.

Kolya raised a hand and the new scooter pulled out, taking the lead. Ahead, the BTRs grumbled and cracked on along the forest road, which, at this point, was only just wide enough to take them.

Half an hour and no change of direction. A faint light spreading over the sky. Then, almost without warning, Bond felt the hairs rise on the back of his neck. Until that moment they had been able to hear the BTRs quite clearly, even above the three scooter engines. Now only their own noise came to his ears. Automatically he slowed, swerving to avoid a rut, and, as he swerved, he saw a clear silhouette of Kolya's new agent in the saddle ahead. Even in the winter gear, Bond thought he recognised the shape of the head and shoulders. The thought jarred for an instant, and in that fraction of time everything happened.

Ahead of them a sudden blaze of light cut through the trees. Bond caught sight of the last BTR and what looked like a vast cliff of snow rising above them. Then the lights grew brighter, shining from all sides – even, it seemed, from above. Great arc lights and spots made Bond feel naked, caught, out in the open. He slewed his scooter, trying for a tight turn in the available space, ready to make a run for it, one hand plunging inside his jacket for the pistol. But the trenches cut in the snow by the BTRs made the turn impossible.

Then they came from the trees – in front, from behind, and both sides: figures in uniform of a field grey with coal-scuttle helmets and long sheepskin-lined jackets, converging on the trio, rifles and machine pistols glinting in the searing lights.

Bond had the automatic out but allowed it to dangle from his hand. This was no time for a death duel. Even 007 knew when the odds were stacked against him.

He stared forward. Kolya sat, straight-backed, on his scooter, but the other agent had dismounted and was walking back, past Kolya, towards Bond. He knew the walk, just as he had thought he recognised the head and shoulders.

Lowering his head against the glare from a spotlight turned full on him, Bond saw the boots of the men now surrounding him. The crunch in the icy snow came nearer, as the boots of Kolya's agent approached. A gloved hand moved out and took the P7 from his hand. Squinting, Bond looked up.

The figure pulled off the scarf, lifted the goggles, then dragged away the knitted hat, allowing the blonde hair to tumble down to her shoulders. Laughing pleasantly, and speaking with a mock stage-German accent, Paula Vacker looked Bond straight in the eyes.

'Herr James Bond,' she said, 'vor you der var iss over.'

# 13

# THE ICE PALACE

The uniformed men closed in. Hands frisked Bond, removed his grenades and his pack. As yet they had not got the commando knife in his Mukluk boot: a small bonus.

Paula still laughed as the men pulled Bond from his scooter and began to urge him forward through the snow. He was cold and tired. Why not? A feigned collapse might bring advantages. James Bond went limp, allowing two of the uniformed men to take his weight. He let his head loll, but followed their progress through half-closed lids.

They had come straight out of the trees into a semicircular clearing which ended in a large backward-raked flat slope, like a mini ski run. It was, of course, the bunker – the Ice Palace – for huge, white-camouflaged doors had opened in the side of the slope. Warmth seemed to pour out from the brightly lit interior.

Vaguely, Bond was also aware of a smaller entrance to the left. This fitted completely with the original drawings Kolya had provided of the place. Two areas: one for storage of arms and maintenance; the other for living quarters.

He heard a motor start up and saw one of the BTRs – the last one – crawl through the opening, then dip to disappear down the long internal ramp, which Bond knew led deep into the earth.

Paula laughed again near by, and a scooter engine revved. Bond's own scooter went past, driven by a uniformed man. Then Kolya muttered something in Russian, and Paula replied.

'You feel better soon,' one of the men dragging him said in heavily accented English. 'We give you drink inside.'

They propped him against the wall, just inside the massive doors, and one of them produced a flask which he held to Bond's lips. Flame seemed to hit his mouth, burning a line down to the stomach. Gagging, Bond gasped, 'What . . . ? What was . . . ?'

'Reindeer milk and vodka. Good? Yes?'

'Good. Yes,' Bond blurted out. He fought for breath. There was no way he could feign unconsciousness after swallowing that firewater. He shook his head and looked around. The smell of diesel fumes floated up from the rear of the cavern, and the sloping wide-ramped entrance descended at a steady angle.

Outside, the uniformed men were being lined up in a column three abreast. All of them, Bond recognised now, wore the same grey uniforms: the short winter boots and baggy field trousers, the loose, fur-lined coats with their slanting pockets, insignia just showing through on the collars of their jackets underneath. The officers wore jackboots and – presumably – breeches under their heavy greatcoats.

Kolya stood by his scooter, still talking to Paula. Both looked intense, and Paula had donned her scarf and hat against the cold. At one point Kolya called out to an officer, his form of address commanding, as though he could, at will, lord it over anyone and everyone. The officer to whom Kolya had spoken nodded and gave a sharp order. Two men detached themselves from the group and began to remove the snow scooters. There appeared to be a small concrete pillbox, large enough to take several scooters, to the right of the main entrance.

The uniformed men were now marched into the bunker, past Bond and the two who guarded him with Russian AKMs: the only note of discord in this weird Teutonic scene. The troop of men disappeared down the ramp, their boots clipping in unison on the reinforced concrete until the order came to break step, as a precaution against constant rhythm causing any structural defects.

Kolya and Paula strolled towards the great opening as though they had all the time in the world. Beyond them, in the trees, Bond saw a couple of the wigwam-like Lapp *kotas*. Smoke came from a fire between them while a figure bent over a cooking pot, a woman in Lapp costume: heavily decorated black skirt over thick, legging-like, trousers, feet wrapped in fur boots, head covered with knitted hat and shawl, mittens on the hands. Before Paula and Kolya reached the entrance, she was joined by a man who also wore the colourful dress, the patterned jacket, and a vividly embroidered black cloak slung over his shoulders. Somewhere behind the *kotas* a reindeer snorted.

From high up in the curved roof came a metallic click followed by a series of high-pitched warning whistles. Paula and Kolya began to move faster, and there was the hiss of hydraulics. The great metal doors slowly began to roll down: a safety curtain against the world.

'Well, James, surprise,' said Paula, pulling off the woollen cap again, and he could now see that she was wearing a leather jacket over some kind of uniform. Behind her, Kolya shifted, moving like a boxer. He certainly knew how to adapt, Bond thought.

'Not really a surprise.' Bond managed to smile. Bluff seemed the only way now. 'My people know. They even have the location of this bunker.' His eyes switched to Kolya. 'Should've been more careful, Kolya. The maps were not really well done. It isn't likely that you'd find two identical areas, with exactly the same topography, within fifteen to twenty kilometres of each other. You're all blown.'

For a split second he thought Kolya's face showed concern.

'Bluff, James, will get you nowhere,' said Paula.

'Does he want to see us?' Kolya asked.

Paula nodded. 'In due course. I think we can afford to take James via the scenic route. Show him the extent of the Führer-bunker . . .'

'Oh my God,' said Bond with a laugh. 'Have they really got

you at it, Paula? Come to that, why didn't you let the goons finish me off at your place?'

She gave an acid little smile. 'Because you were too good for them. Anyway, the deal is to get you alive, not dead.'

'Deal?'

'Shut up,' Kolya snapped at Paula.

She waved an elegant, dismissive hand. 'He'll know soon enough. There's not all that much time, Kolya. The Chief has got what you wanted, as promised. The current stocks have to be moved out in a day or two. No harm done.'

Kolya Mosolov made an impatient noise. 'Everyone's here, I presume?'

She smiled, nodding, stressing the word 'Everyone'.

'Good.'

Paula turned her attention back to Bond. 'You'd like to look over the place? It'll mean a lot of walking. Are you up to it?'

Bond sighed. 'I think so, Paula. What a pity though, what a waste of such a pleasant girl.'

'Chauvinist.' She did not say it unpleasantly. 'Okay, we'll go for a walk. But first,' her eyes moving to the guards, 'search him. Thoroughly. This one has more hiding places than a Greek smuggler. Look everywhere – and I mean *everywhere*.'

They looked everywhere and found everything, and not very gently. Paula and Kolya then took station on either side of Bond. The two soldiers – AKMs at the ready – followed a few paces behind. After a few metres, the ramp started to plunge, angling sharply, and they all headed to the left side where a walkway had been built, incorporating a hand rail and steps.

The bunker had clearly been built with great skill. Warm air surrounded them, and high up on the walls above them Bond was aware of the water and fuel pipes, air conditioning channels, and other underground life-support systems. There were also small metal boxes, set into the concrete at intervals, indicating some kind of internal communications system. The whole place was well-lit, with large strip lights set into the walls and the arched roof. As they descended, so the passage widened. Below, Bond saw that it opened up into a giant hangar.

Even he was shaken by the size of the place. The four BTRs they had seen picking up arms at Blue Hare were lined up with another four – eight altogether, the whole unit of vehicles dwarfed, like toys, by the height and area of the vault.

Crews of uniformed men unloaded the cargo recently brought in. Neat stacks of crates and boxes were being trundled away on fork-lift trucks, then restacked in carefully separated chambers equipped with fireproof doors and large wheel locks. Aarne Tudeer, alias Count von Glöda, was certainly taking no chances. The men worked in soft rubber shoes so there would be no possibility of sparks igniting ammunition. There must – Bond calculated – be enough arms in this place for a sizable war, certainly enough to sustain a carefully planned terrorist operation, or even guerrilla action for as long as a year.

'You see, we have efficiency. We will show the world we mean business.' Paula smiled as she spoke, evidently with great pride.

'No nukes, or neutrons?' said Bond.

Paula laughed again – a dismissive chuckle.

'They'll get nukes, chemicals, neutrons if they ever need them,' from Kolya.

Bond kept his eyes well open, observing everything, from the number of fireproof arms and munitions shelters, to the wide catwalks set half-way up the wall around this area. He also counted off the exit doors making a mental note to try and discover where they led. In the far corner of his mind he thought too of Brad Tirpitz. If Tirpitz had escaped the blast, there was still a chance of his making some vantage point on skis, still a possibility that he would not be far behind, still a hope that he would raise some kind of alarm.

'You've seen enough?' The question – from Kolya – was sharp, sarcastic.

'Martini time, is it?' Bond relaxed – there was no other way. At least he might soon find out the whole truth about von Glöda and the operations of the National Socialist Action Army. Already he knew the bare minimum about Paula, that she was part of von Glöda's quasi-military machine, and that Kolya had somehow become mixed up in the act. There had also been a reference to a deal. He did not like the sound of that. Stay relaxed, get as much information as possible, then try to find a way out.

Bond thought he had spotted the main control booth, behind a catwalk looking down over the great underground store area. The large doors to the bunker would certainly be operated from there, maybe the heating and ventilation systems as well. He had to remind himself, though, that this was only a relatively small part of the entire bunker. The living quarters, which he already knew lay next to this section, would be more complex.

'Martini time?' Kolya answered. 'Maybe. The Count is very big on hospitality. I should imagine there'll be some kind of meal ready.'

Paula said she was sure food would be served. 'He's really most understanding. Particularly with the doomed, James. Like the Roman emperors feeding up their gladiators.'

'I had a feeling it was going to be something like that.'

She smiled prettily, gave him a tiny nod, and led the way across the expanse of concrete, the click of her boots sounding clearly. She took them to one of the metal doors set in the left-hand wall. Paula spoke into a small Entryphone; with a click, the door slid back. She turned, smiling again.

'There's good security between the various sections of the bunker. The interconnecting doors only open to predetermined voice patterns.' The pretty smile once more, then they passed through, the metal door sliding shut behind them.

On this side, the passages seemed as bleak and unadorned as in the outer bunker. The walls were of the same rough concrete – doubtless strengthened with steel, Bond thought. Pipes for the various systems ran, uncovered, along the walls.

It seemed that the living quarters were about the same size as the storage, ordnance, and vehicle bunker. They were also laid out in a symmetrical fashion, with a criss-crossing of passages and tunnels.

The rough entrance corridor led to a larger, central passage, which it crossed at right angles. Glancing to his left, Bond saw metal fire doors, one of which stood open, giving a view back down the passage. From the general layout, he presumed other passages led from the arterial tunnel. On the left there appeared to be barracks for the men. Here be dragons, Bond thought – for to the left would lie the entrance to the living quarters. To get out, you would have to pass through the barracks section, and, most probably, some kind of control by the main door.

Kolya and Paula nudged him to the right. They went through two more sets of fire doors, passing other corridors leading off the main route, and doors on either side. Voices could be heard, and the occasional clatter of typewriters. The security appeared tight, and Bond spotted armed guards everywhere, some in doorways, others at points where the tributary passages joined the main walkway.

Once through the third pair of fire doors, however, the whole ambience changed. The walls were no longer cold, rough stone, but lined with hessian in pastel shades. The heating, water, air and electricity systems were hidden behind curved, decorative cornices, and the doors, on both sides, now had inset windows, through which men and women in uniform were plainly visible – working at desks, surrounded by electronic or radio equipment.

Most sinister of all, Bond thought, were the occasional photographs and framed posters which broke up the line of the walls. The faces were well-known to Bond, and would have been to any student of the Nazi era.

In front of them was another set of metal doors, but once through they trod on deep pile carpet. Paula put up a hand. The little party stopped.

They now stood in a kind of ante-room. A pair of polished

heavy pine doors were set at the far end, flanked by Doric pillars, and two men in dark blue uniforms, peaked caps with skull badges – boots gleaming, the red, black and white arm bands displaying the swastika, a smooth gloss shone on their leather belts and holsters; and the Death's Head silver skull prominent on their caps.

Paula spoke quickly, in German, and one of the uniformed men nodded, tapping on the high doors, then disappearing into the room beyond. The other man eyed Bond with a twisted smile, his hand moving constantly to the holster on his belt.

The minutes ticked by, then the doors opened, and the first man reappeared, giving Paula a nod. Both men grasped the handles of the doors and swung them back. Paula touched Bond's arm and they moved forward into the room, leaving their original guards behind them.

The only thing Bond saw on entering was Fritz Erler's huge portrait of Adolf Hitler, towering over everything else in the room. It took up almost the entire rear wall and its impact was so forcefully shattering that Bond simply stood, staring for the best part of a minute. He was conscious of other people present, and that Paula had straightened herself to attention, raising an arm in the Fascist salute.

'You like it, Mr Bond?'

The voice came from the far side of a large desk, neatly laid out with papers on a blotter, a bank of different coloured telephones, and a small bust of Hitler.

Bond tore his eyes from the painting to look at the man behind the desk. The same weatherbeaten countenance, severe military bearing – even when seated – and well-groomed, iron-grey hair. The face was not that of an old man; Count von Glöda was, as Bond had already noted at the hotel, a man blessed with ageless features – classic, still good looking, but with eyes which held no twinkle of pleasure. At the moment they were turned on Bond as though their owner were merely measuring the man for his coffin.

'I've only seen photographs of it,' Bond said calmly in return. 'I didn't like them, so it follows that, if this is the real thing, I don't really care for it either.'

'I see.'

'You should address the Count as Führer.' The advice came from Brad Tirpitz, who sprawled comfortably in an easy chair near the desk.

Bond had ceased to be surprised by anything. The fact that Tirpitz was also part of the conspiracy caused him merely to smile and give a little nod, as though suggesting he should have known the truth in the first place.

'You managed to avoid the land mine after all, then?' Bond succeeded in making it sound matter-of-fact.

Tirpitz's granite head made a slow negative movement. 'You've got the wrong boy, I'm afraid, James old buddy.'

A humourless laugh came from von Glöda as Tirpitz continued, 'I doubt you've ever seen a photograph of Brad Tirpitz. "Bad" Brad was always careful – like Kolya here – of photographs. I'm told, though, that in the dark with the light behind me, we were the same build. I fear Brad did not make it. Not ever. He got taken out, quietly, before Operation Icebreaker even got under way.'

There was a movement from the desk, a slapping of the hand, as though von Glöda decided he was being neglected.

'I'm sorry, *mein Führer*.' Tirpitz was genuinely deferential. 'It was easier to explain directly to Bond.'

'I shall do the explaining – if there is need for any.'

'Führer.' Paula spoke, her voice hardly recognisable to Bond. 'The last consignment of arms is here. The whole batch will be ready for onward movement within forty-eight hours.'

The Count inclined his head, eyes resting on Bond for a second, then flicking over to Kolya Mosolov. 'So. I have the means to keep my part of the bargain then, Comrade Mosolov. I have your price here at hand: Mr James Bond. All as I promised.'

'Yes.' Kolya sounded neither pleased nor disgruntled. The single word stated only that some bargain had been fulfilled.

'Führer, perhaps . . .' Paula began, but Bond cut across her.

'Führer?' he exploded. 'You call this man Führer – Leader? You're crazy, the lot of you. Particularly you.' His finger stabbed out towards the man behind the desk. 'Aarne Tudeer, wanted for crimes committed during the Second World War. A smalltime SS officer, granted that dubious honour by Nazis fighting with Finnish troops against the Russians – against Kolya's people. Now you've managed to gather a tiny group of fanatics around you, dressed them up like Hollywood extras, put in all the trappings, and you expect to be called Führer! Aarne, what's the game? Where's it going to get you? A few terrorist operations, a relatively small number of Communists dead in the streets – a minuscule success. Aarne Tudeer, in the kingdom of the blind the one-eyed man is king. You're one-eyed and cock-eyed . . .'

His outburst, calculated to produce the maximum fury, was cut short. Brad Tirpitz, or whoever he was, sprang from his chair, arm rising to deliver a stinging backhander across Bond's mouth.

'Silence!' The command came from von Glöda. 'Silence! Sit down, Hans.' He turned his attention to Bond, who could taste the salty blood on his tongue. If he wasn't careful, thought Bond, Hans, or Tirpitz, or whoever, would get a slap himself before long.

'James Bond,' von Glöda's eyes were glassier than ever, 'you are here for one purpose only. I shall explain to you in due course. However,' he took a moment, lingering over the last word, then repeating it, 'however, there are things I wish to share with you. There are also things I trust you will share with me.'

'Who's the cretin disguised as Brad Tirpitz?' Bond wanted to throw as many curves as possible, but von Glöda appeared to be unshakable, used to absolute obedience.

'Hans Buchtman is my SS-Reichführer.'

'Your Himmler?' Bond laughed.

'Oh, Mr Bond, it is no laughing matter.' He moved his head slightly. 'Stay within call, Hans – outside.'

Tirpitz, or Buchtman, clicked his heels, gave the old, well-known Nazi salute and left the room. Von Glöda addressed himself to Kolya. 'My dear Kolya, I'm sorry but our business will have to be delayed for a few hours – a day perhaps. Can you accommodate me in that respect?'

Kolya nodded. 'I suppose so. We made a deal, and I led your part of the arrangement right into your hands. What have I to lose?'

'Indeed. What, Kolya, have you to lose? Paula, look after him. Stay with Hans.'

She acknowledged this order with 'Führer', took Kolya's arm, and led him from the room.

Bond studied the man carefully. If this really was Aarne Tudeer, he had kept his looks and physique exceptionally well. Could it be that . . . ? No, Bond knew he should not speculate any more.

'Good; I can now talk.' Von Glöda stood, hands clasped behind his back, a tall straight figure, every inch a soldier. Well, Bond reflected, at least he was that – not the pipsqueak military amateur Hitler had proved himself to be. This man was tall, tough, and looked as shrewd as any seasoned army commander. Bond sank into a chair. He was not going to wait to be asked. Von Glöda towered over him, looking down.

'To set the record straight, and get any hopes out of your mind,' the self-styled Führer began, 'your Service resident in Helsinki – through whom you are supposed to work . . .'

'Yes?' Bond smiled.

A telephone number – that was all he had as a contact with the resident in Helsinki. Though the London briefing had been precise about his using their man in Finland, Bond had never even thought of it, experience having taught him, years ago, that one should avoid resident case officers like the plague.

'Your resident was – to use the term in vogue – "taken out" as soon as you left for the Arctic.'

'Ah.' Bond sounded enigmatic.

'A precaution.' Von Glöda waved his hand. 'Sad but necessary. There was a substitute for Brad Tirpitz. I had of course to be very careful about my errant daughter, but Kolya Mosolov acted under my orders. Your Service, the CIA, and Mossad all had their controllers removed, and the contact phones – or radio in Mossad's case – manned by my own people. So, friend Bond, do not expect the cavalry to come to your aid.'

'I never expect the cavalry. Don't trust horses. Temperamental beasts at the best of times, and since that business at Balaclava – the Valley of Death – I've not had much time for the cavalry.'

'You're quite a humorist, Mr Bond. Particularly for a man in your present situation.'

Bond shrugged. 'I'm only one of many, Aarne Tudeer. Behind me there are a hundred, and behind them another thousand. The same applies to Tirpitz; and Rivke. I can't speak for Kolya Mosolov because I don't understand his motives.' He paused for a second before continuing. 'Your own delusions, Aarne Tudeer, could be explained by a junior psychiatrist. What do they amount to? A neo-Nazi terrorist group, with access to weapons and people. Worldwide organisation. In time the terrorism will become an ideal, something worth fighting for. The movement will grow; you will become a force to be really reckoned with, in the councils of the world. Then, bingo, you've managed what Hitler failed to do – a worldwide Fourth Reich. Easy.' He gave a dry laugh. 'Easy, but it won't work. Not any more. How do you get someone like Mosolov – a dedicated Party member, a senior officer of the KGB – to go along with you even for some of the way?'

Von Glöda looked at Bond placidly. 'You know Kolya's Department in the First Directorate of the KGB, Mr Bond?'

'Not offhand. No.'

The thin smile, eyes hard as diamonds, the facial muscles

hardly moving. 'He belongs to Department V. The Department that used, many years ago, to be called SMERSH.'

Bond saw a glimmer of light.

'SMERSH has what I understand is called, in criminal parlance, a hit list. That list includes a number of names – people who are wanted, not dead, but alive. Can you imagine whose name is number one on the chart, James Bond?'

Bond did not have to guess. SMERSH had undergone many changes, but as a Department of the Russian Service, SMERSH had a very long memory.

'Mmmm.' Von Glöda nodded. 'Wanted for subversion, and crimes against the state. Death to spies, Mr Bond. A little information before death. James Bond is top of SMERSH's list and, as you well know, has been for a long time. I needed help of a particular kind. Something to get me . . . how would you say it? . . . off a hook, with certain gentlemen of the KGB. Even the KGB – like all men – have a price. Their price was you, James Bond. You, delivered in good condition, unharmed. You've bought me time, arms, a way to the future. When I've finished with you, Kolya takes you to Moscow and that charming little place they have off Dzerzhinsky Square.' What passed for a smile vanished completely. 'They've waited a long time. But come to that, so have we. Since 1945 we have waited.' He dropped his long body into the chair opposite Bond. 'Let me tell you the whole story. Then, possibly, you'll understand that I shall have purchased the Fourth Reich, and the political future of the world, by fooling the Soviet Union and selling them an English spy: James Bond, for whom they lust. Foolish, foolish men, to stake the future of their ideology on one Englishman.'

The man was unhinged. Bond knew that, but possibly so did many others. Listen, he thought. Listen to all von Glöda has to say. Listen to the music, and the words, then, perhaps, you will find the real answer, and the way out.

# 14

# A WORLD FOR HEROES

'When the war was over, and the Führer had died, gallantly, in Berlin,' von Glöda began.

'He took poison *and* shot himself,' interpolated Bond. 'Not a gallant death.'

Von Glöda did not seem to hear him. '. . . I thought of returning to Finland, perhaps even hiding there. The Allies had my name on their lists, but I would, possibly, have been safe. Safe, but a coward.'

As the story came out: the hiding in Germany, then contact with the organised escape groups, Spinne and Kameradenwerk, Bond saw clearly that he was not just dealing with some old Nazi, living with dreams of a past glory which had died in the Berlin Bunker.

'The novelists call it Odessa,' von Glöda almost mused to himself, 'but that was really a rather romantic notion – a loose organisation for getting people out. The real work was done by dedicated members of the SS who had the wit to see what could go wrong.'

Like many others, he had shifted from place to place. 'You know, of course, that Mengele – Auschwitz's Angel of Death – stayed in his home town for almost five years, undetected. In time, though, we all left.'

First, von Glöda and his wife had gone to Argentina. Later, he had been in the vanguard of those to hide in the remote, well-protected camp in Paraguay. They were all there, the wanted

Nazis. But Aarne Tudeer – as he still was then – became dissatisfied with the company he kept. 'They all play-acted,' he snarled. 'When Peron was still in control, and later, they openly showed themselves. Even rallies and meetings: beauty contests – Miss Nazi 1959. The Führer's dream would come true.' He gave an outraged, disgusted snort. 'But it was all talk; idle. They lived on dreams, and allowed the dreams to become their substance. They lost guts; threw away their heroism; became blind to the truth of the ideology Hitler had laid out for them. Hitler was right. If National Socialism was reduced to ashes, a phoenix had to rise from those ashes – otherwise, before the end of the century, Communism would overthrow Europe and, eventually, the world.'

Von Glöda had urged the few who still held on to the dream that the time to strike was at the moment of transition, when the world appeared to lose its bearings, and direction, when everyone cried out for somebody to lead them. 'That would be the time. Inevitably', he claimed, 'the Communist régime would hesitate just before throwing all its might into the domination of the world.'

'It hasn't quite happened like that.' Bond knew his only hope was to establish some kind of common ground with this man – as a hostage must woo his captors.

'No?' There was even a laugh now. 'No, it's better than we ever imagined it could be. See what's happening in the world. The Soviets have penetrated trade unions and governments, right through Britain and America – and much good will it do them. The Eastern bloc is, you'll agree, slowly collapsing in on itself. Last year, we showed the world, by a few well-planned operations – starting with the Tripoli Incident. This year it will be different. This year we are better armed and equipped. We have more followers. We shall gain access to governments. Next year the Party will emerge into the open and within two more years, we shall be a true political force again. Hitler *will* be vindicated. Order *will* be restored, and Communism – the common enemy –

*will* be swept from the map of history. People are crying out for order – a new order; a world of heroes, not peasants and victims of a régime.'

'No victims?' Bond queried.

'You know what I mean, Mr Bond. Of course the dross must go. But, once they're gone, there will be a master race – not just a German master race, but a European master race.'

Somehow, the man had managed to convince some of the older Nazis in Paraguay that all this was possible. 'Six years ago,' he said proudly, 'they allotted me a large sum of cash. Most of what had been left in the Swiss accounts. I had assumed a new name in the late 1960s – or, at least, reassumed it. There are true links between my old family and the now-defunct von Glödas. I returned from time to time, then began work in earnest four years ago. I travelled the world, Mr Bond, organised, plotted, sorted out the wheat from the chaff.

'I planned to start the supposed terrorist acts last year.' Von Glöda was truly in his stride now. 'The problem, as always, was arms. Men I could train – there are plenty of troops, many experienced instructors. Arms are another matter. It would have been difficult for me to pose as PLO, Red Brigade, IRA even.'

By this time, he had moved back to Finland. His organisation was taking shape. Arms and a secret headquarters were his only problems. Then he'd had an idea. 'I came up here. I knew the area well. I found I remembered it even better than I'd thought.'

Particularly he remembered the bunker, built initially by the Russians and improved by German troops. For six months von Glöda had lived in Salla and used the recognised 'smuggling' routes in and out of Russia. Amazingly he found a great deal of the bunker was intact, and he had openly gone to the Soviet authorities, with permission from the Finnish Board of Trade. 'There was some haggling, but, finally, they allowed me to work here: prospecting for minerals. I was not over-specific, but it was a good investment. It cost the Soviets nothing.'

Another six months – with teams brought in from South

America, Africa, even England – and the new bunker was built. And in that time von Glöda had made contact with two ordnance depots near by. 'One was closed down last year. I got the vehicles from them. *I* got the BTRs,' he punched himself in the chest, 'just as *I* did all the deals with those treacherous imbeciles at Blue Hare. Sold themselves for nothing . . .'

'Themselves and a lot of hardware – rocketry you haven't used yet, I gather.' Bond slipped the fact in, receiving a cutting stare in return.

'Soon,' said von Glöda, nodding. 'The second year will see us using the heavy weapons – and more.'

Silence. Was von Glöda expecting congratulation? Possibly.

'You seem to have pulled off a coup of some magnitude,' Bond said. He meant it to sound like a comic book bubble, but von Glöda took him seriously.

'Yes. Yes, I think so: to go out and buy from Russian NCOs, who have no sense of their own ideology – let alone that of the NSAA. Dolts. Cretins.'

Silence once more.

'Then the world catches up with them?' Bond suggested.

'The world? Yes. The authorities catch up with them, and they come running to me for cover. Yes, I really think I can boast of our successes so far. One thousand men and women here, in this bunker. Five thousand men out in the field – throughout the world. An army growing daily; attacks on main government centres all over Europe, and the United States, all planned down to the last detail; and the armaments ready for shipment. After the next assault, our diplomacy. If that does not work, then more action, and more diplomacy. In the end we shall have the largest army, and the largest following, in the Western world.'

'The world fit for heroes?' Bond coughed. 'No, sir. You're undermanned and outgunned.'

'Outgunned? I doubt it, Mr Bond. Already during this winter we've shipped very large quantities of munitions out of here – BTRs, Snowcats, piled high. Straight across Finland, over rough country. Now they're waiting for onward shipment as machine tools and farming implements. My methods of getting supplies to my troops are highly sophisticated.'

'We knew you were bringing them out through Finland.'

Von Glöda actually laughed. 'Partly because I wanted you to know. There are other things, however, you should not know. Once this consignment is on its way, I am ready to move my forces nearer to the European bases. We have bunkers already prepared. That, as you may realise, is one of the problems which concerns you.' Bond frowned, not understanding, but von Glöda was now caught up in the story of how he had dealt with the people at Blue Hare.

A healthy trade with the NCOs at Blue Hare was established and worked well for some time. Then, suddenly, their CO – 'a man of little imagination' – came, in a panic, to the Ice Palace. A spot inspection had been called, and two Red Army Colonels were spinning around like Catherine wheels, accusing anyone and everyone – including the Warrant Officer CO Von Glöda suggested that the Warrant Officer stand on his dignity and ask the Colonels for an investigation by the KGB.

'I knew they'd go for it. If there's one thing I like about the Russians it is their ability to pass the buck. The Warrant Officer, and his men at Blue Hare, were caught. The Colonels were aghast at the amount of matériel missing. They were all trapped in a kind of crossfire. Everyone wanted to drop the problem into someone else's lap. Who better than the KGB, I suggested?'

Count von Glöda, Bond admitted, had shown ideal common sense. An incident like this would be shunned by the Armed Forces (Third) Directorate. The disappearance of vast quantities of weapons and ammunition, in the wastes of the Arctic, would not appeal to the Third Directorate. Whatever else he was, the new-styled Führer understood strategy, and the Russian mind. After the GRU, the job would end up with Department V, and the thinking behind such a move was obvious. If Department V moved in, there would be no trace of anything when they were finished – no missing arms and nobody to question. A clean sweep: probably a terrible accident at an ammunition depot, such as an explosion claiming the lives of all personnel.

'I told the idiot Warrant Officer to alert whoever came from the KGB. Tell him to talk to me. First some GRU people came to Blue Hare. They only stayed for a couple of days. Then Kolya came. We had a few drinks. He put no questions. I asked him what he needed most, in all the world, to enhance his career. We did the deal here, in this office. Blue Hare will cease to exist in a week or so. Nobody will make waves. No money changes hands. Kolya wanted one thing only. You, Mr James Bond. You, on a plate. I simply acted as puppet master, and told him how to get you; deliver you to me; give me a few hours with you. After that, Department V – with whom you have so often dealt as SMERSH – has you. For life. Or death, of course.'

'And you go on to form the Fourth Reich?' James Bond said. 'And the world lives happily ever after?'

'Something like that. But I have delayed matters. My people are waiting now, to talk with you . . .'

Bond raised a hand. 'I have no right to ask, but did you set up the joint operation too? CIA, KGB, Mossad and my people?'

Von Glöda nodded. 'I told Kolya how to do it, and how to substitute people. I did not bargain for Mossad sending my own errant daughter after me.'

'Rivke.' Bond remembered the night at the hotel.

'Yes, that's what she calls herself nowadays, or so I understand. Rivke. Behave yourself, Mr Bond, and I may be tender-hearted and allow you to see her before you leave for Moscow.'

She was alive, then; here in the Ice Palace. Bond willed himself to show no emotion. Instead he shrugged. 'You said people wanted to talk to me?'

Von Glöda returned to his desk. 'Doubtless the authorities in Moscow want you badly, but my own intelligence people also wish to speak to you about certain matters.'

'Really?'

'Yes, really, Mr Bond. We know your Service has one of our men – a soldier who failed in his duty.'

Bond shrugged, his face blank with feigned incomprehension.

'My troops are loyal, and know the Cause comes before anything else. That is why we have been successful so far. No prisoners. All members of the NSAA take an oath, pledging death before dishonour. In all operations last year, none of my men was taken prisoner – except . . .' He let it hang in the air. 'Well, would you like to tell me, James Bond?'

'Nothing to tell.' Bland and flat.

'I think there is. The operation against three British civil servants, just as they left the Soviet Embassy. Think hard, Bond.'

Bond had been way ahead of him. He remembered M's briefing, and the grave look on his chief's face when he referred to the interrogation of the one NSAA man they had in custody at the Headquarters building – the one who tried to shoot himself. What was it M had said? 'His aim was off.' No details, though.

'It is my guess,' von Glöda's voice dropped to almost a whisper, '*my* guess, that any information prised from that prisoner would have been given to you at your briefing, before you joined Kolya. I need to know – *must* know – how much the traitor has given away. You will tell me, Mr Bond.'

Bond managed to draw a laugh from the back of his dry throat. 'I'm sorry, von Glöda . . .'

'*Führer!*' von Glöda shrieked. 'You will be as everybody else, and call me Führer.'

'A Finnish officer who defected to the Nazis? A Finnish-German who has delusions of grandeur? I cannot call you Führer.' Bond spoke quietly, not expecting the tirade that was to come.

'I have renounced nationality. I am not Finnish, nor am I German! Wasn't it Goebbels who proclaimed Hitler's feelings? The German people had no right to survive because they had been found wanting; they could not live up to the ideals of the great Nazi movement. They would be wiped out so that a new Party could eventually rise and carry on the work . . .'

'But they weren't wiped out.'

'It makes no difference. My allegiance is to the Party, and to Europe. To the world. Now is the dawn of the Fourth Reich. Even this small piece of information is necessary to me; and you will give it to me.'

'I have no knowledge of any NSAA prisoner. No information about an interrogation.'

The man who stood erect before Bond suddenly appeared to be convulsed with rage. His eyes blazed. 'You *will* tell all you know. Everything British Intelligence knows about the NSAA.'

'I have nothing to tell you as I know nothing,' Bond repeated. 'In any case, what can you do? To carry on your own struggle you have to hand me over to Kolya – that's your deal for silence.'

'Oh, Mr Bond, don't be naïve. I can get my men, and military materiel, out within twenty-four hours. Kolya has also sold his soul to ambition. He sees a power of his own if he walks into Dzerzhinsky Square with you – the man SMERSH has wanted for so long. Do you think his superiors know what he is doing? Of course not. Kolya has a sense of the dramatic – like all good agents and soldiers. As far as Department V of the First Direct-orate is concerned, Kolya Mosolov is on a mission to sniff out missing armaments in this area. Nobody's going to come look-ing for a while if they don't hear from him. Understand, James Bond? You have bought me time, that's all. A chance to finish my little arms deal, and an opportunity to get out. Kolya Mosolov is expendable. *You* are expendable.'

Bond's mind raced through the logic. Von Glöda's neo-Nazi terrorist army had, indeed, carried out most successful work in the past year. Moreover, M himself was adamant that the National Socialist Action Army was being taken very seriously by all the Western governments. M's gravity, and warning, had followed his remarks about the one NSAA man taken alive, and now incarcerated in the building overlooking Regent's Park. This meant the man must have said enough to provide the Service with high-grade intelligence on von Glöda's strength, and hiding places. The real answer, Bond thought, was that his own Service, if not others, knew exactly where von Glöda's headquarters lay hidden at this moment, and possibly, through interrogation, the location of any future command post.

'So, I'm expendable because of one prisoner,' Bond began. '*One* man who may or may not be held by my people. That's rich, when you consider the millions your former Führer held in captivity, murdered in the gas chambers, killed off with slave labour. Now, one man holds the balance.'

'Oh, a good try, Mr Bond,' von Glöda replied drily. 'Would that it were as simple. But this is a serious matter, and I must ask you to treat it as such. I can take no chances.'

He paused for a second, as though considering how best to convey the situation to Bond. Then: 'You see, there is nobody here, not even on my General Staff, who knows the exact location of my next headquarters. Not Kolya, whose path to great power was handed to him by me, engineered by me, or Paula, or Buchtman – Tirpitz to you. None of them knows.

'Unhappily, however, there are a few people who, however unwittingly, hold this information in their heads. The men and women who await me at the new headquarters, at this moment, of course they are well aware. But there are others. For instance, the unit which carried out the operation in Kensington Palace Gardens, outside the Soviet Embassy, went from here to be briefed – en route for London – at the new Command Post.

'From that new and highly secret headquarters they went out to do their work. All are accounted for but one. My information is that he failed to commit suicide when he fell into the hands of your Service. He is a well-trained man, but even the cleverest officers can fall into traps. You know how two and two can be put together, Mr Bond. I need two things from you. First, if he gave you the location of my new headquarters, where I intend to be established shortly. Second, where he is being held prisoner.'

'I know nothing about any NSAA prisoner.'

Von Glöda gave Bond a blank, completely unemotional look. 'Possibly you are telling the truth. I doubt it, but it is possible. All I want is the truth. My personal feelings are that you do know where he is, and that you are aware of anything he has said. Only a fool would send you into the field without the full facts.'

Clever von Glöda might well be, thought Bond. He certainly had an eye for detail, and a sharp brain; but his last remark left no doubts about his complete ignorance concerning security matters. Bond also took extreme offence at the inference that M was a fool.

'Do you think I would be given access to *all* the facts?' Bond allowed himself an indulgent smile.

'I am certain of it.'

'Then you are the fool, sir. Not my superiors.'

Von Glöda gave a hard, short, one-syllable laugh. 'Have it your own way, but I dare not take risks. I *will* know the truth. We can take a man to the limit here. If you have nothing to say, you will say nothing, and I shall know there is little danger. If you know only where my man is being held, that information can be flashed to London. He may be held in the most inaccessible place, but my team in London will still get him – with time to spare.'

Could one of von Glöda's teams penetrate the Service's Head-quarters? As much as Bond doubted it, he was disinclined to put it to the test.

'And what if I break down and lie to you? What if I say, yes, there is such a prisoner – though I do assure you I know of none – and he has given us all the information we need?'

'Then you also will know the location of the new Command Post, Mr Bond. You see, there is no way you can win.'

Not in your book, Bond thought. The man could see nothing unless it was in clear black and white.

'One other thing.' Von Glöda rose to his feet. 'Here we rely on the older techniques of interrogation. Painful, but very successful. I have yet to trust what friend Kolya would call a chemical interrogation. So know what you face, Mr Bond. Exceptional discomfort, to put it mildly. I plan to take you to the threshold of pain; and doctors tell me that no man has yet been born who will not crack under the method we shall use.'

'But I know nothing.'

'Then you will not crack, and I shall know. Now, why not avoid the worst? Tell me about the prisoner – where he is held; what he has revealed.'

Seconds ticked away, almost audible in Bond's head, and then the outer door opened, and the man Bond had known as Brad Tirpitz came in, followed by the two uniformed men who had been in the ante-room. They raised their arms in salute.

'You know, Hans, what information I require from this man,' said von Glöda. 'Use all your powers of persuasion. Now.'

'*Jawohl, mein Führer.*' The arms raised in unison, heels clicking, then the two men converged on Bond, and took him by the arms. He felt handcuffs encircle his wrists, and the grip of strong fingers as they caught hold, bundling him from the room.

They took him no farther than the ante-room. Tirpitz/Buchtman went over and pressed the hessian-covered wall, revealing a section which swung back with a click.

Buchtman disappeared through the door, followed by one of the officers, his hand grasping Bond's jacket. The other man kept a tight hold on 007's handcuffed wrists. One in front and the other behind. Bond soon found out the reason. Once past the door, they were crammed into a narrow passage, just wide and high enough to take a man.

After half a dozen paces it was clear they were descending; then, quite quickly, they came to a bare stone staircase, lit by dim blue lights set into the walls at intervals, a rope running through metal eyes down one side as a guide rail.

Their progress was very slow, for the staircase went a long way down. Bond tried to work out the depth but gave up quickly. The steps appeared to steepen. At one point there was a small platform, leading to an open chamber. Here Buchtman and the two guards put on heavy greatcoats and gloves. None were offered to Bond who, even in the outdoor winter gear he still wore, began to feel the dreadful uprush of intense cold from the depths below them.

The steps became increasingly slippery and Bond sensed ice-growths on the sides of the walls as they continued down. At last they emerged into a brightly lit cave – circular, the walls of natural rock, the flooring beneath them seemingly pure thick ice.

Heavy wooden crossbeams spanned the cave, passing over its centre. Attached to the beams was a block and tackle mechanism, with a long solid metal chain dangling down and ending in what looked like an anchor hook.

One of the uniformed men took out his pistol, staying close to Bond. The other opened a large, ice-encrusted metal box, from which he took a small, motor-driven chain saw.

The breath of all four men, in this freezing dungeon, thickened the air in clouds. Bond smelled the gasoline from the chain saw motor as it fired. 'We keep it well-protected.' Buchtman had not lost his American accent. 'Okay.' He nodded to the man with the gun. 'Strip the bastard.'

As Bond felt hands starting to undo his clothing, he saw the chain saw biting into the floor of the cell, sending chips of ice flying. Even with his clothes on, the cold had become crippling. Now, as the layers were roughly removed, his body seemed to be enveloped in an invisible coat of sharp needles.

Buchtman nodded towards the man with the chain saw. 'He's cutting a nice bath tub for you, James old buddy.' He laughed. 'We're well below the main line of the bunker here. In summer the water rises quite high. Small natural lake. You're gonna get to know that lake very well indeed, James Bond.'

As he spoke, the chain saw broke through the ice, showing

it to be at least half a metre thick. Then the operator began to chew out a rough circle, the centre of which lay directly under the chain dangling from the block and tackle.

# 15

# DEAD COLD

They unlocked the handcuffs. By that time, James Bond was too cold to resist. The removal of the top half of his clothing, which followed, did not seem to make any appreciable difference. He could hardly move, and it seemed that even his desire to shiver was denied him.

One of the uniformed men pulled Bond's arms in front of his stark naked body, then clasped the handcuffs into place again. The metal on his wrists felt as though it burned.

Bond began to concentrate. Try to remember something . . . Forget the cold . . . Close your eyes . . . See just one spot in the universe, let the spot swell.

The rattle of chains, and Bond heard rather than felt that his handcuffed wrists were being clipped over the hook. Then, disorientation for a moment, as they hoisted the block and tackle. His feet left the ground and he spun and swung as the chain lifted. Acute pain, now, as the handcuffed wrists took the strain. Arms stretched, pulled from their sockets. Then numbness again. It did not matter about the weight on his arms, shoulders, and wrists, for the freezing temperature acted almost as an anaesthetic.

Strangely, the thing that did matter was the swinging and spinning. Bond did not normally react to disorientation, while flying, doing high-speed aerobatics, or the many other stress tests included in his yearly checkout. Now, however, he felt the bile rise in his throat as the swinging became more regular –

pendulum-like – and the spinning slowed, first one way, then the next.

Opening his eyes was as painful as anything else. A struggle against light frost forming on the lids. Necessary though, for he desperately needed some fixed point on which to focus. The ice-streaked sides of the cave turned in front of him, the hard light from above throwing off colour – yellows, reds and blues. It was impossible to keep his head up, with arms stretched above him, taking all the body weight.

Bond's head slumped forward. Below him a wide, dark eye, figures moving on the periphery, the eye turning lazily, squinting, slanting. It was a moment before his numbed brain took in the fact that the eye was not moving. The illusion came from his own swinging motion, at the end of the chain. The needles continued to assault his body. They seemed to be everywhere at once, then localised – clawing at his scalp, moving to a thigh, or rasping against his genitals.

Concentrate: he fought to get a proper perspective, but the cold was like a barrier, a chill wall preventing his brain from working. Harder; concentrate harder.

Finally Bond took in the eye, as the swaying and spinning motion settled. The eye was a circle cut in the ice. Its darkness was the frozen water below. Slowly they were letting out the chain, so that his feet seemed poised directly over the water.

Now a voice. Tirpitz – Buchtman: 'James, buddy, this is going to be dirty. You should tell us now before we go on. You know what we want? Just answer yes or no.'

What did they want? Why was this happening? Bond's very brain felt as though it were freezing. *What?* 'No,' he heard his voice croak.

'Your people have one of our men. Two questions: where is he being held in London? What has he told your interrogators?'

A man? Held in London? Who? When? What had he told? For a few seconds Bond's mind cleared. The NSAA soldier, being held at the Regent's Park HQ. What had he told? No idea, but hadn't he worked it out? Yes, the man must have said a great deal. Tell nothing.

Aloud he said, 'I know nothing about anyone being held prisoner. Nothing about any interrogations.' His voice was unrecognisable, echoing against the walls of the natural cavern.

The other voice floated up to him, each word a struggle for Bond to recognise or comprehend. 'Okay, Jim, have it your way. I'll ask you again in a minute.'

From above, the rattle of something. The chain. His body moving down towards the black eye. For no reason, Bond suddenly thought he had lost all sense of smell. Odd; why no sense of smell? Concentrate on something else. He struggled, setting his mind on a new course. A summer day. The countryside. Trees in full leaf. A bee hovered above his face, and he could smell – the sense of smell was back: a mixture of grass and hay. Far in the distance the sound of some farm machinery peacefully purring. Don't say anything. You know nothing except this – the hay and grass. Nothing. You know nothing.

Bond heard the final rattle of the chain just as he hit the middle of the black eye. His brain even registered that a scum of ice had already re-formed over the water. Then the slack of the chain dropped him into the centre. He must have cried out, for his mouth filled with water. Sunlight. The oak tree. Arms being dragged down by the chain. He could not breathe.

The sensation was not one of biting cold, simply an extreme change. It could have been boiling water just as easily as freezing. Bond's only conscious feeling, after the first shock, was of his body enveloped by a blinding pain, as though his eyes – windows to the brain – had been scorched by white light.

He still lived, though he was aware of it only because of the pain. His heart pumped in his chest and head like tympani.

There was no way of telling how long they had held him under the ice. He gulped and spluttered for air, the whole of his body jerking in spasms, like a puppet controlled by a convulsive master.

Opening his eyes, Bond saw that he was, once more, suspended over the eye cut in the ice. Then the real cold set in – the shaking as he swung to and fro, while the needle-points turned into barbs, excoriating his skin.

No. His brain broke through the pain of cold. No, this was not happening. The grass; smells of summer; sounds of summer; the tractor drawing near, and the soughing of a breeze in the oak tree's branches.

'Okay, Bond. That was just a taste. You hear me?'

He was breathing normally, but his vocal chords did not seem to be working properly. At last: 'Yes, I hear you.'

'We know just how far to go, but don't kid yourself, we'll go further. The limit. Where is our man being held in England?'

Bond heard his own voice, again as though it did not belong to him: 'I don't know of any man being held.'

'What has he told your people? How much?'

'I know of no man being held.'

'Have it your own way.' The chain sounded its death rattle.

They let him stay under, weighted down by the chain, for a long time – or else he remained conscious for longer than before. He fought for breath, the red mist mingling with a white light which seemed to fuse every muscle, each vein and organ. Then the blessed relief of darkness, soon to be blasted apart by the pain as his naked body swung gently, pulled clear again of the ice pool.

The cold air of the dungeon made the second time worse. Not just needles, but tiny animals, gnawing and biting into the numbed flesh; the more sensitive organs alive with agony, so that Bond wrestled with the handcuffs and hook, wanting to get his hands down to cover his loins.

'There is a National Socialist Action Army man being held prisoner in England. Where is he?'

The summer. Try . . . Try for the summer. But this was not summer, only the terrible teeth, small and sharp, biting through the skin into the muscle and flesh.

The NSAA man was at the Regent's Park HQ. Was there harm in telling them? Summer. The green leaves of summer.

'You hear me, Bond? Tell us and things will get easier.'

*Sumer is icumen in,*
*Sing, cuckoo . . .*

'Don't know. Don't know about prisoner . . . Nobody . . .' This time the voice came from right inside his head, the sentence cut short as the chain clattered down, plunging him into the gelid mass.

He struggled, not reasoning what he would, or could, do if the handcuffs became unhooked. This was pure reflex: the body automatically fighting for life, trapped by an element in which it could not possibly survive for long. He was conscious of the muscles not responding, the brain ceasing to operate rationally. Streaking pain. Darkness.

Alive and swinging once more. Bond wondered how near he hovered between life and the unknowing, for the white pain was now centred in his head – a blinding, searing, flashing explosion within the skull.

The voice was shouting, as if trying to get through to him from a distance. 'The prisoner, Bond. Where are they keeping him? Don't be a fool; we know he's somewhere in England. Just give us the place. The name. Where is he?'

My Service Headquarters. Building near Regent's Park. Transworld Export. Had he said it? No, there had been nothing, even though the words were clearly formed in his brain, waiting to leap out.

*The green leaves of summer, Sumer is icumen in; Summertime; The last rose of summer, Indian summer . . .*

Vipers lashed at his brain. Then the words: Bond's voice aloud, 'No prisoner. I don't know about a prison . . .'

The crash of ice around him, the red-hot, blinding liquid, then agony, as the body became aware again. Out, swinging and dripping, gasping, every centimetre of him torn to shreds. The brain which, so far, had computed extremes of temperature, pain like nibbling animals, snakes and needles, had, finally, hit on the real source of pain. Cold. Dead cold. A death by slow freezing.

The sun was dazzling. So hot that the perspiration dripped from Bond's forehead and into his eyes. He could not even open his eyes, and he knew he'd had too much to drink. Drunk as a lord. Why drunk as a lord? Drunk for a penny, dead drunk for twopence.

Balance gone. Laughter: Bond's laughter. He did not usually get drunk, but this was something else. High as a . . . high as something . . . When? On the Fourth of July? At least it made you feel good. Let the world go by. Lightheaded . . . lighthearted . . . darkness. Lord, he was going to pass out. Be sick. No, he felt too good for that. Happiness . . . very happy . . . The darkness coming in, closing around him. Just a hint of what it really was as the night swallowed him. Dead cold.

'James . . . James . . .' The voice familiar. Far, far away, from another planet. 'James . . .' A woman. A woman's voice. Then he recognised it.

Warmth. He was lying down and warm. A bed? Was it a bed?

Bond tried to move, and the voice repeated his name. Yes, he was wrapped in blankets, lying on a bed, and the room was warm.

'James . . .'

With care, Bond opened his eyes – with a stinging of the lids. Then he stirred, slowly because each movement was painful. Finally he turned his head towards the voice. His eyes took a few seconds to focus.

'Oh, James, you're all right. They gave you artificial respiration. I've pressed the bell. They said to get someone in quickly when you came to.' The room was like any other hospital room, but there were no windows. In the other bed, her legs raised in traction and encased in plaster, lay Rivke Ingber, her face alive and happy.

Then the nightmare returned, and Bond realised what he had come through. He closed his eyes, but saw only the dark, cold, circular eye of freezing water. He moved his wrists, and the pain returned where the steel handcuffs had bitten into his flesh.

'Rivke,' was all he could manage, for his mind was assaulted by other demons. Had he told them? What had he told them? He could remember the questions, but not his answers. A summer scene flitted through his mind – grass, hay, an oak tree, a buzzing in the distance.

'Drink this, Mr Bond.' He had not seen the girl before, but she was correctly dressed in a nurse's uniform and held a cup of steaming hot liquid to his lips. 'Beef tea. Hot, but you've got to have hot drinks. You're going to be fine. Don't worry about anything now.'

Bond, propped on pillows, had neither the strength nor inclination to resist. The first sip of the beef tea rolled back the years. The taste reminded him of a far distant past – just as a piece of music will recall a long-forgotten memory. Bond recalled a long-lost childhood: the hygienic smell of school sanatoria, the bouts of winter 'flu at home. He swallowed more, feeling the warmth creeping into his belly. With the inner heat, the horrors also returned: the ice dungeon, and the terrible, terrible cold as he was dunked into the freezing water.

Had he talked? As hard as Bond cudgelled his brains, he could not tell. In the midst of the sharp, satanic pictures of torture, there was no memory of what else had passed between him and his interrogators.

Depressed, he looked at Rivke. She was staring at him, her eyes soft and gentle, just as they had been in that hotel in the early morning. Her lips moved, soundlessly, but Bond could easily read what she was mouthing: 'James, I love you.'

He smiled, and gave her a little nod as the nurse tipped the cup of beef tea so that he could swallow more.

He was alive. Rivke was there. While he lived there was still a chance that the National Socialist Action Army could be stopped and their Führer wiped from the new world map he wanted so badly to draw.

# 16

# PARTNERS IN CRIME

After the beef tea, Bond was given an injection, and the nurse said something about frostbite. 'Nothing to worry about,' she said. 'You'll be all right in a few hours.'

Bond looked across at Rivke and started to say something, but drifted off into a cloud of sleep. Later he could not tell if it had been a dream or not, but there had seemed to be a waking period during which von Glöda stood at the foot of the bed. The tall man was smiling – unctuous and evil. 'There, Mr Bond. I told you we would get all we needed from you. Better than the drugs and chemicals. I trust we haven't ruined your sex life. I think not. Anyway, thank you for the information. A great help to us.'

On finally waking, Bond was more or less convinced that this had been no dream, so vivid was the picture of von Glöda. There were dreams, however, dreams about the same man: dreams in which von Glöda stood decked out in Nazi uniform, surrounded by the trappings of power at a kind of Nuremberg rally.

A wave of terror washed through him as the memory of the ordeal under the icy water returned, then passed quickly. He felt better now, if lulled and dopily disorientated. He was anxious to get going. Indeed, he had little choice. Either find a way out of von Glöda's labyrinth, or take the inevitable trip to Moscow, with its final showdown between himself and what used to be SMERSH.

'Are you awake, James?'

In the few seconds of returning to the world, Bond had

forgotten Rivke's presence in the room. He turned his head, smiling, 'Mixed sanatoria. What will they think of next?'

She laughed, inclining her head towards the two great lumps of plaster, strung up on pulleys, that were her legs. 'Not much we can do about it, though. More's the pity. My stinking father was in here a little while ago.'

That clinched it. Von Glöda's speech had not been a dream. Bond swore silently. How much had he given away to them, under the pain and disorientation of the ice dunking? There was no way to tell. Quickly he calculated the chances of a determined NSAA team getting into the Regent's Park building. The odds would be about eighty to one against. But they would only need to penetrate one man. That would shorten the odds and, if he had given them the information, the NSAA would certainly already have their team briefed. Too late for him even to warn M.

'You look worried. What terrible things did they do to you, James?'

'They took me for a swim in a winter wonderland, my darling. Nothing so dreadful. But what about you? I saw the accident. We thought you were taken away by a genuine ambulance and the police. Obviously we were wrong.'

'I was just coming down the final slope, looking forward to seeing you again. Then, poof – nothing. I woke up with a lot of pain in my legs and my father standing over me. He had that woman with him. I don't think she's here though. But they did have some kind of a hospital organised. Both legs broken, and a couple of ribs. They plastered me up, took me for a long ride, and I finally woke up here. The Count calls it his Command Post, but I've no idea where we are. The nurses are friendly enough but won't tell me anything.'

'If my calculations are correct . . .' Bond eased himself on to his side so that he could more easily talk to Rivke and look at her simultaneously. There were signs of strain around her eyes, and she was in obvious discomfort caused by the casts on her legs and the traction. 'If I'm right, we're in a large bunker, situated around ten to twelve kilometres east of the Finnish border. On the Russian side.'

'Russian?' Rivke opened her mouth, eyes wide with amazement.

Bond nodded. 'Your beloved Papa has pulled a very fast one.' He made a grimace, conveying a certain admiration. 'You have to admit he's been exceptionally clever. We have searched everywhere for clues, and all the time he's been operating from the most unlikely place – within Soviet territory.'

Rivke laughed quietly, the sound tinged with bitterness. 'He always was clever. Who'd have looked in Russia for the headquarters of a Fascist group?'

'Quite.' Bond stayed silent for a moment. 'How bad are the legs?'

She lifted a hand – a gesture of helplessness. 'You can see for yourself.'

'They haven't given you any therapy yet? Let you try and walk – even with crutches or a Zimmer?'

'You're joking. I can't feel much pain. It's just very uncomfortable. Why?'

'There's got to be a way out of this place, and I'm not going alone or leaving you behind.' He paused, as if making up his mind. 'Not now that I've found you, Rivke.'

When he next looked, Bond thought he could detect a moistness in the large eyes. 'James, that's wonderful of you, but if there is a way out, you'll have to try it yourself, *by* yourself.'

Bond's brow creased. If there was a way, could he get back in time? Bring help? He put the answers into words. 'I don't think the clock's on our side, Rivke. Not if I've told them what I think . . .'

'Told them . . . ?'

'Being ducked in almost frozen water, without your clothes on, is slightly disorientating. I passed out a couple of times. They wanted the answers to two questions.' He went on to say that he knew one answer, but could only guess the other.

'What kind of questions?'

In a few words Bond told her about the NSAA man being captured in London before he could commit suicide. 'Your father's got a new Command Post. This fellow has enough information to tip off our people. The devil of it is that the London prisoner probably doesn't realise he knows. Your maniac father had a group sent to his new Command Post for briefing, before leaving for London. Our interrogators, like yours with Mossad, are not fools. The right questions'll yield the answers.'

'So you think your Service already knows where this new place – this second Command Post – is located?'

'I wouldn't put money on it. But if I've told von Glöda's inquisitors we have the man, and that he's been interrogated, they can add up the answers as well as our people. I should think your father's moving everyone out of here pretty damned fast.

'You said there were two questions?'

'Oh, they wanted to know where our people were keeping him. That's no problem, really. There's a chance one man could get at him; but any full-scale assault's out of the question.'

'Why, James?'

'We keep a special interrogation centre in the basement of our Headquarters building in London. He's holed up there.'

Rivke bit her lip. 'And you really think you told them?'

'There's a possibility. You said your father was in here earlier. I can vaguely remember that. He gave the impression they knew about it. You were awake . . .'

'Yes.' She looked away for a second, not meeting his eyes.

Agents of Mossad, thought Bond, tend to opt for a suicide pill rather than face an interrogation which might compromise them. 'Do you think I've failed my own Service', he asked Rivke, 'and this unholy alliance we were supposed to be involved in?'

For a second, Rivke was silent. Then: 'No, James. No. You had no alternative, obviously. No, I was thinking about what my father said – God knows why I call him a father. He's really no father of mine. When he came in, he said something about you having provided information. I was dozing, but he sounded sarcastic. He thanked you for the information.'

Bond felt the lead of despair deep in his guts. M had sent him blind into a compromising situation, though he could not blame his chief for that. M's reasoning would have been the less knowledge the better, as far as Bond was concerned. Like himself, M had almost certainly been duped by what had transpired: the real Brad Tirpitz's elimination, Kolya Mosolov's double-dealing with von Glöda. And then there was the duplicity of Paula Vacker. The despair came from the knowledge that he had let his country down, and failed his Service. In Bond's book these were the cardinal sins.

By now, von Glöda would almost certainly be going through all the standard routines of moving shop: packing, organising transport, loading up the BTRs with all the arms and munitions they could carry, shredding documents. Bond wondered if von Glöda had some temporary base – apart from the major new Command Post – from which he could operate. Now he would want to get out as quickly as possible, but it might take up to twenty-four hours.

Bond looked around to see if any of his clothes had been left with him. There was a locker opposite the bed, though not large enough to contain clothing. The rest of the room was bare, just the formal trappings of a small private hospital ward: another small locker opposite Rivke's bed; a table, with glasses, a bottle and medical equipment standing in the corner. Nothing useful that he could see.

There were curtain-bearing rails around each bed, two lamps – above the bedheads – a strip light set in the ceiling, and the usual small ventilation grilles.

The idea came to him that he might overpower the nurse, strip her, and try to get out disguised as a woman. But the notion was self-evidently ludicrous, for Bond scarcely had the build which lent itself to female impersonation. In addition, just thinking it made him feel dopy again. He wondered what drugs they'd shot him with after the torture.

If von Glöda were to keep his bargain with Kolya – which seemed highly unlikely – Bond's only chance would be an escape from Kolya Mosolov's custody.

There was a sound in the passage outside. The door opened and the nurse came in, bright, starched and hygienic. 'Well,' she started briskly, 'I have news. You'll both be leaving here soon. The Führer has decided to take you out with him. I'm here to warn you that you'll be moving in a few hours.'

'Hostage time,' said Bond, sighing.

The nurse smiled brightly, saying she expected that was it.

'And how do we go?' Bond had some notion it might help to keep her talking, if only to gain a little information. 'Snowcat? BTR? What?'

The nurse's smile did not leave her mouth. 'I shall be travelling with you. You're perfectly fit, Mr Bond, but we're concerned about Miss Ingber's legs. She prefers being called Miss Ingber, I gather. I must be with her. We'll all be going in the Führer's personal aircraft.'

'Aircraft?' Bond did not even realise they had flying facilities.

'Oh yes, there's a runway among the trees. It's kept clear even in the worst weather. We have a couple of light aircraft here – ski-fitted in winter, of course – and the Führer's executive jet, a converted Mystère-Falcon. Very fast but lands on anything . . .'

'Can it take off on anything?' Bond thought of the bleak ice and snow among the trees.

'When the runway's clear.' The nurse seemed unconcerned. 'Don't worry about a thing. We always have ice burners out along the metal runway just before he leaves.' She paused in the doorway. 'Now, is there anything you need?'

'Parachutes?' Bond suggested.

For the first time, the nurse lost her brightness. 'You will both be given a meal before we leave. Until then, I have other work to do.' The door shut, and they heard the click of a key turning in the lock from the outside.

'That's it, then,' said Rivke. 'If you'd ever thought about it, dear James, there'll be no cottage for us, with roses around the door.'

'I had thought about it, Rivke. I never give up hope.'

'Knowing my father, he'll like as not drop us off at 20,000 feet.'

Bond grunted. 'Hence the nurse's reaction when I mentioned parachutes.'

'Shhhh.' Rivke made a sharp noise. 'There's someone in the passage. Outside the door.'

Bond looked towards her. He had heard nothing, but Rivke suddenly appeared alert, if not edgy. Bond moved – surprised that his limbs worked with such ease and speed. Indeed, the action seemed to produce a new and sudden alertness in him. The dopy feeling left him and now Bond cursed himself again, for he realised he'd broken another elementary rule by blabbing his head off to Rivke without making even a rudimentary surveillance check.

Bond sprinted, unembarrassed by his nudity, to the table in the corner, grabbed a glass and returned as quickly to the bed. Whispering, he told Rivke, 'I can always smash it. Surprising how effective broken glass can be on flesh.'

She nodded, her head cocked, listening. Still Bond heard nothing. Then, with a speed and suddenness that took even Bond unawares, the door shot open and Paula Vacker was in the room.

She moved silently – as Bond's housekeeper May would have said, 'like greased lightning'. Before either Rivke or Bond could react, Paula had snaked between the two beds. Bond caught a glimpse of his own P7 automatic raised twice and heard the tinkle of glass as Paula put the bedhead lights out of action with two quick butt strokes from the gun.

'What . . . ?' Bond began, realising that this made little difference to the lighting, as most of the illumination came from the ceiling strip light.

'Just keep quiet,' Paula advised him, the P7 circling the two beds as she moved back towards the door, crouched, pulled a bundle into the room, then closed the door again, locking it behind her. 'The electronics, James, were inside the bedhead light bulbs. Every word – all your conversation with sweet little Rivke here – has now been relayed to Count von Glöda.'

'But . . . ?'

'Enough.' The P7 was pointed at Rivke not Bond. With her foot, Paula pushed the bundle towards Bond's bed. 'Get into those. You're going to become an officer in the Führer's army for a while.'

Bond got up and undid the bundle. There was thermal underwear, stockings, a heavy rollneck and a field grey winter uniform, smock and trousers; boots, gloves, and a uniform fur hat. Quickly he started to dress. 'What's all this about, Paula?'

'I'll explain when there's time,' she snapped back. 'Just get on with what you're doing. We're going to cut it fine in any case. Kolya's taken a run for it, so there's only the two of us now. Partners in crime, James. At least we're going to get out.'

Bond was already nearly dressed. He moved to the door side of his bed. 'What about Rivke?'

'What *about* her?'

'We can't get her out. Whose side are you on anyway?'

'Surprisingly enough, yours, James. More than can be said for the Führer's daughter.'

As she said it, Rivke moved. Paula stepped back and Bond saw a kind of blur as, with alarming ease, Rivke slid her legs from the plaster casts, swivelled sideways, and swung off the bed, one hand clasped around the butt of a small pistol. There was not a single mark on her body, and the supposed broken legs worked like those of an athlete. Paula swore, shouting at Rivke to drop the gun.

Bond, still getting into the last pieces of clothing, saw the whole thing in a kind of slow motion: Rivke, dressed only in a pair of briefs, with the gun arm rising as her feet hit the floor; Paula's arms extending into the full-length firing position; Rivke still moving forward, then the one loud echoing blast from the P7; a cloud of gunsmoke making swirling patterns; Rivke's face disintegrating in a fine mist of blood and bone, as her body, looped backwards by the blast, arced away from them over the bed.

Then the smell of the burned powder.

Paula swore again. 'Last thing I wanted. The noise.'

For one of the few times in his life, James Bond felt out of control. He had already recognised the beginning of emotional feelings towards Rivke. He knew of Paula's treachery. Now balanced on the balls of his feet, Bond prepared to make a last, desperate attempt: a leap towards Paula's gun arm. But she merely tossed the P7 towards him, making a grab for Rivke's small pistol.

'You'd better take that, James. May need it. We could be lucky. I stole the nurse's key, and sent her off on some fool's job. There's nobody in this wing, so the shot may not have been heard. But we're going to need wings on our heels.'

'What are you talking about?' Bond said, suspecting the truth even as he spoke.

'I'll tell you the whole thing later, but can't you understand? You didn't give them anything under torture, so they rigged you up with Rivke. You spilled it all to his daughter because you trusted her. She's Daddy's little helper, always has been. From what I understand she hoped to be the first woman Führer, in due course. Now, will you come on? I've got to try and get you out of here. Partners in crime – like I said.'

# 17

# A DEAL IS A DEAL

Paula wore a heavy, well-cut officer's greatcoat over the uniform Bond had last seen her in. The boots were visible under the coat, and to crown the effect she had added a military fur hat.

Bond glanced towards the bed that had lately contained Rivke. The plaster leg casts were obviously hollow frauds, bearing out Paula's accusations. He was nauseated by the sight of the wall behind, spattered, like some surrealist painting, with blood and tissue. You could still smell Rivke in the room.

He turned away, picking up the officer's fur hat, which Paula had provided for him. Throughout Operation Icebreaker, allegiances seemed to have swerved to and fro in a series of knife-edge uncertainties. He still couldn't be sure of Paula's true intentions, but at least she seemed serious about getting him away from the bunker. This meant putting distance between himself and von Glöda, which was a most appealing prospect.

'As far as the guards are concerned, I'm acting on the Führer's orders,' Paula said. 'There's a standard pass for each of us.' She handed over a small square of white plastic, like a credit card. 'We don't go anywhere near the main workshops or the arms stores. Just keep your head well down in case we run into anyone who's seen you before, and stay close to me. Let me do the talking as well, James. The exit is through the small bunker, and the chances are well above average. They're running around in one hell of a flap since von Glöda gave the movement orders – *after* you spilled the beans to Rivke . . .'

'About that; I . . .' Bond began.

'About nothing.' Paula spoke sharply. 'All in good time. Just trust me, for once. Like you, I'm not in this for fun.' Her gloved hand rested on his arm for a second. 'Believe me, James, they caught you by using that girl, and I had no way to warn you. The oldest trick in the book as well. Shove a prisoner in with some-one he trusts, then listen to the conversation.' She laughed again. 'I was with von Glöda when they brought the tapes. He leaped about ten metres into the air. Idiot – he was so sure that, because you'd survived his torture without saying anything, there was nothing for him to worry about. Now, James, stay close to me.'

Paula unlocked the door, and they stepped out into the passageway, pausing for a second while she relocked the door from the outside. The passage was empty, lined with white tiles – sterile with a hint of disinfectant in the air. Other small hospital wards led off to the left and right, and at the end of the passage – which lay to their left – was a metal door. If nothing else, von Glöda was well-organised.

Paula led the way forward towards the metal door. 'Keep the gun out of sight, but ready for Custer's last stand,' she warned him. 'If we get into a shootout, the chances are not so brilliant.' Her own hand was thrust deep into her right pocket, where she had placed Rivke's pistol.

The corridor, on the far side of the hospital wing, was well-decorated – the hessian covering, with some framed posters and pictures similar to those Bond had seen near von Glöda's personal suite. From this alone, he guessed that they were deep within the bunker, probably parallel to the passages which ran down to the new Führer's offices.

Paula insisted on walking slightly ahead; and Bond, his gloved fingers around the pocketed P7, remained in place, about two steps to the rear and slightly to Paula's left, hugging the wall. Almost the standard position for a bodyguard.

After a couple of minutes, the passage divided. Paula turned right and climbed up carpeted steps. The stairs were steep and led to a very short stretch of passage, at the end of which a pair of double doors, complete with small mesh-covered windows, took them into what must have been an arterial tunnel. Now they were back to the rough walls, with the utility pipes and channels visible. Paula glanced back every few seconds to make sure Bond was with her. Then a left turn, and the simple act of walking told Bond they were on a slight upward slope.

As the slope became steeper, they reached a walkway on the right similar to the one by which they had first entered the bunker, complete with boards, to give a better grip, and a hand-rail. Here, as at the larger entrance, doors and passages led off on either side. For the first time since leaving the hospital section, Bond was aware of noise – voices, the click of boots, an occasional shout or the sound of running feet.

As he glanced into the tributary passages, Bond glimpsed all the signs of hurried, though controlled, activity. Men were carrying personal belongings, metal cabinets, boxes and document files; others appeared to be stripping offices; some even lugged weapons. Most appeared to be heading away towards the left, bearing out Bond's sense of direction. He was now certain they were in the main tunnel, which would take them to the smaller bunker entrance.

A section of six soldiers came down the slope at the double, well-drilled, their faces to the front, the NCO in charge ordering a salute to Paula and Bond.

Now, ahead, a small detachment stood guard on what seemed to be the final hurdle. The tunnel came to an abrupt end, closed off by a massive steel shutter. Near the roof, Bond could see hydraulic equipment for lifting the shutter, but there was also a small, heavily bolted door set low on the right-hand side.

'Now for it,' Paula muttered. 'Look the part. Don't hesitate, and for God's sake let me do the talking. Once we're out, move left.'

As they came nearer to the entrance, he saw that the

detachment consisted of an officer and four men, all armed. Near the door stood a small machine – like a ticket-vending machine in an underground rail network.

Four paces from the exit, Paula called out in German, 'Prepare to let us out. We're under personal orders from the Führer himself.'

One of the private soldiers moved to the door, and the officer took a step forward, standing by the machine. 'Do you have your pass, madam? And you, sir?'

They were close now.

'Of course,' Paula said. She produced the piece of plastic in her left hand. Bond followed suit.

'Good.' The officer had the sour and humourless face of an old army hand who did everything by numbers. 'Do you know anything about this sudden movement order? We've only heard rumours.'

'I know a great deal.' Paula's voice hardened. 'You'll all be told in time.'

They were right up to the officer now. 'They say we have to be out within twenty-four hours. Some sweat.'

'We've all been through sweat before.' There was no emotion in Paula's voice as she offered her card to be checked by the machine.

The officer took both cards, fed them, one at a time, into a small slot near the top, then waited until a series of lights ran their course, sounding a soft buzzer for each pass.

'Good luck, whatever your mission.' He returned their cards. Bond nodded. The private soldier by the door was already opening up the bolts.

Paula thanked the officer in charge, and Bond followed her lead, giving the Nazi salute. Heels clicked and orders were barked as the door swung back.

A few seconds later they were outside, and the biting cold hit them like a fine spray of ice. It was dark, and Bond – with no wrist watch – had lost all sense of time. There was no immediate way of telling whether it was late afternoon or near dawn. The complete blackness gave the impression that it was the middle of the long Arctic night.

They advanced to the left, following tiny blue guide lights which outlined the exterior of the bunker. Under the snow, Bond could feel the hard metal of the long strips of chain-link 'roadway' that must have been laid down around the Command Post. There would be similar wide strips for the runway on von Glöda's airfield.

The main doors of the bunker towered, white, above them, and as they passed them, Bond realised where Paula was taking him – to the small concrete shelter where he had seen the snow scooters being stored. He could just make out the circle of trees to his right, and remembered how when Kolya first lured him to this outpost they had suddenly broken cover from those trees, to be bathed in lights.

Paula seemed to have forgotten nothing. As soon as they reached the small, low structure, built hard against the rock face, she produced a key ring on a thin chain.

The shelter smelled of fuel and oil, while the switch by the door produced only a dim light. The scooters were neatly parked, looking like giant insects huddled together in hibernation.

Paula made for the first one that suited her purpose – a big, long black Yamaha, much larger than those on which Kolya had led them over the border.

'You don't mind if I drive,' Paula was already checking the fuel. In the poor light, Bond could only sense, not see, the cheeky smile on her lips.

'And where're we going, Paula?'

She glanced up, peering at Bond through the gloom. 'My people have an observation post about ten kilometres away.' Her hand waved towards the south. 'It's partly wooded, but on high ground. You can see the whole of the Ice Palace, and the runway, from there.' She heaved at the scooter, pulling it into position so they could run it straight out of the door.

Bond's hand closed around the butt of his P7. 'You'll forgive me, Paula. We've known each other a long time, but my impression is that you're somehow tied up with von Glöda, or Kolya. This operation hasn't been straightforward from the word go. Hardly anybody has been what they seemed. I'd just like to know whose side you're on, and who your "people", as you call them, really are.'

'Oh come on, James. All our files on you say that 007 is one of Britain's best field men. Sorry, you're not officially 007 any more, are you?'

Bond slowly produced the P7. 'Paula? My instincts tell me that you're KGB.'

Her head tilted back and she laughed. 'KGB? Wrong, James. Come on, we haven't much time as it is.'

'I'll come once you've told me. I expect the proof afterwards – even if you are KGB.'

'Idiot.' A friendly laugh this time. 'James, I'm SUPO, and have been since long before we first met. In fact, my dear James, our meeting wasn't a complete accident. Your own Service has now been informed.'

SUPO? Maybe she was at that. SUPO was the abbreviation for Suojelupoliisi – the Protection Police Force. The Finnish Intelligence and Security Agency.

'But . . .'

'I'll prove it within the next couple of hours,' she said. 'Now, for God's sake, James, let's get going. There's a lot to be done.'

Bond nodded. He climbed on to the back of the scooter behind Paula as she started the motor, put the machine in gear, and gently eased it from the shelter. Once outside, she dismounted and went back to close the door behind them. Then, within seconds, they were away into the trees.

For a good minute, Paula did not even bother to turn on the large, broad-beamed headlight. After that, Bond simply clung on for dear life. She rode the Yamaha as though it were part of her body, zig-zagging with an accuracy that took Bond's breath away. She had slipped goggles over her eyes and was well-muffled, but Bond's only protection was Paula's body as the wind ripped around them.

His arms were wound tightly around her waist. Then at one point – with another of her wonderful laughs drifting back on the wind – Paula took her hands off the controls and lifted Bond's arms, so that his hands cupped her breasts through the heavy padding of the greatcoat.

Their route was far from easy. They skirted the bottom of a long rise through tightly packed trees, then made a lengthy run up the slope, swerving among the trees all the way. Yet Paula hardly slowed for anything. Holding the throttle open wide, she took the scooter side on through gaps in the trees, allowing it to ride dangerously, near a forty-five-degree angle on some banks, yet retaining control all the time.

At last she slowed, slewing from left to right at the crest, following what was certainly a natural trail. Then, quite suddenly, two figures rose from the side of the track. His eyes now well adjusted to the night, Bond caught the shapes of machine pistols against the snow.

Paula slowed and stopped, then raised an arm, and Bond found his hand searching for the P7. There was a short, muttered conversation between Paula and the larger of the men, who was dressed in Lapp costume and wore a huge moustache which made him look even more like a brigand. The other was tall and thin, with one of the most evil faces Bond had ever seen – sharp and weasel-like, with small eyes that darted everywhere. For his own sake, Bond hoped Paula had, at last, told him the truth. He wouldn't have enjoyed finding himself at the mercy of either of these people.

'They've been keeping clear of the two *kotas* we've got up here,' Paula said, turning her head towards Bond. 'I've got four men in all. Two have gone in at regular intervals, to check the radio equipment and keep the fires going. It seems that all's safe. The other pair are in the camp now. I've said we'll go straight to the *kotas* – you'll want food, and I've got to get a message off to Helsinki on the short wave. They'll relay it to London. Anything you want to tell your boss – M?'

'Only details of what's been going on, and where I am. Do we know where von Glöda will head for?'

'I'll tell you after I've talked to Helsinki,' she said, gunning the engine.

Bond nodded vigorously. 'Okay.' They advanced at a walking pace, the two Lapps taking station ahead and behind them. Bond leaned forward and whispered loudly, 'Paula, I'll shoot you where you stand if you're taking me for a ride.'

'Shut up and trust me. I'm the only one you *can* trust out here. Right?'

A few steps out of the woods, perched on the ridge, were two *kotas*. The reindeer skin which covered their wigwam-like structures loomed dark against the snow. Smoke drifted up from the criss-cross of forked poles at the top. From below, Bond thought, they would be difficult to spot against the tall firs and pines. Paula stopped the Yamaha, and they both dismounted.

'I'm going to use the radio straight away.' Paula pointed to the right-hand *kota*, and Bond could just make out the aerials among the poles at the top. 'My other two boys are in there. I've told Aslu to stay on guard outside.' She indicated the evil-looking Lapp. 'Niiles will go with you to the other *kota*, where there's food cooking.'

The Lapp with the large moustache – Niiles – grinned, nodding encouragement. His machine pistol pointed towards the ground.

'Okay, Paula,' Bond said. The smell of woodsmoke reached him before they got to within six paces of the *kota*, and Niiles went forward, lifted the hide flap, and peered inside. When he was sure everything was safe, the Lapp waved Bond towards him. Together they entered the *kota*, and immediately Bond felt his eyes sting as the smoke hit him. He coughed, wiped his eyes and looked around. The thin fog of smoke gradually made its way towards the outlet at the top of the tent. Mingled with it was a strong, pleasant cooking smell, and quickly Bond's eyes adjusted enough to make out mounds of sleeping bags, blankets and plates carefully stored within the tent.

Niiles put down his weapon and motioned for Bond to sit. He pointed at the pot bubbling over the fire, burning in a square trench cut into the earth. Niiles then touched his mouth. 'Food.' He gave a pleased nod. 'Food. Good. Eat.'

Bond nodded back.

Niiles took a plate and spoon, went to the fire, bent over it and began to fill the plate with what looked like some kind of stew.

The next moment, the Lapp was sprawled, yelling, in the fire. His feet had been kicked from under him. One of the blankets seemed to take on a human shape, but before Bond could retrieve his pistol, Kolya's voice came quietly from the other side of the fire.

'Don't even think of it, James. You'll be dead before your hand touches the butt.' He then said something in Finnish to Niiles, who had rolled clear of the fire, and now sat nursing his hand.

'I should've known.' Bond spoke as quietly as Kolya. 'It was all too easy. Paula's certainly led me a dance.'

'Paula?' Kolya's face was clear for a moment in the glare from the fire. 'I've just told this bandit here to pass me his machine pistol. I will kill him if he tries anything. Personally, I'd like to be better armed when Paula comes in here. You see, James, I'm on my own. Outnumbered. But I have friends waiting, and I don't intend to go back to Moscow empty-handed.'

Half of Bond's mind began to work on the immediate problem – should he try to warn Paula? How could he deal with Kolya Mosolov, here and now? His eyes moved carefully around the gloomy interior of the *kota* as Niiles – in a state of some agony – gently pushed the automatic weapon towards Kolya with his foot.

'From that, I presume you're taking me with you.' Bond peered through the haze.

'That was the deal I had with that Fascist pig, von Glöda.' Kolya's laugh was genuine enough. 'He really thought he could get away with running a Nazi operation from inside the Soviet Union.'

'Well, he *has* run it. All his terrorist operations have been successful. He's used Russian weapons, and now he's getting out.'

Slowly Kolya shook his head. 'There is no possible way that von Glöda can get out.'

'He was taking me. By air. May even have left already.'

'No. I've been watching and listening. His beloved little private jet hasn't left the runway, and won't even try to get off before dawn. We have a couple of hours left.'

So, it was now only two hours before dawn. At least Bond now had some idea of time. 'How can you stop him?' he asked blandly.

'It's already in motion. Von Glöda has a military force on Soviet soil. They will be blasted at dawn. The Red Air Force will turn that bunker into a boiling kettle.' Kolya's face changed in the fire glow. 'Unhappily our base at Blue Hare will also be taken out. An unfortunate error, but it solves all problems.'

Bond thought for a moment. 'So, you're going to decimate von Glöda and his whole little army. Breaking your part of the deal, but keeping his?'

'My dear James – a deal is a deal. Tough, sometimes it doesn't work out for one of the participants. How could I let you go, my friend? Especially as my department – which you used to know as SMERSH – has tried to catch you off balance for so long. No, my deal with von Glöda has always been slightly one-sided.'

# 18

# THE FENCERS

There was silence for several seconds, then Mosolov spoke a few words to the groaning Niiles.

'No need to let good food go to waste,' Kolya Mosolov said softly. 'I've told him to straighten that pot and stir up the fire. I don't think he'll try anything stupid. You should know that I have some of my men here, and they'll already have taken Paula. So, I think the best thing . . .' He stopped, in mid-sentence, with a sudden intake of breath.

The smoke thickened for a second, then quickly cleared as Niiles urged the fire into flame. Bond saw that Mosolov's head was being forced back. A hand grasped his hair, while another fist held a glinting reindeer knife across his throat. The fire leaped into life again, and the evil face of Aslu became plainly visible behind Kolya's shoulder.

'Sorry, James.' Paula was just inside the leather flap entrance to the *kota*, a heavy automatic pistol in her hand. 'I didn't want to tell you, but my boys spotted Kolya digging his way in here a couple of hours ago. You were my bait.'

'It wouldn't have mattered if you'd told me.' Bond sounded acid. 'I'm quite used to being a tethered goat.'

'Again, sorry.' Paula came right into the *kota*. 'We had other problems as well. Comrade Mosolov brought some playmates. Six of them. Aslu and Niiles dealt with that little group once they saw Kolya safely tucked away in here. That's why I'm a free woman and not a KGB prisoner . . .'

'There are plenty more . . .' Mosolov began, then thought better of it.

'Do be careful, Kolya,' Paula said brightly. 'That knife Aslu's holding to your throat's as sharp as a guillotine. He could sever your head with one well-placed stroke.' She turned to Niiles and spoke a few rapid words.

A grin crossed the big Lapp's face, the expression appearing sinister in the flickering firelight. Holding his burned hand with great care, he moved over to Mosolov, took back his own machine pistol, removed the automatic and began to search the Russian.

'They're like a couple of kids,' Paula said. 'I've told them to strip him, take him into the woods and tie him to a tree.'

'Shouldn't we keep him with us until the last minute?' Bond suggested. 'You say he had men with him . . .'

'We've dealt with them . . .'

'There could be more. He has an airstrike coming in at dawn. Having already experienced Kolya in action, I don't fancy letting him out of our sight.'

Paula thought for a moment, then relented, giving new orders to the Lapps. Kolya was silent, almost sullen, as they tied his hands and feet, placed a gag around his mouth and pushed him into the corner of the *kota*.

Paula gave Bond a nod, directing him towards the exit. Outside, she lowered her voice. 'You're right, of course, James. More of his men could still be around; it's best to keep him here. We'll only be really safe back in Finland. But . . .'

'But, like me, you want to see what happens to the Ice Palace.' Bond smiled.

'Right,' she admitted. 'Once that's over I think we can turn him loose and let his friends find him – unless you want to take his head back to London.'

Bond said taking Kolya Mosolov all the way with them could prove to be an encumbrance. 'Better to get rid of him just before we leave', was his final verdict. In the meantime they had work to do – Paula's message to Helsinki and Bond's to M.

In the radio *kota* Bond began to tap his pockets.

'Are these what you're looking for?' Paula came close to him, holding out the gunmetal cigarette case and his gold lighter.

'You think of everything.'

'Maybe I'll get to prove it later on.' In spite of the presence of the Lapps in the radio *kota*, Paula Vacker reached up and kissed Bond gently; then again, with some urgency.

The radio *kota* contained a powerful short-wave transmitter, with facilities for morse and clear speech. There was also a fast-sending device, allowing a transmission to be taped, and then run through in a fraction of a second, ready for slowing, and decoding, at the other end. These messages often appear as a bleep of static in the earphones of the many listeners who monitor signal traffic.

Bond watched for a few minutes, while Paula organised her own message to Helsinki. There was no doubt in his mind that hers was a thoroughly professional set-up. Paula definitely worked for SUPO – something he should really have known about years ago, considering how far their relationship went back. Already he had asked for her field cryptonym, and was delighted to learn that – for this operation against von Glöda – she was known as Vuobma, the old Lapp word for stockade, or corral, in which reindeer are trapped and herded for breeding.

With all his equipment – except for the Heckler & Koch P7 – either gone, or still in the Saab at the Hotel Revontuli, Bond was without any method of ciphering his signal. While Paula worked at the transmitter, one of the two Lapps who had been in the radio *kota* for most of the time, stood close to her. The other was sent off to keep a watch on the bunker and its airstrip.

Finally, after a few dud tries, Bond composed a suitable clear-language message, which read:

VIA GCHQ CHELTENHAM TO M STOP ICEBREAKER BROKEN
BUT OBJECTIVE SHOULD BE ACHIEVED BY DAWN TODAY
STOP RETURNING SOONEST STOP MOST URGENT FLASH
REPEAT MOST URGENT GET YOUR BEST BOTTLE OUT OF THE
CELLAR STOP I WORK THROUGH VUOBMA ENDS 007.

The 007 would raise some eyebrows, but it could not be helped.
His instructions to move the prisoner were fairly obvious. Not
the best, but if any NSAA listening post picked up the signal,
they presumably already knew where M's prisoner was being
held anyway. This message, if intercepted, would only alert
them to the fact that he would be moved. At short notice, and
without the facilities, it was the best Bond could do.

When Paula had completed her signal, she took Bond's piece
of paper, added a coding of her own to make certain that it
would go on to GCHQ, Cheltenham, via her own Service's
Communications Department, and rattled it off on to tape,
before zipping it through the small fast-sending machine.

When all this was done, they held a conference, Bond suggesting how best a continuous watch could be kept on the bunker.
The dawn airstrike was uppermost in his mind; after that it
would be necessary to get away as quickly as possible, dump
Kolya Mosolov, and clear the frontier without undue hazard.

'Can you find the way back?' he asked Paula.

'Blindfold. I'll give you all the information later, but there's no
problem as far as that's concerned. Except we'll have to move
from here, then wait to make the crossing as soon as it's dark
enough.'

Through Paula, Bond gave orders for the radio *kota* to be
dismantled and packed away – the four Lapps had their large
snow scooters hidden near at hand – and organised periods of
rest, with one of the Lapps briefed to rouse them in plenty of
time to strike the other *kota* before dawn.

'Mosolov's a liability, whatever,' he declared. 'But we'll have
to hang on to him for as long as possible.'

Paula shrugged. 'Leave it to my Lapps and they'll take care of Kolya,' she murmured. But Bond did not want the Russian killed except as a last resort; so the arrangements were made, and the orders given.

While the radio *kota* was being dismantled, they trudged back to the remaining shelter. A blood-chilling howl was carried on the wind through the trees, long and drawn out, followed by another, similar sound.

'Wolves,' Paula said. 'On the Finnish side, our border patrols have had a bumper year: at least a couple of wolves a week for most of them, and three bears since Christmas. It's been a particularly hard winter and you mustn't believe all you hear about wolves not being dangerous. During a bad winter, when food's scarce, they'll attack anything: man, woman or child.'

Niiles, his hand bandaged, had already fed Kolya, whom he'd propped in the corner of the *kota*. Previously, Bond had cautioned Paula that they should not, under any circumstances, discuss plans in front of him. They ignored the Russian, though there was always one armed Lapp near by making certain he was well-guarded.

Niiles's reindeer stew proved to be delicious, and they ate with enjoyment – the Lapp nodding and smiling at their pleasure. In the short time spent at Paula's observation post, Bond had acquired a great admiration for her tough resilient Lapp assistants. As they ate, Paula produced a bottle of vodka, and they drank a toast to final success, knocking the little paper cups together and chanting '*Kippos*', the Finnish equivalent of 'Cheers'.

After the meal, Paula settled down with Bond in one of the larger sleeping bags. Mosolov seemed to have dozed off, and soon the couple, after several tender embraces, also slept. Eventually, they were wakened by Aslu urgently shaking Bond's shoulder. Paula was already awake and had been told by Aslu that there was some activity at the bunker. 'And a good half hour to go before dawn,' she announced.

'Right.' Bond then took charge. The *kota* would be dismantled here and now, after which one of the Lapps would stay – in the cover of the trees – to guard Mosolov, while the rest could gather at the observation point.

Within five minutes, Paula and Bond had, themselves, joined Niiles who lay among rocks and snow on the rise, scanning the view below through a pair of night glasses. Behind them, Paula's other Lapps went quietly about the business of striking camp, and Bond glimpsed Kolya being hustled away into the trees – Aslu prodding him along with a submachine gun.

Bond was amazed at the sight, even in the gloom of half-light, which now heralded a dawn that would come in twenty minutes or so. From Paula's observation post the view down to the small clearing among the trees, and the huge rocky area of the bunker's roof, was unimpeded. It was plain now that the entrance to the Ice Palace itself was built into a rising wall of rock, like a giant stepping stone forming a rough crescent in the centre of a thick forest. The trees had been expertly cleared to allow only minimal open space in front of the main entrances, while other paths were cut – through trees, rock, and ice – as routes around the bunker to the higher, more open, ground above.

To the south, and above the huge spur of rock, the thick forest was broken by carefully prepared clear tracks, through which a wide runway pointed a long grey-white finger, disappearing into the heart of the surrounding forest. There was no sign of an aircraft. Bond presumed the Mystère-Falcon Executive Jet and the two light aeroplanes were tucked away in concrete pens, built into the rock which helped form the roof of the bunker itself.

In the present light, and at this distance, it was not possible to make an accurate calculation about the length of the runway. All Bond considered was that a take-off, among trees, left little margin for error. Yet von Glöda had already proved his ability in most things, so it was unlikely that the runway would present a genuine hazard, for landing or take-off.

Below them von Glöda's private army was about to get under way. The floodlights were on under the trees, and the big doors, leading to the vehicle ramp running deep inside the Ice Palace, were open, sending a sharp-angled flood of light out over the trees.

Paula spoke a few words to Niiles, then turned to Bond. 'Nothing's come out yet. No vehicles or aircraft sighted, though Niiles says there's a lot of troop activity among the trees.'

'Let's hope Kolya was specific,' Bond replied, 'and the Russians are going to hit them on time.'

'When they do get here we'd better dig ourselves into the snow and pretend to be rocks,' murmured Paula. 'I think Kolya's instructions would be accurate enough, but we don't want to catch a stray missile up here.'

She had hardly said the words before the sound of a jet-whine became audible, a fair distance away – like a wail carried on the wind. Just then the sun glowed blood-red in the east. They looked at each other, and Bond lifted his hands, showing gloved fingers crossed for good luck. Shifting slightly, all three watchers tried to dig themselves deeper into the snow. Bond shivered. He had not realised how cold he was – the elements forgotten as he concentrated on the bunker far below, and about a kilometre away. Then, even that brief moment of discomfort was gone as a great double crump seemed to blast the air around them. Far off to the north-east there was a series of brilliant orange flashes, and a plume of smoke rose from the close-knit trees.

'Blue Hare,' Paula said loudly, as though she had to shout against the noise. 'They've . . .' Her next words were truly drowned. The supersonic shockwaves from the aircraft travelled ahead of the machines. A consuming, growling roar surrounded Paula, Bond and Niiles – a terrifying harbinger of what was to follow, in the new, clear dawn.

The first pair of strike aircraft came in level with the trees, crossing to the hiding trio's right, neither firing nor dropping anything. They streaked through the cold air, little eddies of steam surrounding the wings, as the sub-zero temperatures produced contrails even at this low level. They looked like silver darts, precision-built arrows, with large box-like air intakes, high tails, and wings folded back into a delta configuration, joining the elevators to make one long, slim, lifting surface. As if controlled by one man, the two aircraft tipped noses towards the sky and screamed upwards in a terrifyingly fast climb until they were only tiny silver dots, banking away to the north.

'Fencers,' Bond breathed.

'What? Fencers?' Paula scowled.

'Fencers. It's the NATO code name for them.' Bond's eyes moved constantly, watching the sky for the next wave which, he knew, would bring in the first attack. 'They're Su–19s. Very dangerous. Ground attack fighter-bombers. They pack a nasty punch, Paula.' In the back of his head Bond could almost hear the details of the Fencer clicking through, like a computer read-out. Power: two afterburning turbofans, or jets, of the 9,525 kg thrust class. Speed: Mach 1.25 at sea level; Mach 2.5 at altitude. Service ceiling: 60,000 feet; initial climb 40,000 feet per minute. Armament: one 23 mm GSh–23 twin-barrel cannon fitted on lower centreline, and a minimum of six pylons for a variety of air-to-air, and air-to-ground, guided, and unguided, missiles. Combat radius: 500 miles with full weapons. That all added up to a most efficient, and lethal, piece of warplane. Not even the most optimistic of NATO airmen could deny it.

Having spotted their target, the two leaders would call up the rest of their squadron – or even wing – and pass on the co-ordinates and instructions, probably tapping them out on a small keyboard. Already the pilots would have been briefed on the order of attack, and the fast reconnaissance assured it would come in a series of angled dives, around forty-five degrees – maybe from different directions, the pairs of aircraft vectored, and controlled, to come in with split-second timing, one after the other. Bond thought of the Soviet pilots – top men to be flying the Fencers – concentrating on their electronics, speed, height, timing, and angle of dive; priming their weapons; glancing constantly at the sky, sweating under their G-suits and helmets.

The first approach growl came from their left, followed, almost immediately, by a second from what seemed to be directly above. 'Here we go!' Bond saw Paula's head turn as he looked up, and the twin streaks came tearing out of the now clear bluish sky to their left. He had been right. The Fencers came in pairs and with noses down in a classic ground-attack dive. Quite clearly they saw the first missiles flash away from the wings – long white flames shooting back, then the orange trails as the deadly darts ripped through the air. Two from each aircraft, all four catching the front of the bunker, boring in and exploding with wide orange blossoms of fire reaching their eyes before the heavy zoom and thud hit their ears.

As the first two aircraft whipped to the left, flick-turning away, so the second pair came down from Bond's and Paula's right. Identical plumes of flames shot out, then fire bloomed from within the target area. The missiles were digging well into the rock, steel and concrete before exploding. Bond watched, fascinated, trying to identify the weaponry. As the third pair came in, from the far right, he was able to follow the missiles through their complete trajectory – AS-7s, he thought, Kerries to NATO, and the Kerry came in several specifications, both guided and unguided. They also had changeable warheads – straight HE, or armour- and rock-penetrating delayed charges.

Below, after just three attacks – using twelve Kerry missiles – the Ice Palace looked ready to be broken in two. The thunder of the explosions still echoed, and through the inevitable pall of smoke, they could see the terrible crimson glow of fire begin to sweep out of the open main doors, up from the arms stores and vehicle parks.

Then a fourth and fifth wave of Fencers hurtled out of the cold sky, their rockets seeming to hang in the air for a moment as the aircraft turned away and lifted in a whining climb, before shooting forward – straight as ruled lines of fire until they disappeared into the smoke and flame, to explode, a few seconds later, with twin roars which seemed to grow louder with each rocket.

From their grandstand view, the Lapp, Paula, and Bond could not draw their eyes from this sight of deliberate destruction. The sky now seemed full of aircraft – one pair following another, with the accuracy of some crack air display team. Their ears were pounded with supersonic shock waves and their eyes with lightning strikes as the rockets found their marks again and again.

The bunker became almost invisible, its presence marked by the tower of black smoke and the constant crimson fists punching within the dark cloud. The attack, which could have taken only seven or eight minutes, seemed to go on for hours. Finally a pair of Fencers came in, from the left, at an unusually low angle of attack. The aircraft had exhausted their missiles and began to rake the smoke and flame with cannon fire.

Both aircraft pulled up short, their track taking them low and directly through the rising smoke. Just as they disappeared into the black cloud there was a great rumble, followed by an almost volcanic roar. At first, Bond thought the Fencers had touched wings and collided over the target; then the black smoke turned into a huge fireball, spreading outwards, growing in size, first orange, turning to white and, last, to a bloody crimson. The ground shook, and they could feel the snow and earth moving under them, as though an earthquake had, against all the laws of nature, suddenly been activated.

Heat scorched their faces as the fireball rose past them. Tongues of flame reached out for them or wound themselves around the trees. Then the updraught came like a twisting tornado, the whole engulfed by a colossal noise as the sound of the explosion hit them. Bond's hand shot out, banging Paula's head into the snow as he buried his face, holding his breath.

The heat receded at last. The two aircraft had gone. Disappeared. Above, they could see other planes gaining height and circling. It was when Bond looked down that the picture became clear.

Where the bunker had been there was now only a huge crater, surrounded by burning or bent trees. Fires spouted from deep down in the ground, and you could see the uncanny sight of odd pieces of masonry, steps and steel girders hanging free above a maze of open walls and broken passages. The wreckage looked like a bombed building that had been dropped into a chasm.

The explosions and fires, caused by the constant penetration of the Kerry missiles, had, eventually, detonated all the loaded ammunition, bombs, gasoline and other war matériel in one comprehensive explosion. The result was the total destruction of von Glöda's Ice Palace.

Smoke billowed up and then drifted away; there was the occasional spurt of flame, mixed with fires already burning well. Apart from the odd crackling noise, though, there was no other sound. Only the terrible smell of devastation wafted up towards their perch, above what had once been a deep and seemingly impregnable fortress.

'Kristos,' breathed Paula. 'Whatever else happens to Kolya, he's had his vengeance.' It was only when she spoke that they realised their own sense of hearing had returned.

Still slightly dazed by what they had witnessed, they made their way back to the site of Paula's encampment, and Bond headed towards the point where Aslu was guarding Mosolov within the woods.

He spotted it before anyone else, reacting sharply with a quick order to the Lapps to fan out and get down. Dropping to the ground himself, he pushed Paula with him.

'You stay here.' Bond spoke quietly, all his senses now alert, and the P7 heavy in his hand. 'Tell your people to cover me if anything happens.'

Paula nodded, her face pale even against the snow, as though she also knew something very terrible had happened.

Bond ran forward through the trees, crouching and ready for anything. The evil-faced Aslu appeared even more bizarre in death. By the marks in the snow, Bond reckoned that four of them had taken him, using knives for silence. The Lapp's throat was slit, but there were other wounds, signifying this was only the final act in a struggle. Aslu had fought, even though taken by surprise.

Of Kolya Mosolov there was no sign, and even the most dim-witted person would quickly realise this was not the most healthy place to linger. As he made his way back to Paula, Bond wondered if the scooters had been left intact, and whether Kolya would launch his counter-attack straight away.

Later Paula was to tell Bond that Aslu had worked with her for many years, and had been one of her most loyal operators on the Russian side of the border. But now she passed the news to the others without even a shake in her voice. Only by looking closely could you see how badly Aslu's death had hit her.

Bond issued the orders – quiet, fast, and clear. One of the Lapps was to check out the snow scooters. If they were still hidden and working, Bond decided the party would have to go for a fast getaway. The main, and obvious, fear was that the men who had rescued Kolya were still near by, and ready to pounce.

'Make sure your boys are prepared to fight now – and I mean fight their way out if necessary,' he told Paula.

Niiles went forward, returning in a matter of minutes with the news that the scooters were untouched, with no tracks to indicate they had been found.

Bond understood now why the Lapps had been such a formid-able enemy against the might of the Russian army in 1939. They moved through the trees with speed and cunning, leapfrogging, covering each other as they went and becoming at times almost invisible even to Bond.

Paula stayed close, for she was to lead the party out. As Bond reached the scooters with her, the three Lapps were just starting the engines. The roar of four scooters seemed to shake the trees, and Bond expected bullets to rain in on them at any moment.

Paula was in the saddle of the big Yamaha – with Bond behind her – in a matter of seconds, and they were away, gathering speed, and zig-zagging through the trees, heading south. No trouble so far.

The ride took the best part of two hours, and Bond – even in the cold and uncomfortable position behind Paula – was aware of the three Lapps circling them, spreading out, moving forward, covering against ambush all the way. There was a moment, as they slowed through some particularly rough ground, when Bond imagined he could hear the sound of other engines – other scooters. Of one thing he was certain, Kolya Mosolov would not let them get away scot-free to Finland. He had to be following, near by, or already waiting for them, calculating at which point Paula intended to make the last long dash to freedom. There was, Bond presumed, even the remote possibility that Kolya would call up another air strike.

Finally they stopped, taking up station among trees above the great open valley which separates Russia from Finland, running like a dry artificial river from north to south.

Bond decided they should immediately take up defensive positions. He stayed, with Paula, beside the big Yamaha while the three Lapps disappeared further into the trees, forming a triangle around Paula and Bond. There they would wait until it was dark enough to make the run back into Finland.

'You're confident about making it?' Bond asked Paula, smiling, testing her own nerve and will. 'I mean, I'd rather not end up by going over a mine.'

Paula was silent for a few seconds. 'If you want to walk it by yourself . . .' she began, with an edge to her voice.

'I've every confidence in you, Paula.' Bond leaned over and kissed her. She was trembling, but not from the cold, and James

Bond knew well enough how she felt. If Kolya was going to act while they were still on the Russian side, it would be soon.

Slowly the light began to go, and Bond felt the tension starting to build within him. Niiles had settled himself into a high point among the branches of a pine tree. Bond could not see him – indeed had not even spotted him making the ascent – but knew only because the Lapp had told Paula exactly where he was going. Try as he would, straining his eyes, Bond could not see the man, and the fast-fading light made it constantly more difficult. Suddenly, the 'blue moment' was on them – that blue-green haze reflected off the snow, changing perspective.

'Ready?' Bond turned to Paula and saw her nod.

In the second his eyes left the pine in which he knew Niiles was hidden, they heard the first shot. It came directly from the pine tree, so the Lapp had got in before Kolya's men. The sound still echoed in the air when the next shots followed. They seemed to be coming from a semi-circle to the front, within the trees: single rounds followed by the lethal rip of machine-gun fire.

It was impossible to gauge the enemy strength, or even if they were making progress. All Bond knew was that a fire fight of some vigour appeared to be developing to their front.

Though the 'blue moment' had not entirely dropped them into darkness, there was no point in waiting. Paula had already said that the Lapps were prepared to hold off anything Kolya sent in, while they tried to make their escape. Now was the time to put the promise to the test.

'Go,' Bond shouted at Paula.

Like the professional she was, Paula did not hesitate. The Yamaha's engine fired, and Bond was up behind Paula as she slewed the machine diagonally into the open, and down the bare icy slope towards the valley, naked of trees, that would lead to safety.

The gunfire was louder, and the last thing Bond saw, through a fine spray of snow, was a figure falling, toppling from the branches of the pine. It was not the right moment to tell Paula that Niiles had joined his friend Aslu.

By the time they had covered half a kilometre, darkness surrounded them, and the noise of firing still came from behind. The last two Lapps were putting up a strong fight, but Bond knew it would only be a matter of time, and a great deal depended on Kolya Mosolov's strength. Would he try to follow on high-powered scooters? Or, as a tactician, would the Russian prefer to spray the valley with fire?

The answer came as they neared the valley floor, with three or four kilometres of hard riding to go before they reached the far slope and the safety of the trees. Above the engine noise Bond detected a sound high above them. Then the terrain was lit by a parachute flare, throwing an eerie, dazzling light across the packed snow and ice.

'Is it safe to zig-zag?' he yelled in Paula's ear, thinking of the minefields.

She turned her head back, shouting, 'We'll soon find out,' hauling on the handlebars so that they slewed violently sideways, just as Bond heard the ominous crack of bullets breaking the air to their left. Again Paula heaved the handlebars, working with a strength drawn from those hidden reserves people find in desperate moments. The scooter skidded and swerved, sometimes zig-zagging, then moving broadside on, then straight, with throttle wide open.

The first flare was dying, but the bullets still cracked around them, and twice Bond watched the long, almost lazy lines of tracer falling in front of them – reds and greens – first left, and then to their right.

They both automatically crouched low on the scooter, and Bond felt an odd sense of mingled anger and frustration. It took him a moment to detect the cause, then he realised his instincts had been to stay on the Russian side of the ridge and fight Kolya Mosolov instead of running. His head buzzed with the old jingle, 'He who fights and runs away, lives to fight another day'. But it was not natural to Bond's character to run from a fight. Deep inside him, though, he was aware that it was necessary. Both Paula and he had a job to complete – to return safely – and this was their only chance.

The tracer still kept coming, even though the flare had gone out. Then another small explosion heralded a second flare, and this time the guns ceased firing. Instead came the terrifying noise of a fast-approaching express train: at least that was what it sounded like until the mortar bomb landed, well behind and to their left. It made a solid, ear-ringing crump, followed by a second and third: all behind them.

Paula was taking the Yamaha to its limit, still using avoiding action, but relying on the straight runs for speed. There were moments, as Bond clung to her, when he thought they would leave the ground completely.

The screech of mortar bombs came again; this time to their right and ahead – three violent orange flashes played havoc with the eyesight in the dark, the dazzling after-flash lingering on the retina.

The thing that worried Bond most, was the placing of the mortar bombs. First they had fallen behind; now they were in front. It meant only one thing: that Kolya's men were bracketing their target. Chances were that the next bombs would fall at least level with them, unless Paula could outrun the range: she was certainly doing her best: throttle wide open, the Yamaha skimming ice and snow, flat out.

Through the white gloom, the far rise – into the trees and Finland – was already becoming visible.

There was one more nasty moment as they heard the distant thump, and the hiss of falling bombs for the last time. But Paula's burst of speed had given them the lead. There were half a dozen explosions this time, but all were behind, and well off line. Unless the scooter hit a mine – and there had already been plenty of opportunity to do that – they would make it.

\*

While Paula and Bond were making their desperate dash for the Finnish border, two men climbed from the rocks to the left of the flaming ruins of von Glöda's Ice Palace. There was no one to observe them in the gathering dusk.

Since the horrors of that morning's attack, the men had worked frantically in the only tiny fragment of the bunker that had remained, miraculously, intact – one steel and concrete pen housing a small, grey Cessna 150 Commuter, with ski attachments on its tricycle undercarriage. As the light failed, so they finally managed to swing the buckled doors free.

The aircraft seemed undamaged, though the runway ahead had been gutted and strewn with débris. The taller of the men gave a few friendly instructions to his companion, who had worked so hard. Willingly, the man trudged out on to the runway, shifting what he could, clearing a few hundred yards of makeshift pathway in front of the Cessna.

The plane's engine started with a sporadic cough, then settled down to warm into its comfortable hum.

The other figure returned, climbed in beside the taller man, and the little aircraft gingerly moved forward, as though its pilot were testing the strength of the runway beneath him. Then the pilot turned to his companion, giving him the thumbs-up sign, and pushed down the flap control to give maximum lift. A second later, he gently opened the throttle. The engine rose to maximum revolutions, and the Cessna bumped forward, gathering speed, the pilot craning, slewing the aircraft from side to side to avoid the worst sections of the runway. With a bump, the Cessna hit a short, straight patch of ice, seemed to snatch at an extra few kph of ground speed, and began to skim the rough surface.

Trees loomed ahead of them, growing taller by the second. The pilot felt that moment of response from his craft as the weight transferred safely to the wings. Gently he eased back on the yoke. The Cessna's nose came up. She seemed to hesitate for a second, then thrust forward, balanced only a short distance from the ground but gaining airspeed with every second. The pilot eased back a little more, his right hand pushing the throttle fully open, then winding back on the trim to give the aircraft a shade more weight in the tail. The propeller grabbed at the sky. The nose fell slightly, then the propeller grabbed again, clawed at the air and sent it barrelling back over the flying surfaces until the small plane was stable, nose up and climbing. They cleared the top of the fir trees by a matter of inches.

Count Konrad von Glöda smiled, set a course, and headed the Cessna towards his next goal. This day might have been a defeat, even a crushing one, but he was not through yet. There were men, legions of men, waiting to come under his command. But first, there was one score to be settled. Gratefully, he nodded at the craggy face of Hans Buchtman, whom Bond had known as 'Bad' Brad Tirpitz.

Paula and Bond reached the Hotel Revontuli at two o'clock in the morning, and Bond went straight to the Saab to send a carefully worded cipher back to M. When he got to Reception there was a note waiting for him. It read:

> We are in suite No. 5, my darling James. Can we sleep in please, and not leave for Helsinki until the afternoon? All love, Paula.
>
> P.S. I'm not really all that tired at the moment, and have ordered champagne and some of this hotel's rather excellent smoked salmon.

With a certain amount of satisfaction, Bond remembered Paula's hidden delights and particular expertise. Spryly he walked to the lift.

# 19

# LOOSE ENDS

They talked almost the whole way back to Helsinki in the Saab.

'There are a lot of things I still need to know,' Bond, now fresh, showered and changed into clean clothing, had begun soon after they left Salla.

'Such as?' Paula was in one of those cat-who's-licked-the-cream moods. Dressed in furs, looking more like a woman than what she had called 'a bundle of thermal underwear', she shook out her lovely blonde hair and snuggled her head against Bond's shoulder.

'When did your Service – SUPO – first suspect Aarne Tudeer, or Count von Glöda, as he likes to call himself?'

She smiled, looking very pleased with herself. 'That was my doing. You know, James, I've never worked out why you didn't cotton on to me years ago. I know my cover was good, but you didn't even suspect?'

'I was foolish enough to accept you at face value,' Bond said, taking a deep breath. 'I did have you checked out once. Nothing came back. It's easy to say it now, but there were times when I wondered how we managed to bump into each other so often in far away places.'

'Ah.'

'And you haven't answered my question,' Bond persisted.

'Well, we knew he was up to something. I mean, all that business about me being a schoolfriend of Anni Tudeer is absolutely true. Her mother *did* bring her back home, and I did meet her. But when I heard, officially, long after SUPO had recruited me, that Anni had joined Mossad I just couldn't believe it.'

'Why?'

For a second Bond's mind drifted away from the road. Any mention of Anni Tudeer was bound to bring back unpleasant memories.

'Why didn't I believe she was a genuine Mossad agent?' Paula did not hesitate. 'I knew her too well. She was the apple of Aarne Tudeer's eye. She also loved him dearly. I knew only as a woman can know. Partly it was some of the things she said; partly intuition. Everyone knew about her father – of course they did – there was never any secret. Anni's secret was that she had been brainwashed by him. I think that, even as a child, he had mapped out what part she would play. Almost certainly he was in constant touch with her, advising and instructing her. He was the one person who could teach Anni how to penetrate Mossad.'

'Which she did very well.' Bond glanced at the pretty face next to him. 'Why did you mention her name to me? That first time – when I questioned you, following the knife fight at your place?'

She sighed. 'Why do you think, James? I was in a very difficult situation. It was the only way I could pass on some kind of clue.'

'All right. Now, tell me the whole story.'

Paula Vacker had been in on the entire NSAA affair from the start – even before the first incident at Tripoli. SUPO, through informers and observation, knew that Tudeer had returned to Finland, taken the name of von Glöda, and appeared to be up to something just over the border, in Russia. 'After every possible intelligence agency had been called in on the National Socialist Action Army, I suggested it could be the work of Tudeer,' she told him. 'For my pains, my masters ordered that I infiltrate. So I put myself in the right places and said the right things. It got back, I was a good healthy Aryan Nazi.' Eventually, von Glöda had made contact. 'I was finally appointed to his staff as resident in Helsinki. In other words, I was doubling with the full know-ledge of my superiors.'

'Who refrained from passing information to my Service?' There were many things that still puzzled Bond.

'No. SUPO was, in fact, preparing a dossier. Then the storm broke at the Ice Palace – over Blue Hare – and there was no need to make any reports. Kolya's superiors set up Icebreaker and I was supposed to be there for your protection. I gather your Service was put in the picture – late on – after you'd left for the Ice Palace.'

Bond pondered on this for a few kilometres. Eventually he said, 'I find it hard to swallow – the whole business about Ice-breaker and the deal with Kolya.'

'It would be difficult to believe unless you were actually there, unless you really got to know von Glöda's deviousness, and Kolya Mosolov's cunning mind.' She gave her delightful laugh. 'They were both egomaniacs, and power mad – though each in his own way, you understand. I did the journey from Helsinki to the Arctic and across to the bunker a dozen times, you know. I was also there, and trusted, when the balloon went up.'

'What? Blue Hare?'

'Yes. That was all absolutely genuine. You have to take your hat off to von Glöda. He had nerve. Incredible nerve. Mind you, I think the Soviets were keeping more of an eye on him than he imagined.'

'I wonder.' Bond took an icy bend a little fast, swore, left-footed the brake, came out of the skid with power, and had the car under control all in a matter of seconds. 'You know a British General has said that the Russians should be awarded the wooden spoon for ineptitude? They can do the most stupid things. Tell me what happened with Blue Hare.'

'I was completely accepted within the, so-called, Führer's inner circle. He seldom let us forget how clever he was in bribing those stupid NCOs at Blue Hare. He really did pay them a pittance for the equipment; and they didn't seem to think about being caught.'

'But they were.'

'Indeed they were. I was there when it all happened. The fat little Warrant Officer came dashing up to the bunker. Like the rest of them, he was really only a peasant in uniform. Stank to high heaven, but von Glöda was terrific with him. I have to admit the man could be exceptionally cool in moments of crisis. But of course he believed in his destiny as the new Führer. Nothing could go wrong, and every man had his price. I heard him tell the Blue Hare CO to get the army people to call in the GRU. He knew they would pass it on to the KGB. Oddly, it worked. Quicker than a wink, Kolya Mosolov was there.'

'And asked for my head on a charger.'

Paula gave a secretive smile. 'It wasn't quite like that. Kolya had no intention of ever letting von Glöda get away with it. He simply played along, gave him some rope. You know the Russians; Kolya's one chink was that he wanted to bury the problem of Blue Hare. On the other hand, I think von Glöda saw himself as the Devil tempting Christ. He actually offered Kolya his heart's desire.'

'And Kolya said: J. Bond, Esquire?'

'Von Glöda's mad dream was of power to control the world. Kolya did not think that big. All he wanted was to bury Blue Hare – which meant doing away with von Glöda's set-up. He could have dealt with it all in a couple of days, on his own. But von Glöda, being the kind of man he was, set his own delusions of grandeur to work. In turn they fired Kolya's imagination.'

Bond nodded. 'Kolya, what do you want in all the world? Kolya thinks: *You* swept out of the way, Comrade von Glöda; and the Blue Hare business hushed up. Fame and promotion for me. Then, aloud, he says Bond – James Bond.'

'That's it. The old SMERSH – Department V as they now are – wanted you. So he asked for you.' She began to laugh. 'Then von Glöda had the gall to do a deal which meant that Kolya had to work very hard. After all, it was through Kolya that the CIA, Mossad and your Service were brought in; it was through Kolya that you, James, were asked for personally; it was Kolya who set everything up.'

'Under the instructions of von Glöda? It somehow doesn't ring true.'

'No. No, James, it doesn't, until you take into account the personalities involved, and their motivations. I told you, Kolya had no intention of letting von Glöda get away with it. But his own private thirst for power and advancement allowed him to use the whole of von Glöda's organisation for the one purpose of luring you into Russia. It took a lot of doing – the specially printed maps, the replacement of Tirpitz . . .'

'Getting Rivke appointed to the team?' Bond suggested.

'Von Glöda suggested that Kolya should ask for her, just as he suggested Tirpitz from the Americans. Kolya, of course, wanted you – he spent hours using von Glöda's telephone, talking to Moscow Centre. They were sticky about it to begin with, but Kolya concocted some kind of tale. His superiors agreed, and put in their formal requests to America, Israel and Britain. Everyone was furious when you couldn't be brought in straight away. The fellow Buchtman arrived first. He was some contact of von Glöda's, and they sent him off to meet the real Tirpitz and dispose of him. Then Rivke arrived in Finland. That was very worrying. I had to keep clear most of the time. Von Glöda appointed me as liaison officer for Kolya, which was handy, and by this time Moscow Centre had given Kolya a free hand. They thought he was simply clearing up some nest of dissidents on the Finnish border and wiping the slate clean of Blue Hare, using the Americans, British and Israelis as fall guys if anything went wrong. I suppose they imagined that the NSAA was only a small cell of fanatics.'

She paused, took one of Bond's cigarettes, then continued. 'For me, Rivke was the most difficult part. I did not dare see her, and Kolya wanted messages passed to her in Helsinki. I had to do it through a third party. Then everyone was really waiting for a chance to have you brought out. Rivke came into play, when von Glöda hatched his little scheme, as a standby . . .'

'Which particular scheme?'

She sighed. 'The one that made me very jealous. That Rivke should worm her way into your heart, then disappear in case von Glöda needed to use her to trap you. The business on the ski slope took one hell of a lot of organisation – and not a little nerve on Anni's part. But, then, she was always a good gymnast . . . As you certainly discovered,' she added pointedly.

Bond grunted. 'You think von Glöda had any idea that he wasn't going to be allowed to get away with it?'

'Oh, he suspected Kolya enough. He didn't trust him. That was why I liaised with the Russians. Von Glöda had to know everything. Then, of course, we got to the point where our noble Führer needed to know about the man your people captured in England. You were already under sentence of death. So was Kolya. Von Glöda's plan was to get all his people out to Norway.'

'Norway? That was where his new Command Post had been built?'

'So my chiefs tell me. But they also knew of another hiding place he had in Finland. I should imagine that was where everyone was going when Kolya's airstrike was called in.'

They travelled in silence for a long way, Bond going over the facts in his mind. 'Well,' he said finally, 'my trouble is that von Glöda's the first real enemy against whom I've had to pit my wits at long range. Most of my assignments allow me to get close; to know the man I'm dealing with. Von Glöda never let me really come near him.'

'It was his strength. He didn't let anyone gain his complete confidence – even that woman he took around with him. I think Anni – Rivke – was the only one who really knew him.'

'And you didn't?' Bond's voice was laced with suspicion.

'What do you mean?' Paula's tone turned cold, as though offended.

'I mean there are times I'm not completely certain of you, Paula.'

Paula gave a sharp intake of breath. 'After all I've done?'

'Even after all you've done. For instance, what about the pair of thugs at your place? The knife merchants?'

She nodded, quietly. 'I wondered when you'd get back to them.' She edged away, turning her body towards him. 'You think I set you up?'

'It crossed my mind.'

Paula bit her lip. 'No, dear James.' She sighed. 'No, I didn't set you up. I let you down. How can I explain it? As I said, neither von Glöda nor Kolya were playing it straight. Everyone was in a no-win situation, as they say. I worked under SUPO's instructions, and also von Glöda's orders. The situation became impossible once I was put in charge of liaison with Kolya. He was always in and out of Helsinki. You turned up out of the blue, and my chiefs had to be told. I let you down, James. I shouldn't have said anything.'

'What you're trying to say is SUPO ordered you to inform Kolya? Right?'

She nodded. 'He saw a way to get you in Helsinki, then whip you up to the Arctic and into Russia all on his own. Sorry.'

'And what about the snow ploughs?'

'What snow ploughs?' Her mood changed. A few moments before, Paula had been on the defensive, then contrite. Now she was plain surprised. Bond told her about the trouble on the way from Helsinki to Salla.

She thought for a minute. 'My guess would be Kolya again. I know he had the airport and hotels watched by his own people – in Helsinki, I mean. They would know where you were heading. I think Kolya would have gone to a lot of trouble to tuck you under his arm and get you into Russia without using any of von Glöda's formulas.'

By the end of the journey Bond was virtually convinced by Paula's explanations. As he said, there had never been time for him to get really close to the autocratic, iron-haired von Glöda; and he understood from past experience the strange power clash between two determined men, like von Glöda and Kolya.

'Your place or mine?' Bond asked as they reached the outskirts of Helsinki. He was almost satisfied with Paula's answers, true, but a niggling doubt remained in a corner of his mind, for nothing in Operation Icebreaker had been what it seemed. Time now to play his trump card.

'We can't go to my place.' Paula gave a small cough. 'It's in a hell of a mess and roughed up – it got burgled, James, for real. I didn't even have time to report it to the police.'

Bond pulled the car over to the side of the road and stopped. 'I know.' He reached across to the glove compartment, taking out von Glöda's Knight's Cross and the Campaign Shield and dropping them on Paula's lap. 'I found these on your dressing table when I called there and discovered the place wrecked, on my way to the party in the Arctic.'

For a second, Paula was angry. 'Then why the hell didn't you use them? You could've shown them to Anni.'

Bond patted her hand. 'I did. She identified them. Which made me concerned, also very suspicious. Of you. Where did you get them?'

'From von Glöda, of course. He wanted them cleaned up. The man was obsessively proud of them, just as he was obsessive about his destiny.' She made a disgusted noise in the back of her throat. 'Oh hell, I might have known that bitch would turn them on to me.'

Bond took the medals and threw them into the glove compartment. 'Okay,' he said, relieved. 'You pass. Let's give ourselves a treat. We'll take the honeymoon suite at the Inter-Continental. How about that?'

'How *about* that?' She squeezed his hand, running a finger across the palm.

They had no difficulty checking in, and the Inter-Continental's twenty-four hour room service provided food and drink with the minimum delay. The drive, the explanations, and their long relationship together seemed to have removed all the barriers.

'I'm going to shower,' Paula announced. 'Then we can enjoy ourselves to our hearts' content. I don't know about you, but I think there's no need for either of our Services to hear we're back in Helsinki for at least another twenty-four hours.'

'You don't think we should call in? We can always say we're still on the road,' Bond suggested.

Paula thought it over. 'Oh, maybe I'll dial my answering service later. If my controller has anything urgent he leaves a number for me. What about you?'

'Have your shower, then I'll follow you. I don't honestly think M would appreciate anything from me until the morning.'

She gave a dazzling smile and headed for the bathroom, lugging her one small overnight case.

# 20

# DESTINY

James Bond dreamed. It was a dream he often experienced: sun, and a beach, which he recognised only too well as the seafront at Royale-les-Eaux. It was the five-mile promenade as it used to be, of course, not the garish package-tour resort it had since become. In Bond's dream, life and time stood still, and this was the place he remembered from both childhood and his younger years. A band played. The tricolour beds of salvia, alyssum and lobelia bloomed in a riot of colour. And it was warm, and he was happy.

The dream often came when he was happy; and that night had certainly brought happiness. Together Bond and Paula had escaped from the clutches of Kolya Mosolov, made their way to Helsinki, and there – well, things had gone even better than they themselves expected.

Paula returned from the bathroom dressed only in a see-through nightdress, her body glowing and her scent as seductive as Bond had ever known it.

Before showering, Bond tapped out a call to London – a number reserved especially for taped messages from M. If there was anything new – in answer to the cipher sent from the Saab at Salla – he would hear it now. Sure enough, M's voice was on the line: a brief double-talk message which came quite near to congratulating Bond, and also confirmed that Paula was known to be working for SUPO. There could, Bond thought, be no more surprises.

Paula had taken the initiative, making love to him as a kind of hors d'œuvre; then, after a short rest, during which Paula talked and laughed about their brush with disaster, Bond started where she had left off.

Now there was peace, safety and warmth. Warmth, except for a cold spot developing on his neck, behind the ear. Still half asleep, Bond brushed at the cold spot. His hand came into contact with something hard, and vaguely unpleasant. His eyes snapped open and he felt the cold object pressed against his neck. Gone was Royale-les-Eaux, replaced with uncompromising reality.

'Just sit up quietly, Mr Bond.'

Bond turned his head to see Kolya Mosolov stepping away from him. A heavy Stetchkin – made even more bulky by a silencer fitted around the barrel – pointed, out of reach, at Bond's throat.

'How . . . ?' Bond began. Then, thinking of Paula, he turned to see her sound asleep beside him.

Mosolov laughed – a chuckle, almost out of character; but Kolya was a man of so many voices. 'Don't worry about Paula,' he said, soft and confident. 'You must have both been very tired. I managed to deal with the lock, administer a small injection, and move around without disturbing either of you.'

Bond cursed silently. This was so unlike him, to drop his guard and allow sleep to take over completely. He had done everything else. He even recalled sweeping the room for electronics the moment they arrived.

'What kind of an injection?' Trying not to sound concerned.

'She'll sleep peacefully for six or seven hours. Enough time for us to do what has to be done.'

'Which is?'

Mosolov made a motion with the Stetchkin. 'Get dressed. There's a job I have to see completed. After that we're going on a little journey. I even have a brand new passport for you – just to be certain. We leave Helsinki by car, then helicopter, and later there'll be a jet waiting. By the time Paula can alert anyone, we'll be well on our way.'

Bond shrugged. There was little he could do, though his hand moved unobtrusively to the pillow, under which he had placed the P7 before finally going to sleep. Kolya Mosolov reached inside his padded jacket, which he wore open, to show Bond the P7 tucked into his waistband. 'I thought it safer – for me, that is.'

Bond put his feet on the floor. He looked up at the Russian. 'You don't give up easily, do you, Mosolov?'

'My future rests on taking you in.'

'Dead or alive, it would seem.' Bond got to his feet.

'Preferably alive. The business at the frontier was exceptionally worrying in that respect. But now I can finish what was started.'

'I don't understand it.' Bond began to move towards the chair on which his clothes were folded. 'Your people could have had me at any time in the past few years. Why now?'

'Just get dressed.'

Bond began to do as he was told, but continued to talk. 'Tell me why, Kolya. Tell me why now?'

'Because the time is right. Moscow's wanted you for years. There was a period when they wanted you dead. Now, things have changed. I'm glad you survived. I admit to using bad judgment in letting our troops fire on you – the heat of the moment, you understand.'

Bond grunted.

'Now, as I said, things have changed.' Mosolov continued. 'We wish simply to verify certain information. First we'll do a chemical interrogation, to clean you out. Then we'll have a nice little asset to exchange. You've got a couple of our people who've done sterling work at General Communications Headquarters in Cheltenham. In due course an exchange will be arranged, I'm sure.'

'Is that why Moscow went along with all this in the first place? The games played with von Glöda and his crazies?'

'Oh, partly.' Kolya Mosolov jerked his pistol. 'Look, just get on with it. There's another job to be done before we leave Helsinki.'

Bond climbed into his ski pants. '*Partly*, Kolya? *Partly?* Bit of an expensive operation, wasn't it? Just to get me – and you damned near killed me doing it.'

'Playing along with von Glöda's wild schemes helped get rid of other small embarrassments.'

'Like Blue Hare?'

'Blue Hare, and other things. Von Glöda's death is a foregone conclusion.'

'*Is?*' Bond looked up sharply.

Kolya Mosolov nodded. 'Amazing, really. Wasn't that some display our ground attack boys gave? You wouldn't have thought anybody could survive. Yet von Glöda managed to get out.'

Bond found it difficult to believe. Certainly M had not known. He asked where the would-be leader of the Fourth Reich was now hiding.

'He's here.' Mosolov spoke as though the information were obvious. 'In Helsinki. Regrouping, as he would say. Reorganising. Ready to start all over again, unless he is stopped. I have to do the stopping. It would be embarrassing, to say the least, if von Glöda were allowed to continue his operations.'

Bond was now almost dressed. 'You're taking me out – back to Russia. You also intend to deal with von Glöda?' He adjusted the collar of his rollneck.

'Oh yes. You're part of my plan, Mr Bond. I also have to get rid of friend von Glöda, or Aarne Tudeer, or whatever he wishes to call himself on his tombstone. The timing is good . . .'

'What is the time?' Bond asked.

Kolya, always the professional, did not even glance at his watch. 'About seven forty-five in the morning. As I was saying, the timing is good. You see, von Glöda has some of his own people here, in Helsinki. He leaves for London, via Paris, this morning. I gather the madman imagines he can stage some kind of rally in London. There's also the question of an NSAA agent being held by your Service, I think. Naturally, he wants to take his revenge on you, Bond. So, I consider it best to offer you as a target. He cannot resist that.'

'Hardly,' Bond answered crisply. Already he had felt a tidal wave of depression sluice over him at the thought of von Glöda being still alive. Now he was to be used as bait – not for the first time since all this began. Bond's whole spirit revolted against the idea. There had to be a way. If anyone was going to get von Glöda, it would be Bond.

Mosolov was still speaking. 'Von Glöda's flight leaves at nine. It would be a nice touch if James Bond were to be seated in his own car, outside Vantaa Airport. That very fact should lure Comrade von Glöda from the departure building. He will not know that I have my own ways – old-fashioned perhaps – of making certain that you will sit quietly in the car: handcuffs, another small injection, a little different to the one I gave Paula.' He nodded towards the bed where Paula still slept soundly.

'You're mad.' Though he said it, Bond knew he was the one person whose presence could lure von Glöda. 'How would you do it?'

Mosolov's smile was sly now. 'Your motor car, Mr Bond. It's fitted with a rather special telephone, I believe?'

'Not many people know about that.' Bond was genuinely annoyed that Mosolov had found out about the telephone. He wondered what else the Russian knew.

'Well, I do, and I have the details. The base unit for your car telephone needs to go through an ordinary phone, linking the system to that of the country in which you operate. For instance, the base unit can be fitted to the phone in this room. All we do is wire in your base unit here, and drive out to the airport. By the time we get there you will be handcuffed, and unable to move. But, just before we arrive, I use the car phone, call the information desk, and ask them to page von Glöda. He will receive a message – that Mr James Bond is outside, in the car park, alone and incapacitated. I think I could even leave the message in Paula's name; she wouldn't mind. When von Glöda comes out, I shall be near him.' He patted the silenced Stetchkin. 'With a weapon like this, people will think it's a heart attack – at least to begin with. By the time they get to the truth we shall be well away. I already have another car standing by. It will all be very quick.'

'No chance. You'll never get away with it,' Bond said aloud, though he knew there was every possibility of Mosolov getting away with it. This was the cool, audacious act which so often works. But Bond grasped at a straw. Mosolov had made one error – that of believing the Saab's telephone required a base unit fitted to the main phone system. This would be a local call, and the electronics in the car had an operating range of around twenty-five miles. An error like this one was just what Bond needed.

'So,' Kolya hefted the Stetchkin in his hand, 'just give me the car keys. We'll go together. You can tell me how to get at the base unit.'

Bond pretended to think for a full minute. Mosolov repeated.

'You have no alternative.'

'You're right,' Bond said at last, 'I have no alternative. I resent coming to Moscow with you, Mosolov, but I am also anxious to see von Glöda out of the way. Getting the base unit's a tricky business. There are various routines I have to go through with the locks to the hiding place, but you can have me covered all the time. I'm ready. Why don't we do it now, straight away?'

Kolya nodded, glanced at the prostrate Paula, then thrust the Stetchkin inside his jacket. He gestured for Bond to take out the car keys and the key to the room, then to go on ahead of him.

All the way down the corridor, Mosolov stayed a good three paces behind Bond. In the lift, he remained in one corner – as far away as possible. The Russian was well-trained, no doubt about that. One move from Bond and the Stetchkin would make its muffled pop, leaving 007 with a gaping hole in his guts. They went down to the car park, heading for the Saab. About three paces from the car Bond turned.

'I have to take the keys from my pocket. Okay?'

Kolya said nothing, just nodded, moving the big pistol inside his coat to remind Bond it was there. Bond took the keys, his eyes darting around. Nobody else was in the car park, not a soul in sight. Ice crunched under his feet, and he felt the sweat trickle down from his armpits inside the warm clothing. It was fully light.

They reached the car. Bond unlocked the driver's door, then turned back to Kolya. 'I have to switch the ignition on – not fire the engine, just put on the electrics to operate the lock,' he said.

Again Kolya nodded and Bond leaned across the driver's seat, inserted the key into the ignition, and told Kolya he would have to sit in the driver's seat to open the telephone compartment. Once more Kolya nodded. Bond felt the eye of the automatic pistol boring through the Russian's jacket, and knew that surprise and speed were his only allies now.

Almost casually, Bond pressed the square black button on the dashboard, while his left hand dropped into position. There was a tiny hiss of gas, as the hydraulics opened the hidden compartment. A second later the big Ruger Redhawk dropped into his left hand.

Trained to use weapons with both hands, urged on by speed, Bond's body turned only slightly, the flash of the Magnum cartridge burning his trousers and jacket as he fired almost before the big revolver was clear of its hiding place.

Kolya Mosolov knew nothing. One minute he was ready to squeeze the trigger of the silenced Stetchkin, hidden under his coat; the next moment a blinding flash, a fractional pain, then darkness and the long oblivion.

The bullet lifted the Russian from his feet, catching him just below the throat, almost ripping head from body. His heels scraped the ice as he slid back, turning as he hit the ground, and sliding a good one and a half metres after he had fallen.

But Bond saw none of that. The moment he fired, so his right hand slammed the door closed. The Redhawk went back into its compartment, and the key was fully twisted in the ignition. The Saab burst into life, and Bond's hand moved with calm, expert confidence – pushing the button to close the compartment housing the Redhawk. He slid the gear lever into first, clipped on his inertia reel seatbelt, released the brake, and smoothly moved away as his fingers adjusted the hot air controls and the rear window heater. As he pulled away, Bond got the merest glimpse of what remained of the Russian: a small huddle on the ice, and a swelling pool of crimson. He swerved the car on to the Mannerheimintie, joining the sparse traffic heading for the Vantaa Airport road.

Once settled into the road pattern, Bond reached down and activated the radio telephone – which had proved to be Kolya Mosolov's fatal mistake. This was a simple local call, needing no base unit, for the resident agent, under whose control Bond officially worked, should be at a number situated less than ten miles from where the Saab sped towards the airport.

Bond punched out the number, by feel rather than looking down, for his eyes had to be everywhere now. In the handset he heard the number buzz at the far end. The buzzing continued, unanswered. In some ways Bond was pleased. The resident was away from his phone, but at least Bond had gone through the official motions.

He drove with care, watching his speed, for the Finnish police are extremely vigilant when it comes to the breaking of the speed limit. The clock on Bond's dashboard, which had been adjusted to Helsinki time, said five minutes past eight. He would be at Vantaa by eight-thirty all right – possibly just in time to catch up with von Glöda.

*

The airport was crowded, like any other international terminal, when Bond entered. He had parked the Saab in an easily accessible place, and now carried the awkward Ruger Redhawk inside his jacket, the long barrel pushed into the waistband of his trousers and twisted sideways. Never, the training schools taught, imitate the movies and shove a gun barrel straight down inside your trouser leg; always turn it to one side. If there should be an accident, straight down would mean losing part of your foot, if you were lucky. An unlucky man would lose what one instructor insisted on calling his 'wedding tackle' – a term Bond thought oddly vulgar. Twist the weapon sideways, by the butt, and you would get a burn, though the unfortunate person beside you would catch the bullet.

The big clock in International Departures stood at two minutes to eight-thirty.

Moving very fast, elbowing through the throng, Bond made the information desk and asked about the nine o'clock flight to Paris. The girl hardly looked up. The nine o'clock was Flight AY 873 via Brussels. They would not be calling it for another fifteen minutes as there was a catering delay.

As yet there was no need to put out a call for von Glöda, Bond decided. If the man's colleagues were around to see him off, there would still be a chance to corner him on this side of the terminal. If not, then Bond would simply have to bluff to get him back from the air-side.

Keeping behind as much cover as possible, Bond edged his way past the kiosks, trying to position himself near the passage on the extreme left of the complex which led to passport control and the air-side lounges.

At the far end of this section of the departure area, set in front of high windows, was a coffee shop – separated from the main complex by a low, flimsy trellis barrier covered with imitation flowers. To the left of it, very close to where Bond now stood, was the passport control section, each of its little booths occupied by an official.

Bond started to look at faces, searching through the crowds for von Glöda. Departing passengers were constantly moving through passport control, while the coffee shop was crowded with travellers, mainly seated at low, round tables.

Then quite unexpectedly – almost out of the corner of his eye – Bond saw his quarry: von Glöda rising from one of the coffee shop tables.

The would-be heir to Adolf Hitler's ruined empire appeared to be just as well-organised in Helsinki as he had been at the Ice Palace. His clothes were immaculate, and even in the grey civilian greatcoat, the man had a military look about him – a straightness of back and a bearing that singled him out from the ordinary. No wonder, Bond thought momentarily, that Tudeer imagined the world was his destiny.

He was surrounded by six men, all smartly dressed – each one of them looking like an ex-soldier. Mercenaries, perhaps? Von Glöda spoke to them in a low voice, punctuating his words with quick movements of the hands. It took Bond a second or two to realise the movements were similar to those of the late Adolf Hitler himself.

The radio announcement system clicked and played its little warning jingle. They were about to announce the Paris flight, Bond was certain. Von Glöda cocked his head to listen, but he'd also apparently decided, before the jingle finished, that it was his flight. Solemnly he shook hands with each of his men in turn and looked around for his hand baggage.

Bond moved closer to the trelliswork. There were too many people in the coffee shop to risk taking von Glöda there, he decided. The best place would be as the man walked clear of the coffee shop towards passport control.

Still maintaining cover among the constantly changing throng, Bond edged to the left. Von Glöda appeared to be looking around him, as if alerted to some danger.

The jingle died away, and the voice of the announcer came from the myriad speakers – unusually loud and clear, almost unbearably so. Bond felt his stomach churn. He stopped in his tracks, eyes never leaving von Glöda, who also stiffened, his face changing at the words:

'Would Mr James Bond please come to the Information Desk on the second floor?'

They were on the second floor. Bond quickly looked around, eyes searching for the Information Desk, aware that von Glöda was also turning. The voice repeated, 'Mr James Bond, please go to the Information Desk.'

Von Glöda turned fully. Both he and Bond must have spotted the figure, standing by the Information Desk, at roughly the same moment – Hans Buchtman, whom Bond had first known as Brad Tirpitz. As their eyes met, so Buchtman moved towards Bond, his mouth opening, words floating, lost in the general noise and bustle.

For an instant, von Glöda stared at Buchtman, scowling, incredulous. Then, at last, he saw Bond.

The whole scene appeared to be frozen for a split second. Then von Glöda said something to his companions. They began to scatter as von Glöda grabbed for his cabin baggage and started to move quickly from the coffee shop.

Bond stepped into the open in an attempt to cut him off, aware of Buchtman elbowing his way through the crowd. Bond's hand touched the Redhawk's butt as Buchtman's words finally reached his ears: 'No! No, Bond! No, we want him alive!'

I'll bet you do, Bond thought, as he hauled on the Redhawk, closing towards von Glöda who was crossing in front of him, moving rapidly. There was no stopping Bond now. 'Halt, Tudeer!' he shouted. 'You'll never make the flight. Stop now!'

People began to scream, and Bond – only a few paces from von Glöda – realised that the leader of the National Socialist Action Army held a Luger pistol low in his right hand, half screened by the small case in his left.

Bond still hauled on the Redhawk, which would not come free from his waistband. Again he shouted, glancing back to see that

Buchtman was bearing down on him from behind, thrusting people out of his path. In the midst of the panic erupting around him, Bond heard von Glöda shouting hysterically as he turned full on towards Bond.

'They didn't get me yesterday,' von Glöda yelled. 'This is proof of my mission. Proof of my destiny.'

As though in answer, the barrel of the Redhawk came free. Von Glöda's hand rose, the Luger pointing towards Bond, who dropped to one knee, extending his arm and the Redhawk. Von Glöda's hand and the Luger filled Bond's vision as he called again, 'It's over, von Glöda. Don't be a fool.'

Then the spurt of flame from the Luger's barrel, and Bond's own finger squeezing twice on the Redhawk's trigger.

The explosions were simultaneous, and a great hand seemed to fling Bond sideways. The passport control booths spun in front of him and he sprawled across the floor while von Glöda twisted and reared like a wounded stag, still screaming, 'Destiny . . . Destiny . . . Destiny . . .'

Bond couldn't understand why he was on the ground. Vaguely he caught sight of a passport control officer diving for shelter behind his booth. Then, still sprawling, he had the Redhawk zeroed in on von Glöda, who seemed to be trying to aim again with his Luger. Bond squeezed off another shot, and von Glöda dropped the Luger, then took one step back as his head disappeared in a thick red mist.

It was only now that pain began to overtake Bond. He felt very tired. Someone held his shoulders. There was a lot of noise. Then a voice: 'Couldn't be helped, Jimmy. You got the bastard. All over now. They've sent for an ambulance. You'll be okay.'

The voice was saying more than that, but the light ebbed away from Bond's eyes, and all sound disappeared, as though someone had deliberately turned down the volume.

# 21

# THIS CAN'T BE HEAVEN

The tunnel was very long, its sides white. Bond wondered if he was back in the Arctic Circle. Then he was swimming. Warm and cold by turns. Voices. Soft music, and the face of a girl leaning over him, and calling his name, 'Mr Bond . . . ? Mr Bond . . . ?'

The voice seemed to sing, and the girl's face was truly beautiful. She had blonde hair and appeared to be surrounded by a halo. James Bond opened his eyes and looked at her. Yes, a blonde angel with a shining white halo.

'Did I really make it? I couldn't have. This can't be heaven.'

The girl laughed. 'Not heaven, Mr Bond. You are in hospital.'

'Where?'

'In Helsinki. And there are people here to see you.'

He suddenly felt very tired. 'Send them away,' he said in a slurred voice. 'I'm too busy now. Heaven is great.' Then he retreated, back down the tunnel which had turned dark and warm.

He could have been asleep for hours, weeks, or months. There were no guidelines. But when Bond finally woke, he was conscious only of the pain down the right side of his body. The angel had gone. In her place a familiar figure sat quietly in a chair near the bed.

'Back with us, 007?' asked M. 'How do you feel?'

The memories returned like a series of clips from an old movie. The Arctic Circle; snow scooters; Blue Hare; the Ice Palace;

Paula's observation post; the bombs; then the last hours in Helsinki. The eye of the Luger.

Bond swallowed. His mouth was very dry. 'Not bad, sir,' he croaked, then remembered Paula, prostrate on the bed. 'Paula?'

'She's fine, 007. Right as rain.'

'Good,' Bond closed his eyes, recalling all that had happened. M remained silent. In spite of himself, Bond was impressed. It was rare enough for his boss to leave the safe confines of the building overlooking Regent's Park. Eventually, Bond opened his eyes again. 'Next time, sir, I trust you'll give me a full and proper briefing.'

M coughed. 'We thought it better for you to find out for yourself, 007. Truth is we weren't sure about everyone ourselves. The general idea was to put you in the field and draw the fire.'

'There you appear to have been successful.'

The blonde angel came in. She was, of course, a nurse. 'You're not to tire him,' she chided M in impeccable English, then disappeared again.

'You stopped two bullets,' M said, seemingly unconcerned. 'Both in the upper part of the chest. No serious damage done. On your feet again in a week or two. I'll see you get a month's leave after that. Tirpitz was going to bring Tudeer to us, but you had no alternative in that situation.' M, uncharacteristically, leaned over and gave Bond's hand a fatherly pat. 'Well done, 007, Good job well done.'

'Kind of you, sir. But I *was* under the impression that Brad Tirpitz's real name is Hans Buchtman. He was a crony of von Glöda's.'

'It was what I had to let you think, Jimmy.' For the first time, Bond realised that Tirpitz was also in the room. 'I'm sorry about the way it turned out. Everything went wrong. I had to stay with von Glöda. I guess I waited a hair too long. It was pure dumb luck that we weren't killed with the rest. The Russian Air Force did some kind of number on us. Jesus Christ Almighty. It was the worst I've ever been in.'

'I know. I watched it,' said Bond, feeling, in spite of his condition, an irritation with the American. 'But what about the whole Buchtman business?'

Tirpitz went into a lengthy explanation. About a year before, the CIA had instructed him to make contact with Aarne Tudeer, whom they suspected of doing arms deals with the Russians. 'I met him in Helsinki,' Tirpitz said. 'I speak German well enough, and I had a phony background all set up, under Hans Buchtman. I got to know him under the name of Buchtman and insinuated myself as a possible arms source. I also dropped some pretty heavy hints that I bore a strong physical resemblance to a CIA guy called Brad Tirpitz. That was for insurance, and it paid off. I guess I'm one of the few people living who got to kill themselves, if you see what I mean.'

The nurse returned with a large jug of barley water and warned them they only had another few minutes. Bond asked if he could have a martini instead. The nurse gave him an official smile.

'There wasn't a hell of a lot I could do about the torture, or getting you out any earlier,' Tirpitz continued. 'I couldn't even warn you about Rivke, because I knew nothing. Von Glöda didn't confide much, didn't tell me about the hospital set-up until too late. And the information from my own people was pretty half-assed, to say the least.'

*Half-assed indeed*, Bond thought vaguely. Then he drifted off again, and when he came to, a few moments later, only M was in the room.

'We're still rounding up the remnants, 007,' M was saying. 'The N-S-Double-A, We've scuttled them for good, I think.' M sounded pleased. 'I can't see anyone else reactivating what's left of it now – thanks to you, 007. In spite of the lack of information.'

'All part of the service,' Bond replied sarcastically.

But the remark ran off M's back like water from the proverbial duck.

After M left, the nurse returned to make sure Bond was comfortable.

'You are a nurse, aren't you?' he asked suspiciously.

'Of course. But why, Mr Bond?'

'Just checking.' Bond managed a smile. 'How about dinner tonight?'

'You are on a restricted diet, but if you fancy something I'll bring you our menu . . .'

'I meant you – dinner with me.'

She took a step away from the bed and looked him full in the eyes. Bond thought she was built from a mould long broken. Rarely did they make figures like that any more. Only occasionally. Like Rivke. Or Paula.

'My name's Ingrid,' the nurse said coolly. 'And I'd love to have dinner with you as soon as you're fully recovered. And I mean *fully* recovered. Do you remember what you said to me when you first became conscious after you were shot?'

Bond shook his head on the pillow.

'You said, "This can't be heaven." Mr Bond – James – maybe I'll show you it is heaven. But not until you're quite better.'

'Which will not be for a very long time.' The voice came from the door. 'And if anyone's going to show Mr Bond what heaven Helsinki can be, it will be me,' said Paula Vacker.

'Ah.' Bond smiled weakly. He had to admit that, even next to the impressive nurse Ingrid, Paula had the edge.

'Ah, indeed, James. The minute I turn my back, there you are, getting shot at, flirting with nurses. This is my city, and while you're here . . .'

'But you were asleep.' Bond gave a tired grin.

'Yes, but I'm wide awake now. Oh James, you had me so worried.'

'You should never worry about me.'

'No? Well, I've arranged things. Your chief – he's rather cute, by the way – he says I can look after you for a couple of weeks once they let you out of here.'

'Cute?' Bond said, incredulous. Then he put his head back, drifting off once more as Paula bent over to kiss him.

That night, in spite of all the memories – the Arctic, the terrors, the double and triple crosses – James Bond slept without dreams or nightmares.

He woke around dawn, then drifted into sleep again. This time, as always when content, he dreamed of Royale-les-Eaux. As it had been.